the way home

A Novel By
Judy Norwood Enter

This book is a work of fiction. Real people, places, and incidents have been blended into a story that is purely fiction. The actual historical events and facts are not represented here as true. All names with the exception of Sam McPhee, used with his permission, are fictitious products of the author's imagination. Any resemblance to actual events or locales or persons, living or dead, is entirely coincidental.

Copyright © 2012 Judy Norwood Enter
All Rights Reserved.

ISBN-10: 0615646565
ISBN-13: 9780615646565

*Special thanks to Lorie Apperson Moore
for permission to adapt a painful experience in her life
for this work of fiction.*

*Thank you to my friend, Clint Goddard, who shared his passion and
love of Haiti.
January 6, 1935 - July 28, 2012*

PROLOGUE

The following was reportedly inscribed on the wall of Shishu Bhavan, Mother Teresa's children's home in Calcutta, and attributed to her. However, an article in the *New York Times* has since reported on March 8, 2002 that the original version of this poem was written by Kent M. Keith. In fact, Kent M. Keith is the author as he published these "commandments" in a booklet when he was a student at Harvard around 1968.

Mother Teresa's *Anyway* Poem

People are often unreasonable, illogical and self-centered;
Forgive them anyway.

If you are kind, people may accuse you of selfish, ulterior motives;
Be kind anyway.

If you are successful, you will win some false friends
and some true enemies;
Succeed anyway.

If you are honest and frank, people may cheat you;
Be honest and frank anyway.

What you spend years building, someone could destroy overnight;
Build anyway.

If you find serenity and happiness, they may be jealous;
Be happy anyway.

The good you do today, people will often forget tomorrow;
Do good anyway.

Give the world the best you have, and it may never be enough;
Give the world the best you've got anyway.

You see in the final analysis, it is between you and your God;
It was never between you and them anyway.

one

Five years have passed since I looked down on Charleston from ten thousand feet or, actually, any elevation. My father is obliging me from his watery grave to return to South Carolina. He enjoyed flying almost as much as he loved boating and fishing, and he had headed south to Eleuthera in his Cessna for a little of all his favorite sports with his only brother in tow. According to records provided to the United States Coast Guard and the Bahamas Air and Sea Rescue, he methodically filed a flight plan for leaving Marsh Harbour, Abaco, Bahamas, in the late morning of July 10, 2008, for Rock Sound Airport on the southernmost part of the island of Eleuthera. Although my father was an experienced pilot with many hours of flight time to his credit, he was unprepared for the confluence of two oceanic storms that assaulted him and his brother in his small plane on that same afternoon. The National Oceanic and Atmospheric Administration reported the unexpected collision of the storms produced strong squalls igniting winds in excess of seventy miles per hour that continued into the night and abated early the next day. Bahamas Air and Sea Rescue was first to respond when they failed to arrive at Rock Sound. The United States Coast Guard immediately joined the operation, its scope immense over a wide area of land and sea. No sign of wreckage was found.

His disappearance nine months ago has hung in legal limbo, and now South Carolina state law declares Robert J. Chapin Sr.

the way home

officially dead. This legal declaration of death entitles his widow to collect his life insurance, settle the sizable estate, and generally move on to a new future unencumbered by a husband not dead but not living. And evidently such a declaration of the law has the power to roust me back to this inexhaustible, vintage city I never wanted to see again. It is an enigma how you can attach misery and aversion to a place when it's actually people who cause you the pain you are fleeing. Adding to the unceasing churning of my stomach at awakening old ghosts in the city of my childhood is the dread of seeing my father's second wife again, another discarded piece from the past I had no plans to pick up. My father, in his questionable wisdom, legally appointed Rachael and I co-executors of his estate, which means we have to agree on how to execute his last written instructions. This ominous alliance with Rachael has all the ingredients necessary to kindle a fire storm. I have no interest in anything of my father's, especially Rachael.

He married Rachael about ten years ago, when my brother and I were barely men. It was confusing to all involved because Jeff and I grew up with Rachael's family, and we spent summers together on Pawleys Island in the Low Country of South Carolina. Rachael and Jack, her husband, were my parent's best friends since college at the University of South Carolina. They referred to themselves as "the four chickens" after their beloved Gamecocks. Our family and theirs were inseparable at least until Jack drowned, and two years later my father left us. My mother's response to Jack's death and my father's abandonment was to hide out in plain view in her own home. After these two prodigious men vacated our lives, one in death and one in life, an implosion of seismic proportions changed the landscape of all our futures. But my brother and I had given up on our parents long before our father walked out the door of our home for the last time. His emotional and physical absences required that we take care of each other and our mother. And, as the human condition tends to make one who has been deprived of care and consolation do, we searched for substitutes. Drugs and alcohol became pseudo-parents for Jeff and me about the same time my mother started downing food and prescription pills. I crawled out of the wreckage of my drug-riddled life nine years ago. Jeff and my mother didn't make it out alive.

My father never spoke to me about his assets as he knew I didn't care. Adding to my lack of any intimate knowledge with regard to his life's accumulations is that I have spoken little to him since my mother and Jeff died. I've allowed him scarce opportunity to speak to me about anything. His attempts to contact me through the phone and e-mail were regular, though, so it seems he never gave up. As a last resort to force me to communicate with him, he drove to Asheville a couple of years ago, but the shouting match between us in my driveway had neighbors peeking out their windows and standing bug-eyed on their porches. That was the last time I saw him.

Some of the more obvious benefits of my father's wealth are a fine old home on the harbor, a yacht in the Bahamas, a successful, respected law practice on Meeting Street in venerable Charleston, South Carolina, a Cessna airplane, and a few other things that fed his voracious material appetite. The large settlement of a much publicized class-action lawsuit early in his career put Robert J. Chapin Sr. on the "Who's Who" list of the law profession, driving fear into the collective hearts of any large corporations dallying with screwing the public. This enigmatic man was a renegade of his profession, and his basic business philosophy was to take no prisoners. Unfortunately for his family, his merciless plan seeped into the business of his fatherhood like gas from a leaking fuel line.

Precisely because of his "take no prisoners" style, however, he became sought after in many controversial and nationally relevant class-action lawsuits. His legal rhetoric became fodder for stories of legend. The man's character appeared invincible. Everything he touched turned to gold for others as well as himself, and he was not reluctant to bathe in the limelight. He liked the money, no doubt, but what he enjoyed more was publicly flexing his formidable muscle to sway juries into transferring voluminous amounts of money from offending corporations to poor, unsuspecting consumers injured by the greed of corporate America. His notoriety was born with his television debut on a local station in Charleston, and as his inimitable reputation spread nationally, he soon graduated to major network

the way home

interviews on the coveted morning shows. Unapologetic because he was not a suave and refined man as many expected him to be, he used his superior intelligence and wily street smarts as well as his folksy sense of humor to win people over. One well known morning talk show host once asked him pensively what troubled him most in this world, and to this seriously posed question he thoughtfully replied, "Warm beer and Democrats."

During our school breaks, Mother would dress my brother and me in our Sunday best and drag us to my father's courtroom, where we could observe his bellowing over the injuries of his clients. In the evening over elaborate dinners my mother prepared, we were expected to partake in intelligent and interesting discussions on what we had witnessed in court. We grew to despise school breaks when he was conducting cases in Charleston and were relieved when his cases took him to other cities. One insufferable summer, when Jeff and I should have been sailing and swimming with our friends, Mother required us to dress and sit hour after hour in a stuffy courtroom in Charleston to witness my father dismantle piece-by-piece a tobacco company. His wheezing clients carted their oxygen bottles into the courtroom, and when my father had ripped the overstuffed and overpaid corporate moguls to bits, the gallery exploded. My Father was a savior in the eyes of all the afflicted and aggrieved suckers who ever drew a breath on a cigarette. Jeff and I were doomed to forever be shrouded by the vainglory of our father.

Even in death my father's storied life looms large in Charleston. My plans are to meet with his lawyer, sign on the dotted line, and get out of there.

I am nothing like my father. I have a modest home in Asheville, North Carolina, where Jill teaches third grade, and where twin girls with blonde hair and blue eyes can break their father's heart in all the right places. My dream is to give them all the unconditional love, significance, and security they deserve and to protect them and guide them into living for the things in life that really matter. I have a satisfying sales career that provides well for my family, but I do not allow the job or money to become more important to me than this little gathering place on a cul-de-sac in this sweet mountain town

judy norwood enter

where my girls come home every night. The travel required by the sale of wholesale pharmaceuticals is more than I want or is healthy for my family, and I'm negotiating with the company I work for out of Chicago to modify that. Not making my career first is something I have to try hard to do every day, because I've always been a salesman at heart and do love the pursuit. In fact, I've realized lately that it's not the kill that gives me that rush I need—it is the hunt.

Although I guess my father loved me, I never felt I was important in his life, like I was a mere spec on the lens of his glasses. The shadows his sons cast were tenuous compared to the titanic scope of his, and we gave up growing them when we were just boys. Our father was not cruel or abusive unless you tag absence or disappointment in us as those things. He blew in and out of our lives like a great wind, always loud, laughing and reveling in his victories. He tried to instill the same killer instinct for success in school and sports in his sons, but we frequently defeated him. Sometimes his ire, but always his disappointment in either our failures as young men or our pure rebellion in refusing his admonitions would find their way to our tender, formative ears. I remember one warm winter when Jeff and I purchased plans from a sailing catalog to build a sailing dinghy we dreamed of racing on the harbor in the spring. We purchased the materials with money we had earned during the previous summer and set up shop in the old carriage house. Most evenings after chores and homework, we headed out back to our makeshift boatyard to construct and varnish to a keen shine our own sleek sailing vessel which we imagined would win every race of the summer. On the evenings when our father was home, he would cross the yard from the house to the shop with his coffee cup in hand and proceed to inspect our work with a critical eye.

"Boys, this piece of wood is warped. You should return it and insist on its replacement. Jeff, you're not using that plane correctly on the wood. Rub your fingers over the planed wood as you work and you can feel the rough spots. Bobby, use a light touch when you brush the varnish on the wood. Are you fine-sanding between every coat? How are you securing the mast? It looks like a stiff breeze that catches your sails could snap it off."

the way home

And so we learned to work in the afternoon and early evening before he came home. But he would wander out late at night and perform his inspection, then report to us at breakfast how we should and should not be building the sailing dinghy. One afternoon in early spring after I returned home from baseball practice, I saw the doors open to the carriage house. I called out to Jeff, but no answer. What I saw was the complete destruction of our little sailboat chopped into a hundred pieces by the ax lying on the floor next to it. I ran to the attic to find Jeff smoking a joint. All he said was, "Hell, I don't want to give him the satisfaction of watching us win races on the harbor this summer and believe he had something to do with building our boat."

But in every childhood, some inalterable division must occur, I suppose. Had my mother and Jeff not died and had I not held my father chillingly responsible, I may have forgiven his failures as a parent and enjoyed at least a fragile bond with him in adulthood.

I have no grievous feelings of loss but rather only the weight of the legalities of this estranged man's life and death. Am I stone cold? I also cannot locate a grain of sympathy for Rachael. More than once she invited Jill, the girls, and me on his boat for a week in the northern Bahamas. I wasn't sure of her motive, but I had no plans of allowing my family to spend a week with these two traitors anyplace in the world.

My stepmother insists on meeting me at the airport, and I'm vigilant for an ambush. I have qualms about this initial meeting but no reason to initiate an argument this early. I can do anything for twenty-four hours—that's all I'm giving her and Louis, my father's law partner and attorney in the dispensation of the Last Will and Testament. She's standing near the exit gate wearing my father's money well in breast implants and Botox injections, all nipped and tucked. She has maintained her girl-like, petite figure, with medical help I suppose, and her clothes are straight off a designer's rack. Game on.

Rachael is waving a stylish, French-manicured hand. "Bobby, Bobby. Here! Oh my gosh, you look just like your daddy. The resemblance to your father is just breaking my heart. But looking so much like your daddy is probably a burden to you, isn't it, Bobby?" Rachael can always chide you effectively with her formidable arsenal of

judy norwood enter

sarcasm. She stands on tiptoe in her four-inch designer heels and brushes my cheek with an awkward, light kiss. I am grateful to see nothing of my father when I look into the mirror. I am my mother's son.

Rachael sighs theatrically. "We have so much to catch up on and so many issues to deal with but so little time since you can only give us a day. Let's get going to the house. I have prepared the carriage house for you. Thought you might be more comfortable staying there than in the main house with me."

"You're putting me in the old carriage house with tools and yard equipment and paint cans?"

"No, silly. We were finally able to obtain the necessary permits from the city a few years ago and remodel the existing carriage house. It turned out beautiful! Your father believed that you might come and bring your family if you didn't have to actually stay in the main house with us. Maybe too many memories of your mother and her passing—he wasn't sure. It was his constant hope you would bring Jill and the girls for a visit, but sadly for us all, you did not."

Why are women so good at greasing you down with guilt? Among themselves, southern women call it just that: *guilt grease*. It's their primary motivational weapon to get their men to slide easily into submission. I swear that even my mother, who I hold in near sainthood, kept an invisible pantry from which she could easily gather the right amount of guilt to goad Jeff and me into reluctant obedience. Sometimes it even worked on my father. I crawl hesitantly into Rachael's new silver Lexus.

"Rachael, I can make short work of all these 'issues' you are worried about. I told you when you called that I have no interest in anything of my father's. I plan to sign over everything with my name on it to you. So what issues are you talking about?"

"Bobby, first, the house is so full of personal effects your father and mother saved—books, pictures, toys, trophies, and the like. You should decide who gets what. It isn't fair for me, an outsider, to make the decisions and just ship them off to you or Jeff's kids or my own children. Remember, in your mind, I went from a beloved 'insider' to a despised 'outsider' when I married your father. And, anyway, what

the way home

does Jill think about you forfeiting your inheritance? Are you willing to snatch away your children's future with a few strokes of a pen?"

Her sarcasm eludes me because it is the truth.

She rants on. "Then there is the business of you and I executing his will. It's just not that simple. But we'll talk about these things later. Let's get you home and settled in and have a beer on the portico overlooking the harbor. It was your father's and my favorite spot to watch the sun go down. And I really want to hear about Jill and the twins."

Pulling into the cobblestone drive at the plantation-style house with its towering magnolias, memories that I wish belonged to someone else begin to surface. I have got to get out of here. She has the gardener take my one bag to the carriage house, and I don't follow him. I slowly stroll to the enormous, columned front portico overlooking a portion of Charleston Harbor that is a marked channel of the Intracoastal Waterway running from Norfolk to Miami. Boats ply this water on their odysseys north from Florida and the Bahamas this time of year. In October they reverse the trip, fleeing the cold north and sailing to warmer climes. They sail or motor away on shiny yachts, hopefully on fair winds and light seas, to the Keys, the Bahamas and Caribbean, or the east coast of Florida or the Gulf of Mexico through the Okeechobee Waterway. Wherever their charts lead them, they are all in search of the land of no worries.

Seduced by the view, we both stand watching a shining navy-hulled sailboat, the wind propelling its bow north through the calm water of the harbor. A two-seat kayak is lashed to the lifelines on the starboard side, and two slightly rusted bicycles are tied securely to the port side. A grill, a large cooler, jugs of fuel and water, and some laundry drying in the breeze are on deck. The bronzed couple is working in tandem in the cockpit, she at the helm and he adjusting the yards of white fabric snapping and catching the stiff wind that propels them forward toward their northern destination. I fantasize about them—retired but young at heart and healthy. They're still best friends, laughing and loving after all these years. Watching these glistening boats moving in perfect symphony with the radiant water on Charleston Harbor, some of the old, familiar languor returns. This

judy norwood enter

tranquil place of tides and salty ocean breezes still speaks restfully to me. Jeff and I used to retreat to the sea and the varied boats of our youth, running away from the failure to meet the expectations our parents had set for each other and us.

"My father stood here often with his dreams of being on one of those boats heading to nowhere. In a way I guess he got his wish."

Rachael drops her head, abruptly leveling it again and staring at me with what appears to be disdain. "That is an insensitive thing to say and makes light of his death. And for all the things your father wanted out of life, it was never his dream or his destiny to head 'nowhere.'"

A smile slowly congeals on her face, and the more urbane Rachael appears. "Your father's hapless death has been devastating to many people. In his career he helped literally thousands of people injured by the callousness of others. Our entire community has lost a friend and ally. He always possessed a streak of advocacy for the least of the least, and the largesse he poured into charity has been sorely affected. He was a father, a grandfather, a husband, a crusader, and a friend to so many, and in the blink of an eye, that well-lived life vanished. And I will not have you diminishing his memory."

"His memory is only diminished in my eyes."

Ignoring me she stares out over the shimmering water. "And I lost my best friend. Our relationship was forged on just that—friendship. His big heart and his capacity to love knew no limits. I know you don't understand how with all our history we could wind up married, but we did. As strange as this may sound to you, our relationship as husband and wife became an extension of the friendship of the four of us throughout all those years. At the risk of sounding didactic, your prejudices or your unwillingness to accept our relationship washed away some of the joy of life for your father. The gulf that separated the two of you seemed impenetrable to him. He missed you. And he missed Jill and those little girls."

"If he didn't care about his own boys, I figured he couldn't care about my girls."

"Neither of those things are true. You are a hateful, hurtful man to believe and say that about Robert. Your father loved you and Jeff

the way home

very much, and he experienced insurmountable grief and remorse over Jeff's death as well as over the estrangement between you and him. Your absence from his life troubled him every day. And he missed being a part of his granddaughters' lives. But know that your father and I had a wonderful life together, living his dreams. As we all do, he had regrets, but he determined to be happy with what he was granted and to share it. But so much grief shrouded his life. He once told me that it seemed he could easily have riches, but having what he wanted and loved most, his family eluded him."

"If he wanted his family, he could have had us. It seemed to me that other things, his accomplishments and celebrity, meant more to him than us."

"That was never true. You cut yourself out of this time of his life, believing his attempts to reconcile with you were some sort of cheap trickery he contrived to manipulate you. He respected your choices and was proud of you just the way you are. He didn't want to infringe on your life. He just wanted to share in it."

"My father didn't share in anyone's life. He had to own and control everything and everyone he touched."

The disappointment and grief are carved into her face. "Your father shared everything he had, his life and his wealth. If we had to lose him, it is better it was while he was doing what he loved than some other way. And, Bobby, just so you know, I made your father happy, too. Let's finish our drinks and go inside. The temperature is starting to drop."

On the grand, columned, Confederate portico of my childhood, I stand too close to her in the near dark and stare directly down into her moist eyes. "Rachael, let's understand this—it has never been and never will be your place to tell me my father loved Jeff and me. His regret or remorse or whatever tripe he invented to assuage his guilt was an act, just like his courtroom antics. He never made restitution to our mother for the decay of our family, as far as I know. I never even saw him cry for Jeff at his funeral. So don't ever speak to me about what my father was feeling or not feeling about us. Understood?"

Rachael sets her drink down on the table a little too hard. "So much of what you believe and say is simply not true. It's a lie. Your father grieved for Jeff as well as your mother. You weren't around to see. But I emphatically understand this is not the time or place to articulate these things to you. Truth will have its day in time."

The familiar contempt in me continues to emerge. "And another thing. I don't give a damn whether 'Saint Robert' was happy or not. As far as I'm concerned, he alone was the incontrovertible source of all of my mother's unhappiness. He loomed above us all, and his life overshadowed hers. He cared nothing for her happiness. So don't try to tell me about my family. You don't know."

She hesitates. Her voice is soft and almost consoling. "It's all quite convoluted, and you understand so little. You make your bitter judgments looking from the outside in without all the facts, and what happened in the relationships of Jack and me and your father and Mary Elizabeth needs to be known from the inside out. The unbreakable bond that was forged between the four of us over many years really defies any model I see today in modern relationships. It held up under unusual pressure and any loss we faced. We were friends in spite of our wrongdoings, our differences, our geography, our jobs, our deaths, and your father and Mary Elizabeth's divorce. We shared our broken lives with abandonment to one another. And death and divorce could not erase the bond. The bedrock of genuine, lasting relationships is forgiveness. Our love and forgiveness of each other was the glue that held us together."

"Rachael, don't believe for one minute that I will lighten your load of regrets and grief by forgiving you or my father. Screw you for screwing my mother and me and Jeff."

Her snippy sarcasm returns. "Well, I can see that you still enjoy colorful language. Although I will say that bitterness doesn't become you. You've kind of soured like the starter for sourdough bread, brooding over time. The difference is that the bread starter morphs into something useful, whereas you've just spoiled to no good. You and I find ourselves in the kitchen together again, like when you were a boy, and we're back here in this place to complete some unfinished business for your father. So you can continue with this diatribe, but it's just going to make the task at hand more difficult. We have a little journey to travel together, Bobby. Call it an odyssey, an adven-

the way home

ture. And while we're together, my hope is that you and I can make peace as a sort of bridge between you and your father, with the past."

"Peace! For me or for you, Rachael?"

"My attempt at peacemaking is for all of us. It's what your father desperately wanted and couldn't achieve while he was alive because you wouldn't allow him. We can make peace with the dead as well as the living, and you need to do a little of both."

Her voice turns tender and motherly, and her accent grows more pronounced, as only can happen with a southern woman. "Remember, when you were growing up, we were all like family. Those were good times, living those summers at the beach like one big family. Trudy and Trent and you and Jeff were like brothers and sisters. They say you don't even stay in touch with them. Why did you turn on them, too? It's me you're mad with. That old, sour part of you is trying to throw away all the sweet parts of our lives together and hold on to the bitter. Every family has some 'bad'. It's what you do with it that matters. If you must blame me, then I accept that for now. You need someone to rail against, and I'm the only one left. So blame me, but eventually truth will trump that lie you believe about all of us and yourself. You were always the caretaker for your mother and Jeff but never yourself. It's time for you to take care of you by going on a hunt for the truth. When you find it, you're going to wrestle with it for a while because it's hard to let go of old pain and exchange it for the new pain that can eventually make you well. But the Bobby I know is a fighter, strong and smart, and has a good heart. You'll win the struggle between denial and reality. And if you'll let me, I'll help you."

"What an eloquent load of bullshit. You make it sound like some storybook adventure I'm about to embark on. Here's the truth, Rachael. Jeff died because my father couldn't see beyond the end of his narcissistic nose and notice what he was doing to his own children and to our mother. Jeff's loneliness, his darker side, his self-mutilation, and his drug use all fall at my father's feet. His self-centered pursuits—building that damn law practice, traveling, spending time with his friends excluded his family."

"Stop it! You have become so foul. And you defile your family's memories. I won't have it in our conversation."

judy norwood enter

"Conversation! In case you haven't noticed, this passes for a pretty hot contentious argument. And what I'm arguing is the truth, what you are defending is your version of the truth."

"There are no 'versions of the truth', my poor delusional boy. The truth is the truth. Please don't tell me you no longer know the truth from a lie."

"The truth, my former friend, is that you fouled everything more when you married my father. As if our lives weren't screwed enough, you became my father's wife and our stepmother. You broke my mother's heart when she saw her best friend take her place with my father. You killed her, and my father killed Jeff. You and my father were complicit in your deeds, so don't hold your breath waiting on me to forgive you. Nor will I forgive my father just because he is dead."

two

Dinner is shrimp and grits, another reminder of the things I've tried to forget, but I am helpless to say I'm not hungry. Quite naturally, Rachael and Jack became the summer's chefs at the beach house our families rented each summer on Pawleys Island. Their family-style restaurant in Myrtle Beach was a favorite of locals and tourists. During those summers at the beach, both the children and the adults frequently requested shrimp and grits. Part of the enjoyment was netting the shrimp in the tidal saltwater creek behind the house. Taking the Jon boat into the creek on those lazy, scorching afternoons and casting the nets and us kids squealing as the haul was dragged into the boat were all ingredients of the ritual. When the boys were older, we got to take the boat into the creek alone and do that glorious work of harvesting big, fat, juicy shrimp straight from the saltwater creek on Pawleys Island fed by the Atlantic Ocean. Heck, I've seen my father snatch one of those succulent shrimp from the net, pop the head off, and eat him right out of the creek! After the haul the men drank beer and peeled the shells from the shrimp on the back deck while we kids buried our feet up to our knees at low tide in the decay that was pluff mud in the fertile creek. And with the sounds of beach music drifting into the kitchen while they worked, the women boiled a big pot of stone-ground grits with butter and milk over the flame on the old stove. My mother was the biscuit maker. Her mother had taught her how to make the best but-

the way home

termilk biscuits on the planet. The smells of briny shrimp cooking in butter and Old Bay spice, warm bread fresh from the oven, and the gooey buttery grits cooking and popping in their boil—if only life could have stayed like that. That place and time fed our souls as well as our bellies.

Rachael serves generous helpings for both of us at the big pine table in the kitchen. It sits where it always has, before a big bay window overlooking the harbor, and a bench seat and six bulky chairs are still arranged around it. This is the same oversize table with its scratches and stains, some of which my brother and I put there. Today, after being shipped down to an antique shop on King Street in Charleston, it would be a prized antique. You have to ask why some people are willing to call "antique" and pay so much money for furniture bruised by others' pasts. Rachael is sitting across from me at the other end of the table in what was traditionally my father's chair. She's speaking, but all I can see and hear is my father.

"Now, Bobby, you and Jeff need to look after your mother. I'm heading out to Los Angeles for a meeting on this class-action case tomorrow morning. Don't know when I'll be back. I'm trying to negotiate a nice settlement from these sons of bitches. They're real close, I can feel it. Big pharmaceutical companies are nothing but profit-mongers pretending to research and develop drugs to help the sick. Hell, they hurt about as many people as they help."

"Robert, please. Watch your language in front of the boys."

"Tomorrow morning! But, Dad, Jeff's game for the basketball championship in his league is Friday night. You can't miss that. Their team came from behind and rolled over two teams who thought they had the spot sewed up. I guess Jeff's coach has done a real fine job bringing them this far, sir. And Jeff is high-scorer for the season. He'll get an award for sure. Coach is asking all the families to come out and support them." I laughed a little nervously as I tried to sell him on staying.

Jeff sat silently twirling his fork and staring at his plate of uneaten chicken and rice. Mother continued to eat, stuffing the white rice and boiled chicken into her mouth with a vengeance. Her fork found the bottom of the pile of food hitting her plate regularly.

16

judy norwood enter

"Now, Bobby, I don't hear anybody complaining except you. Business comes first, and everybody understands that. I have clients depending on me. You understand they've been hurt and are counting on me to help them. I'll call after the game and see how it went. And when this is settled, we boys will go down to Wadmalaw Island for a little camping trip and some fishing." He turned to Jeff. "Is it all right with you, buddy, if I call after the game?"

Jeff put his fork down and stood off his end of the bench seat facing dad. "No, sir, it isn't. Don't call because you really don't give a shit about me or my game or anybody else here at this table, except yourself. And I am not your 'buddy.'"

Mother had placed a dull knife beside Jeff's plate for cutting the chicken and spreading the butter on his biscuit. Jeff stood motionless, allowing the anger to build and never taking his eyes off my father. He suddenly grabbed the knife, lifted it high into the air, and heaved it into the soft wood of the big table in front of my father's plate. All our eyes landed on the erect and motionless knife standing on its end.

Jeff seemed to have transferred all of his rage into the knife and bludgeoned table. He glared at my father once more and then walked away without another word. My parents locked eyes, and my father silently shook his head from side to side in her direction, registering his disappointment. He wiped his mouth, stood tiredly, and went upstairs to pack. Mother, who had watched the entire scene with her fork in mid-air, resumed eating. I followed Jeff to the attic room and found him digging out our stash of marijuana from beneath the heart pine floorboard.

"Bobby, Bobby, you listening to me? I said you will hear the entirety of your father's Will tomorrow, but there are a couple of things you need to know. Your father is leaving this house to you with the understanding that I'm to be allowed to live here as long as I wish or until I die. I am receiving a percentage of stock and his life insurance as well as a little cash, and he's seeing that I will be well cared for, as he has assured these last many years."

My eyes are still attached to the scar on the table where Jeff plunged the knife. I'm wondering how Mother felt when she cleared the dishes alone and pulled the knife out of the table.

17

the way home

"Well…good for you, Rachael. But you can have the house. I don't want this mausoleum of memories."

"Neither do I, Bobby. This was never my home. It belongs in your family. I moved back here with your father after your mother died because that's what she wanted."

Rachael and my father moved back into our old home a few months after Mother died. Mother loved this house, and in her last years, she seldom left it. She holed up inside, feeding her obesity until a massive stroke claimed her as she was climbing the grand staircase in the foyer. She was only fifty years old, and I blame my father for killing her. Bit by bit, piece by piece, he robbed her of who she was. I remember her beauty and how refined she was in speech and exquisite style from my childhood. Even as a young boy, I was always proud to have her take my hand when we strolled through the eloquent shops in the historical districts of Charleston. Why a person of her beauty and refinement married a boor of a man like my father, I never understood. Mother's family was of old Charleston society and inherited money; my father was brash and of new money he earned the old-fashioned way, by working. The money might be spent the same, but new money in Charleston doesn't gain you access to the socioeconomic status old money does. Her parents never endorsed their marriage, and my father always knew he was an outsider to the Charleston elite. However, the wealthier my father became, the more her parents and Charleston seemed to accept him, especially when he purchased this ostentatious house on Waterview in the historical district.

Rachael stands to clear our plates, refills her wine glass, and snaps it off the table. "Follow me. Let's go the attic."

I sit locked in place. Memory can be a terrible thing, and at this moment I wish to magically develop amnesia. Hundreds of times Jeff and I had taken refuge in the attic, which wasn't really an attic but an attic-type room on the third floor with an old, rumbling AC unit to cool us in the hot Charleston summers. That room became our lone sanctuary because our parents hardly ever went there. It was as if between the main house and the attic there grew a physical fissure representing the emotional separation between our parents and us.

judy norwood enter

It was where we would hide from their arguments and all our father's expectations of us, play games, and smoke cigarettes. Rachael leads up the stairs, after I'm finally able to move, and she is chattering away about how wonderful this is going to be—remembering. She throws open the aged wooden door and touches a light switch. Hundreds of white lights—the kind people hang at Christmas—are strung near where the clapboard walls meet the peaked ceiling. They produce a sort of surreal glow that dances across the big room as the light wind from an open window tickles the strings of lights. Rachael, anticipating our visit here tonight, has opened these windows facing the ocean, and the warm salt air mixes with the blended smells of old pine, musty rugs, and just plain age.

The moving reflections of the rattling Christmas lights on the old, whitewashed clapboard walls and heart pine floor shines soft and a little eerily, creating the perfect setting for meeting old ghosts. Other than the luminous lights, little else seems to have changed since we were children. Our pinball machine is still here, and the old TV with rabbit ears and the air hockey and ping-pong tables are just like we left them. Our old bunk beds are in the corner where Jeff and I preferred to sleep (instead of in our rooms). Rachael has choreographed this dramatic scene, as the large walk-in closet at the end of the long room is open, and she is already pulling the boxes that hold the pieces of our fractured lives onto the threadbare rug in the light-dappled room. Some of the remnants of our pasts are lying like skeletons on shelves in the closet, and she stands barefoot on tiptoe to reach them. Here we find my football pads and Jeff's model airplane, the tip of one of the wings gone where our father crashed it showing us how to fly it. The blankets lovingly quilted by our grandmother are sealed in clear plastic and hung over a dowel rod to preserve them. Rachael is silently working like a deranged elf dragging out gifts at Christmas.

I pivot in place and scan the room. The framed awards Jeff and I earned in sports are hanging on the walls. I walk slowly, examining them and finding every award has been newly framed and arranged according to date. When Jeff's team won the basketball championship, he was given the award for MVP that hangs here now. Wooden

the way home

shelves are symmetrically mounted down the long wall on the other side of the room, displaying the trophies awarded for every game my father never attended.

It's a big closet, and Rachael continues to push and pull boxes of homemade Christmas tree ornaments, school pictures, toys, baby albums, and family photos into the heap. Each box is carefully marked with printed labels. My eyes fall on one marked *Pawleys Island—Summer of 1994*. That was the year before Uncle Jack drowned.

Rachael notices my interest in that particular box and pulls it out of the heap toward me. We both kneel down on the worn rug, she waiting for me to open it. In the soft glow of white lights, I catch a glimpse of the woman I had once grown to love like a mother, the woman I was most apt to run to for a Band-Aid as a child or to receive help with coping with heartache as a teenager. This was the woman I liked playing practical jokes on, and she on me, the woman I could drop to the floor and tickle until she threatened to pee in her pants. I reach for the tape on the box and slit it with a box cutter Rachael has brought with us to this time machine of a room.

Inside the big box, there aren't yellowed photos thrown randomly into shoe boxes or envelopes but albums that contain real, old-time photos someone chose and painstakingly glued in to capture all our lives. We open the first one and are transfixed by the photo of Jeff and I holding up shiny, waxed surfboards. We were all smiling goofily with white teeth and had tanned faces and hair bleached by the summer sun. We each stood tall and skinny, my brother only a few inches shorter than me. We looked as though we came from the Beaver Cleaver family on that old television show. No one could ever look at this photo and recognize the depth of emptiness and destruction already taking root inside us.

Rachael smiles, shaking her head from side to side at the memory. "You two boys were like my own. Remember that picnic Jack and I prepared and hauled down to the wide beach on Pawleys in front of the old house? A few sandwiches and chips and pickles wouldn't do for Jack. We cooked made-from-scratch pizzas and tucked them into insulated bags we'd brought from the restaurant. We loaded the beach cart at the house with the cooler and pizzas. Remember,

judy norwood enter

Bobby, we spread everything out on the big beach blanket and called everyone in from surfing and swimming. Had it all ready, and all of a sudden a big wave on the incoming tide hit the shore, spreading seawater and foam onto the blanket. It scooped up all the insulated bags with the pizzas, and there they were, floating out to sea. You and Jeff grabbed four of the bags, and Trent grabbed the other two. Trudy was laughing so hard she didn't notice a wave coming that knocked her off her feet. There you all were, standing in the water eating the soggy pizza you could salvage! Your mother almost wet her pants laughing at you guys!"

I do remember the two families who had lived and loved like one. For entire summers, we romped in the surf by day and competed in Scrabble and Monopoly and card games by night. Kids scared one another with ghost stories in their rooms in the dark while their parents sat on the big front porch on the ocean or on the back deck on the creek sipping libations and talking softly in the night. My mother, Rachael, and Jack were all best friends. On many of those summer nights, my father would drive up from Charleston and return the next morning for work. He came. Jeff and I liked to lie in bed upstairs on those warm, humid summer nights with our windows open to the briny sea breeze and listen to their low voices and laughter and the soft, familiar sounds of beach music drifting out from the living room. It was like we felt normal when the four of them were together and had a sort of strength in the belief that our families would last, that nothing could shatter us that couldn't be picked up and put back together.

Rachael and I sit on the faded, frayed rug, rummaging through boxes and looking at more of the albums. It never occurs to me to ask who put all this together. But she seems very familiar with it all.

"Bobby, I need more time with you. We need to go through all this and settle your father's business. Please. I can't do it alone. And we need to plan a memorial service for him together."

"You can get Trent or Trudy to help you."

"Robert is your father, not theirs. They've already been down this road when Jack drowned." Rachael's eyes glaze as though she's recounting past grief and speaking to no one in particular. "Trent

the way home

watched his father die, and to this day he has some sort of survivor's remorse for not being able to save his dad. But we could have lost them both. If Jack had not put on those damn fishing waders that cool fall morning, he could have swam back to the overturned boat. They filled with water and just dragged him down to his death. All those years fishing, and on this one fateful day, it kills him. Who can possibly understand life? I sure can't. How different all our futures might have been had he lived."

I slam the album shut, and my agitation declares the implied truce we had made during dinner over. "What do you want from me, Rachael? I mean, I haven't been in this house since Mother died and you and my father moved back in. And I resent the hell out of having to be back now. This room is a setup. Someone is pulling me back into a place and time I'm trying to forget. This shrine or museum should be sealed up and never opened again. My brother is dead, and none of this stuff will bring him back. My mother wasted her life on my father, and none of these artifacts can undo her loss. I can't see sitting on the floor of my home in Asheville sipping a glass of sweet tea and opening boxes with my wife and the girls while pretending my childhood was anything but counterfeit."

"Bobby, this is a moment in time you've been walking toward all your life, and continuing to run away from it is no longer an option. You'll see better tomorrow. When you were growing up, you trusted my counsel. I helped you through some very rough spots and even kept your secrets from your parents. And I loved you enough to keep your parents' secrets from you. Why can't you trust me again?"

"In a word, you betrayed me, Rachael."

"Because I married your father or because you believe I killed your mother? Yes, I did marry your father, but I did not kill your mother. I loved your mother. She was like my own sister. As children, there are elements of your parents' lives you cannot understand or grasp and others you should not be told. Your mother wrestled with depression most of her adult life. I took her to doctors and to treatment centers, held her in some of her worst hours, and begged her to take her meds. I pleaded with her not to use food as consolation. She just gave up and abused the very medications that could help

judy norwood enter

her. In the end, when she wouldn't leave the house, she said the kindest thing I could do for her would be to bring food to the house so she wouldn't have to leave its relative safety. I knew she was tired of living, so I guess you could say I helped her. It was her choice. Just like Jeff made his choices. Your mother's depression seemed to affect Jeff more than you. He was so sympathetic to her that, in a way, she transmitted that negative vibe to him as a child. They were the ones always in the background. Don't you remember how shy he was at accepting these awards and trophies?" She sweeps both sides of the room with her arms. "He loved the games and would practice and play until he was exhausted, but he was shy when it came time for recognition. Your mother once told me I knew her better than anyone else. I think that was true. And when I saw Jeff coming up with all those same traits of highs and lows and depression, it frightened me. Knowing the truth can be painful, but living like a lie is the truth can destroy you and all you love. Basing your life on a lie is like building a house on a slowly disintegrating foundation. That house will eventually fall and injure its inhabitants."

"Rachael, there's nothing wrong with the house I've built. And I don't know what your real motives are for bringing me back here. But I can't trust you again."

"Can't or won't, Bobby?"

23

three

The smells of warm cinnamon buns and strong coffee draw me from the carriage house to the kitchen and the big pine table once again. After leaving the attic and Rachael around midnight, the night was a fitful one. Rachael's homemade buns smell just as sweet as my mother's, but she constructs them in a more health-conscious size. My mother, the designer of fist-sized buttermilk biscuits, could turn out the same remarkable dough interlaced with cinnamon and sugar and rolled into buns so sticky and sweet one bite gave you a sugar buzz.

"You take cream and sugar in your coffee?"

"I'll take the half-and-half, but Jill cut my sugar out."

"Good for her watching your diet. But you spend a lot of time on the road in sales, don't you, Bobby? Guess it's a little harder to watch your diet out there in restaurants than at home. Or at least that's what your father and I experienced."

Now Rachael is petite and as trim as a rail, but she still eats like a horse like she always has. I can't imagine she is concerned about her diet. Rachael is using the international language of food as well as light, normal conversation to try to ease us back into a truce. She sits at the table, again in my father's place. I wish she would sit somewhere else. There are four other chairs.

the way home

The coffee is bitterly strong and hot, the full-fat half-and-half is flavored with amaretto, and my first bite of cinnamon ecstasy explodes in my memory as much as in my mouth.

"Mary Elizabeth, honey, why don't you cut down on the size of these cinnamon buns you've been making all these years? The boys' metabolism can take 'em, but mine and yours can't. I'm going to have to buy a new belt and bigger pants."

"Robert, I've been making these cinnamon buns just like my mother for over two decades, and I can't make them any other way. If you don't want the whole thing, here's a knife. Cut the thing in half and stop complaining. The rest of us like them just the way they are, don't we, boys?"

"Yes, Mama, don't change the buns just because he says so." Jeff always sided with Mother regardless of whether she was wrong or right. And Mother's pattern for combating my father unwittingly evolved into an uncommon alliance with my brother I was not invited into.

As she said this about the knife, she rose from her chair and picked one off the kitchen counter, which she cleaned on the front of her apron. She slammed it down on the table in front of my father, almost squarely on top of the scar left on the table by Jeff. Jeff, mouth full of warm, sugary dough, laughed hysterically and, to keep from choking, drained his milk from his glass.

Jeff swept up another whole bun from the plate in the center of the table and walked away. I didn't see anything funny about it, and neither did my father. My father picked up the knife and sliced firmly through his bun, placing half back on the serving plate.

Always the diplomat, my father said, "Here you are, Mother. That half can be yours."

My mother picked up the half left for her by my father and then another whole bun, which she laid beside the reduced portion on her plate, and she began to eat. It was an act of pure, unredeemable defiance.

"Don't tell Jill I'm feeding you these homemade southern treats while you're visiting."

"Well, today is my last day here so you won't have to fret about my diet any longer. And this is not a visit. I'm here on business."

judy norwood enter

Rachael takes two long sips of her coffee, peering at me over the rim of the cup. "Let's talk about your leaving after the Will is read this morning. You may feel differently about staying for a while."

While my mouth is stuffed with this spicy, sweet goodness, I rudely speak. "Rachael, make no mistake. There is absolutely nothing I will hear from my father this morning that will keep me here."

. . .

When we arrive at my father's law offices, his longtime partner and friend Louis Chandler is waiting. The offices are bustling with running fax machines, copiers, computers, and telephones. There are pretty, little secretaries-turned-servants and paralegals and impressive attorneys in their tailored suits shouting orders as if whether the world will keep spinning on its axis lies completely in their godlike hands. I hate lawyers, and I love every joke I've ever heard at their collective expense. I've even made up a couple of my own. Louis steers us into my father's office. Photographs of our family are hanging on the wood-paneled walls, strung gallery-style. Many of them are from the summers at Pawleys, but some are from my father and mother's life before us. They are standing in front of the bakery in Charleston above which they opened their first law practice together. Their youth and apparent happiness is startling. My mother is tall and beautiful and has dark brunette hair, shimmering brown eyes, and creamy white skin. She is simply but fashionably dressed in what I suppose is attire for a female attorney for what was, in the mid-seventies in Charleston, South Carolina, a man's profession. Other pictures of them, some extraordinary black-and-whites, were taken in the surf, but I don't exactly know where. I can't help emphasizing how startled I am by her sublime beauty. I feel a little embarrassed for admiring my mother's legs, but they are model-perfect, extending graciously from beneath a white bathing suit. She is laughing and seems to be teasing my father, who is reaching for her. I don't think I ever knew the woman in this photo. She bears no resemblance to the woman my mother became.

27

the way home

Louis takes my father's chair behind his desk, and Rachael sits in one of five chairs on the front side facing him. I take an empty chair as far away from her as possible. This configuration around my father's old desk makes me feel like I'm in a class in school I haven't prepared for and would like to skip. Louis wants to make small talk and, of course, talk about my father and his death. He tells us how devastating my father's death has been for him. And I actually offer him my condolences. A heavy air hangs in the room as if to portend the weight of what's to come. Louis tells us we are waiting on Trent and Trudy and Brenda Grace, Jeff's wife. I'm told they are named in the Will.

"Louis, I've booked a flight for late today and need to get back to Asheville. So if we can just move along and get this thing done, I'll be grateful."

"I understand your scheduling difficulties, Bobby, but we must wait on the others. They'll arrive shortly."

If the truth must be told, I'm dreading to encounter more faces from the past. We've exchanged the occasional Christmas cards with Trudy and Trent as well as Brenda Grace, but I haven't seen or spoken to them since Jeff's funeral five years ago. And I have never seen Jeff's son since Brenda Grace was pregnant with the boy when my brother died. As I process this timeline, I realize Jeff's death placed an impregnable seal on this place and these people, preventing their entry into my life. I neither want anything from them nor have anything to give them.

Brenda Grace arrives first, followed by Trent and Trudy. We all remark about how we've aged and exchange curt smiles and handshakes. The women share warm, familiar hugs.

Louis lightly clears his throat. "Let's begin. We are trying to stay within Bobby's schedule, as he has a late afternoon flight."

Trudy, in her best exaggerated southern accent, says, "Well, since our little stray 'brother' has come all this way for his money, I presume, we want to fit into his schedule and not hold him up. After all, coming to Charleston once every five years surely burdens his travel itinerary. And I don't know who's next to die, but that seems

judy norwood enter

to be the only thing that brings him back. But on the bright side, my 'deah' brother, it is good to see you somewhere besides a funeral."

"Ah, Trudy, I see you've inherited your mother's talent for sarcasm," I say.

Her brother, Trent, ever the passive peacemaker, touches her on the knee to silence her, and if looks could kill, mine would be the next funeral they would all attend.

Louis ignores the tension and hands us all a copy of my father's Last Will and Testament in a file folder. He asks us not to read along with him, however, but to allow him to read portions of it aloud. He says it's complicated in parts and we can all take a look at those parts that involve us together but also that much of it is straightforward and simple. We skip the introductory legal jargon and get right to the dispensation—the "meat," as he calls it.

"To Rachael, who is the sole beneficiary of my life insurance and 50 percent owner of stocks and investments held with Bennett & Bennett, I direct the allowance to live in our house at 6003 Waterview Street, Charleston, South Carolina, until such time of her death or at her choosing of another residence. This same house is hereby bequeathed to my son, Robert J. Chapin Jr., under these same conditions. It is my wish and my request that the home remain in the Chapin family at the direction of my son, Robert J. Chapin Jr."

OK, so far, this is just like Rachael says. No surprises there.

"To Louis Chandler, my partner and longtime trusted friend, I leave intact our law practice. All benefits from that practice are directed to him at my death."

Louis stops here and tells us that he and my father took care of the legalities necessary for either of them dying first. I shrug my shoulders and check my watch.

"To the children of my son, Robert J. Chapin Jr., I leave in two trusts the sum of two million dollars to be managed by Louis Chandler of Chapin & Chandler Law Offices. The trusts will be managed and invested separately for Mary Chapin and Elizabeth Chapin, each trust having one million dollars."

I noticeably gasp for air, and Louis reacts.

29

the way home

"Bobby, I will go into the details of these trusts for your children at a later date. It was your father's desire that this might be used for college or the start-up of a business or whatever your children need." Louis says this haltingly as he appears to gauge my mounting reaction.

"Louis, I can take care of my children. Neither I nor my children need my father's money."

"Bobby, no one questions your ability to take care of your family, least of all your father. He raved about you and your accomplishments often. This is a gift and in no way portends your present or future ability to provide for all your family's needs. In this you have no say. It is a trust, and it belongs to your children, not you."

I violently slam the arm of my chair. "Damn! He's controlling my life again when he has no right. I won't have it!"

Louis stands at his desk, smoothing invisible wrinkles from his expensive, custom-tailored suit jacket. Since I last saw him, he has gone completely gray but still has a thick head of hair that seems not to have lost a strand in his advancing age. He looks down at me, still in my chair, from his position standing behind the desk, and he smiles as though he's about to give a convincing closing argument to a jury in a trial he knows he's going to win.

"Robert J. Chapin Jr., you will do well to conduct yourself with a little decorum at the reading of your father's last wishes and directions. In deference to him, gather your good manners as a benefit to us all and listen to his last written words to his family. Can you do that? Because there is more to come that might cause you to call upon every source of good conduct and manners I know your mother taught you as a proper southern boy."

At the mention of my mother, I shrink like a child. "Yes, sir. I'll try to control my temper in order to cause no disgrace to her. I will try, Mr. Chandler. But you and I are going to have to talk later about this."

"My boy, we will talk. Oh, yes, we will talk later." Louis adamantly assures me.

I shift in my seat and adjust the lapels of my navy sports jacket for no good reason. I glance at Rachael to my right beyond Trent,

judy norwood enter

Trudy, and Brenda Grace. Her injected lips are pursed, and she won't look at me. Nor will anyone else.

"To the children of my late son, Jeffrey Hargrave Chapin, I leave the sum of two million dollars to be managed by Louis Chandler of Chapin & Chandler Law Offices. This will be left in trusts that will be managed and invested separately for Sarah Sinclair Chapin and Hargrave Crawford Chapin, each having one million dollars."

Louis pauses and looks at Brenda Grace, who is smiling and slightly nodding her head in agreement. He takes a deep breath, telling us he will continue.

"To my daughter-in-law, Brenda Grace Chapin, there should remain in place an allotment of five hundred thousand dollars, paid in two installments per year. Should Brenda Grace remarry, that amount will be reduced to one hundred thousand dollars annually, with the remaining four hundred thousand dollars held in trust for her should she ever require it in the event of becoming widowed or divorced. Dispensation of the resulting invested funds, should she never be widowed or divorced, is at the discretion of Louis Chandler."

Louis turns the page slowly and glances my way, waiting for any reaction, and then continues. Since Louis preached his sermon to me, I've managed to conjure up a stoic face and refuse to display any discernible response to anything he reads.

"To Trent Crawford, Rachael's son, I bequeath the sum of five hundred thousand dollars. To Trudy Crawford Benedict, Rachael's daughter, I bequeath the sum of five hundred thousand dollars. And I will say this is a token of my love: yours and your children's greatest tangible inheritance will come to you at the proper time from your mother."

My eyes tell me that Trent and Trudy are pleased, and they both extend affectionate, sympathetic smiles toward Rachael.

Louis draws a deep breath and glances at me expectantly.

"To my son, Robert J. Chapin Jr., I bequeath the following: 50 percent ownership in any and all stocks and investments at the time of my death; one sixty-one-foot Viking sports fishing yacht, *Game On*, owned by me at the time of my death; the Jeffrey Chapin Drug

the way home

Rehabilitation Clinic in Charlotte, North Carolina, owned by me at the time of my death; the Jack Crawford Medical Center in Port-au-Prince, Haiti, owned by me at the time of my death; and the Robert J. Chapin Jr. Children's Home in Port-au-Prince, Haiti, owned by me at the time of my death. I also bequeath my lifetime place on the Board of Directors of the Mary Elizabeth Hargrave Treatment Center at the Medical University of South Carolina in Charleston, South Carolina. Lastly, I bequeath the sum of thirty million dollars to be enjoyed at his discretion with faith it will be invested and used for good.

"To Louis Chandler, I bequeath one Cessna airplane, owned by me at the time of my death."

Louis knows the plane now does not exist because it became my father's tomb, and I think he tacks this unrelated, moot information onto the end of the shocking list as a temporary diversion.

"Does anyone have a Tylenol?" I rub my temples with my head down, and since no one answers, I say more loudly, "Does anyone have a damn Tylenol?"

I hear the women grabbing their purses and rifling through their contents. At the same time, Louis is on the intercom with an assistant, asking for water for everyone and a bottle of Tylenol.

I grasp the leather chair's polished arms and use them to stand up. I test my legs as I walk around the room, staring at the pictures on the walls again. An intern rushes into the office with the Tylenol and water. Louis doles out two tablets to me while the others murmur to one another like people do at a viewing of the deceased. Rachael says to Louis, still holding the bottle of pills, "Give me two of those." She throws them into her mouth with a flourish and washes them down with bottled water. I see Louis shake two more pills out of the Tylenol bottle and swallow them without water. Still wandering through the gallery of photos, I come upon one ornately framed picture of Jeff in his cap and gown—his graduation picture from high school. He has an athlete's youthful, ruddy complexion, and it shines too much from the light of camera. His cap is slightly crooked, and he is smiling sadly beneath it. Is Rachael right? Were he and Mother bent on destroying themselves because of some darkness they couldn't or wouldn't fight? If that's true, why didn't the people who love them fight for them? When they were dying, did they know they were taking a part of us with them?

Trent and Trudy give hugs and good-byes to the others. Trudy, petite like her mother, reaches upward and puts both hands on my shoulders. "Sorry I gave you such a hard time, but you always were such a prick. Now you're a rich prick. But I love you anyway, Brother." She winks.

"You are so your mother's daughter."

"Thank you. You just play the cards you're dealt."

Brenda Grace playfully bumps Trudy aside with her hip. "My turn." She embraces me firmly and kisses my cheek. "We miss you, Bobby, all of us. Bring Jill and the girls and come to Charlotte to see us sometime."

I smile. "You look great. How are the kids?"

"They're wonderful! Come to Charlotte and see for yourself."

Rachael hears our conversation and reaches out to hug Brenda Grace tightly like one of her own. Probably because I didn't respond to Brenda Grace's two invitations to visit, she feels the need to fill the void and declare in my presence she is coming to Charlotte this month to see the kids.

As Rachael is finally escorting the richer trio to the door, I call out to Trent to come to the mountains sometime for a little fishing. I say it unthinkingly since I had blown off the others. He shakes his head and replies to me with sad eyes, "I don't fish anymore."

Rachael returns and joins Louis and me, who are now standing awkwardly alone. Louis begins his little oration.

"Bobby, you are a person your father thought very highly of. He admired your guts and your unrelenting pursuit of your dreams. He knew his dreams weren't necessarily yours, but he is asking you to test the waters to see if father and son share any of the same thirst for life. Your father has laid at your feet an enormous challenge. Perhaps as a man and as a father, I understand that even more than Rachael. It is all yours, and you can choose to give it away, both the money as well as the responsibility. But I'm asking you, not as your father's advocate but as yours, to take some time and not make any rash decisions. What you have heard today is unalterable. What you do with it

the way home

is up to you. No one is taking away your right to do with these things what is best for your life."

I am incredulous. A yoke, this Will of my father's, is around my neck. The rage I want to express is repressed, and I understand that it's because the one I want to unload it on is gone. I want to scream and shout obscenities at him—I want to laugh at this contrived joke, but only a fool would laugh at this mess. I should cry at the sad loss of my life, but I'm not sure I can still cry. I'm a weak, empty, helpless shell of a man when words on a piece of paper have more power over me than my own will. How ironic this is called a "Last Will and Testament". My father is usurping my own will to carry out his own. And I still have a raging headache.

Louis continues when I say nothing. "Bobby, the complex part of this Will is your responsibility to these organizations being built as memorials or honorariums to the people your father loved. And that includes executing management over them."

"Wait. 'Being built'? What are you saying, Louis?"

"Well, the new wing at MUSC in your mother's memory is complete and fully staffed. But chairing the board of directors there is ongoing."

"Chairing the board of directors?"

"Yes, your father has a lifetime position, although you can appoint someone else chair and merely serve on the board as a member."

"And what about these…these." I grab my file folder with the Will and wildly rifle through pages where the names of the other agencies appear.

"The Jeff Chapin Drug Rehabilitation Center in Charlotte. The Jack Crawford Medical Treatment Center and the Robert J. Chapin Jr. Children's home in Port-au-Prince, Haiti. Haiti! What in the name of everything reasonable and sane is my father doing in Haiti? It's a third world country!"

I shake off my unanswered question, staring wild-eyed at both Rachael and Louis. "My father is trying to whitewash his life. I won't have any part of it. His alleged benevolence as outlined in this Will is just words on paper. My mother ate and medicated herself to death in that house because he left us emotionally and physically. Jeff drugged himself for most of his life, and it finally killed him. He left a wife and two babies to struggle with the same damn things we struggled with—missing parents. And my father's money can't fill that emptiness. OK, I give him this: that it was and is a decent thing to provide for Jeff's family. But it doesn't change Jeff's death or restore that missing father and husband to his family."

Louis ignores the anger and pain I'm exuding and continues his tactical course to get me back on his track. "Bobby, the medical clinic and the children's home are under construction. Your father suffered some setbacks. Let's just say, and I'll explain completely later, misuse of construction funds as well as thefts on-site held up the projects. He was just getting underway again when…well, he died in a plane crash. These projects are on hold as there has been no dependable leadership on the ground."

"Get this straight, Louis. I am not my father. And he is not a sacred cow because he's dead. His life is still under my scrutiny, and Robert Jr. is not assuming any facet of Robert Sr.'s life. I'll work out the house with Rachael and work with you on the girls' trusts, and I can't even think about what to do with stocks and cash. But his soul-cleansing projects in the names of those he hurt—I'll have nothing to do with."

Rachael is plainly piqued. She looks strong and ready to attack, so I assume her Tylenol is working. "I've never known anyone with as much hatred for their father as you, Bobby. If someone possessed the power to rip it from you, I don't know if there would be enough substance remaining to keep you on your feet. You tell me you have this perfect family in Asheville where nothing sinister can touch them. Well, I don't believe you. No one can bring home that kind of nurtured, cultivated bitterness at night to their family and not damage them eventually. You've made hating your father your primary identity. Do you really think no one in your circle of influence and trust observes, through your sarcasm and bravado, your virulent feelings about your father? That abhorrence for Robert lives deep

35

the way home

within you, and you seem to thrive on it. You've come to love hating your father."

Rachael is jerking up her purse and the file folder containing her copy of the Will while continuing to chastise me. "No one gives you a book on how to raise your children perfectly. Did anybody give you one? Overall, adults are selfish and damaged by their own parents, or else they become victims of an event or circumstance in life they can't control and unwittingly pass on its horrific effects to their children. Some parents are more willing than others to look at the reasons behind their behavior and make some changes. And some are just so damaged they can't make it any better for themselves or their children. All of your life you have kept a mental record of your father's deficits rather than his assets as a man. How well did you really know him? Do you know anything about what shaped the young boy he used to be? Or what broke his heart as a man and a husband and a father? What about his successes as an adult? The people he helped in his life? Are you willing to risk knowing both his friends and his enemies? If you bail on this, I think you're a coward. Afraid to face your own demons, you would rather entertain your father's."

"Damn it, Rachael! You should have been a therapist. Who gave you the right to tell me how to live my life? Get off my back. I'm not a boy any longer who you can manipulate. I'm not doing this, you know. It's my choice, and I've made my decision - I'm not assuming any part of my father's life."

She makes no rebuttal to me. "Louis, he is like my son, and I apologize for his behavior in your presence today—for both of us. Call me, and we'll meet again."

"I am not your son."

In the doorway, Louis kisses her lightly on the cheek, and as an afterthought, she turns toward me again.

"Oh, and one more thing. For all our sakes, find your sense of humor. You used to possess one."

Her pungent words hang in the air. I still have a sense of humor. I'd like to find it right about now. Louis drops into a nearby chair, looking sad and still clutching his file folder while also holding the original copy of the Will. He appears way older than an hour prior.

36

judy norwood enter

"Bobby, you and I will need time together, lots of time, to hammer this out. When can you return?"

"I don't know."

• • •

My flight is delayed, and I sit at the bar near my gate. Flying here from my home office in Chicago made sense, but Charleston to Asheville doesn't. I could drive to Asheville faster than this. Louis offered to charter a flight for me, using my new money of course, but I stubbornly refused. The closed file folder labeled "Robert J. Chapin Sr. Last Will and Testament" is lying on the polished bar in front of me. I have been shadowboxing with my father for years in life, and now he has produced a very real target for fighting him in his death.

four

The girls are in bed when I arrive. Jill is wearing my favorite pajamas and is curled up on the sofa grading papers. A remnant of a fire she has built is smoldering in the fireplace. The mountains are still cool at night in early April.

I flash a tired smile and an air kiss across the room, toss my sports coat in the chair, and take my carry-on into the bedroom. I go to the girls' rooms and tuck their covers in tighter and kiss each of them on the cheek.

"I love you."

Each of them rouses slightly and smiles sleepily. "Love you, too, Daddy." And Elizabeth asks if I have to leave again soon. I tell her no to comfort her, but I know it's not true.

I go back into the family room and kiss Jill on the forehead. "How was your day?"

She wrinkles her brow and lays down her red pen. "Better than yours."

I want a drink, but I had two in the airport. "And how do you know this?"

"Well, it's etched into your face in tired frown lines and the downward curve of what should be a smile. And Rachael called."

"Damn it! Why is she calling you?"

"Because she's my friend and your stepmother, and she's concerned about you. Rachael and I talk once in a while. Just to check

the way home

up, you know. She keeps up with the girls. I've told you this before, but you chose to ignore it. We're family, right?"

I decide for that third drink. "I should have known. You women stick together and are too fragile to choose sides. I'm too tired to argue about this mess with you tonight. I was blindsided by my father one last time, and I don't want to talk about it."

"Why? Because he provided an immeasurable gift for our girls? And you became a multimillionaire? I'll bet every person living would wish this was their worst day."

"What are you saying? That I'm ungrateful?"

"I don't know what you are. And choosing sides in a family spells war. It's destructive. You're my husband and my allegiance is always with you. But my love is for all our family. You already know this."

Jill crosses the room and gives me a tenuous hug. "Thank you. I needed that."

"You're going to have to return to Charleston, aren't you?"

"Yes. Eventually. What am I saying? I'll have to return immediately to confer with Louis over the assets and these agencies."

"Looks like it has taken your father's death to get you back to Charleston." Jill moves around the room, picks up the girls' strewn toys, and stows them in a toy box I built, painted, and stenciled with Dora the Explorer cartoon characters.

"Yep. He always wins, doesn't he?"

"That's an awful thing to say. Your father died so he could win? Win what? What's wrong with you?"

"What's wrong with me? You tell me. That's what you really want to do - tell me how to feel and how to react and basically fix what's wrong with Bobby."

Jill is familiar with this stage, exhales, and concedes. "You're right. You're tired and we can talk tomorrow."

"I want to talk about it now. It pisses me off that you and Rachael have been talking behind my back. Did my father know you two were conspirators?"

"This conspirator theory of yours is ridiculous. And venting at me because you're angry with your father and Rachael is not constructive. You've managed to tamp down that temper of yours mostly, but it simmers just below the surface. I'm not wise enough to know if your father's death will put to rest what boils inside you or if it will exacerbate your feelings about him. And speaking of feelings it's just not normal for a son not to grieve his father's death. Robert died a horrific death along with his brother and these last nine months you wouldn't talk about it. And still tonight after the reality of the Will, there seems to be no grief, only anger."

"Are you finished?"

"Yes, I believe I am. Spring break is next week, and I'm taking the girls to my parents in Savannah. I need some time at the coast near tides and white sand and beach umbrellas. I'm not abandoning you. Call it a time out. I'll come back when school reconvenes.

The phone rings and Jill picks up. "Hey, Rachael. Yes, he made it home safely. Well, he's understandably tired and a little rattled."

"Stop talking about me like I'm not in the room."

"Here, Rachael, talk to the old bear yourself."

Jill thrusts the phone in my direction. "Rachael, it's too late for phone calls. I'm tired and I don't want to talk to you about anything tonight. Good-night."

Jill says, "That was rude."

"Good, I meant to be rude."

"I don't like this side of you. If you could be this detached and mean-spirited to our family, you could behave that way toward us one day."

"I would never hurt you or the girls. And besides Rachael is not real family."

"This estrangement from your family does hurt us. It follows you into all your relationships. We've built a pretty good home together, but I don't have all of you nor do the girls. You and I have begun to just go through the motions, and we don't connect on a deep level. This 'perfect' family you've tried to construct is for you, not for us. Life is about recognizing one another's frailties and weaknesses, as well as loving and forgiving and building relationships that survive the hard times. And, Bobby, we never laugh anymore."

"I laugh, damn it. I still have a sense of humor."

the way home

"You'll feel better after a good night's rest. Let's go to bed. We'll talk tomorrow morning."

"I smell like the stale air in an airplane and need a shower, but I'm too exhausted to take one. I'll just sleep on the couch."

I retrieve my pillow and blanket from the closet, kick off my shoes, and sink into the couch fully clothed. Jill stands in the doorway leading to our bedroom and turns off the light. She lingers in the dark and I can see her in silhouette. "Good-night, Bobby. I love you."

five

Before I return to Charleston, I announce my conditions to Louis. I will not meet in my father's old office. I will not stay with Rachael. I will give him two weeks before I have to return to my job and my home in Asheville.

"Bobby, Bobby! Thank you for returning. I hope Jill and the girls are well and they will forgive you this little absence. How is your room at the Vendue Inn? You know Rachael would be happy to let you to use the carriage house. Actually, she is already packing up her personal things from Waterview for her move. You wouldn't be in the way."

"Really? Where is she moving?"

Louis, who has now become the Sword of Damocles in my life, says, "She has purchased the old beach house in Pawleys Island and is going to live there permanently. She actually rented it last November and has been dividing her time between it and the house on Waterview. Now that the estate is settled, she used a portion of the money to buy it. Says she loves that big, old, rambling beach house."

"Our old beach house? I mean, the one we used to rent every summer?"

"Yes, I think that's the one. Says Charleston was never her style and that she's a beach girl. Says she was happiest there and wants to live out her remaining years there."

the way home

Louis excuses himself to go for files we'll need on this first day of work together. My father's old office is just down the hall. I'm thinking of the photographs on his wall and wonder if they've been removed to ready the office for new staff.

I smile and greet staffers in the hall, gracefully accepting some condolences. His office is just as we left it a week ago when I sat here to hear the Will read. I peruse the walls and wonder at the pictures, many of which I've never seen. In all of my years at home, I never saw my parents' wedding photos. Mother is elegant, and Father is trim and handsome. It's a Charleston socialites' wedding, and in the background an orchestra can be seen playing alongside a many-tiered wedding cake. If my father was uncomfortable with the high-society wedding, he hid it well. He's laughing and has both his arms wrapped around my mother's tiny waist.

Several photographs in a collage seem to have been taken on either the beach or the creek on Pawleys Island. Jeff, Trent, and I are sitting in the Jon boat in one, fishing rods and nets in hand. In another Jeff is holding up a big flounder he has gigged in the creek at dark, while someone shines a light on it. Adults and children alike are tanned and laughing, and some of us are stuffing our faces with cotton candy and corn dogs on a stick. This was probably up in Myrtle Beach on a Pavilion outing.

In another photograph Rachael and Jack are holding hands and standing in front of their restaurant, the Shrimp Boat. It seems unimaginable that these four friends enjoyed a life before they had children. They are fresh-faced and with a kind of recklessness about them, so young and free of responsibility.

"Bobby, I can have your father's things boxed up for you while you're here." Louis is standing in the door with his arms full of files.

"The photographs, Louis, if you could have them packed up and delivered to Rachael's house in a box marked 'The Attic,' I would appreciate it."

"You mean your house on Waterview?"

"Yes, I guess so…my house."

Back in Louis's office, we begin the prodigious work my father has thrown over me like a heavy saddle on a tired horse. The enormity of it overwhelms me, and regardless of my decision about how involved in it I want to be, I can see right now this is going to be a marathon, not a sprint.

"Louis, I want to deal with these clinics first. How did my father wind up in Haiti? I thought the Bahamas was more his style."

"Your father's connection to Haiti began with the Bahamas, actually. Phillipe, the groundskeeper at the marina where he keeps his boat, is Haitian. I met Phillipe when your father invited me for a fishing trip in the Bahamas. He's an interesting and industrious fellow. Told me he had been living in Abaco in the Bahamas about twenty-five years but still wants to return to his homeland. He has a couple of kids in Haiti he supports and a family in Abaco. Turns out there's a large contingent of Haitians who have fled their country living in Marsh Harbour on Great Abaco Island. Immigrants heading to the Bahamas for work still risk their lives on small, overcrowded boats leaving Haiti and crossing hundreds of miles of ocean. Phillipe took your father to the 'Mud,' one of their squatter developments. Robert was aghast that people were living in squalor on an island in the northern Bahamas that attracts so much money in second homes and yachts from the United States and Europe. It set him to thinking why these people risk so much to come live in a slum so far from home. You would have to talk to Phillipe to get the whole story. I just know that, for your father, it became an obsession to know about these displaced people and why they ran so hard to an unfriendly land to have seemingly no more than they had in Haiti. Your father was sort of a global thinker, so he got it in his head to go to Haiti and see what they were fleeing."

Louis opens a file, but before we begin, I remind him I'm only here for information. I'm making no commitments and will more than likely ask him to help me dispose of all of this.

Louis, referring to my father's information, tells me that the Jack Crawford Medical Treatment Clinic is wholly funded by my father's investments. The clinic is currently under construction but having a myriad of problems. Government interference, a shortage of doctors and medical staff, endangerment of staff, building materials being stolen, and lack of approval for shipment of AIDS medications

the way home

as well as meds for malaria and tuberculosis are just a few of the obstacles. Interruption by theft of shipments of pharmaceuticals is a continuous stumbling block to medical treatment centers such as the one he's building. The only thing I really hear is 'endangerment of staff.'

It seems like there's an abyss of regulations and a departure from any norm I've developed for coping with the pharmaceutical business. The purchase and shipment of prescription drugs within the United States is highly regulated and international shipments are complicated. "Louis, the sale and movement of pharmaceuticals is my game. But international shipments are steeped in a whole different world of regulations. And shipments to a third world country—you're just asking for trouble."

"Well, in all the decades I've known your father, I never knew him to undertake anything easy. We started late today on these things, Bobby. Think about what we've talked about thus far, and we'll start again tomorrow. And talk to Rachael about these interests of your father's. She knows his heart more than I do. She traveled to Haiti with him and fell in love with the people and the work your father was doing. I know where the investments are and how they're managed, but she can be a wealth of personal information. Please talk to Rachael."

six

"Rachael, if you can hear this, pick up. I would like to use the carriage house after all. The bed in this hotel is breaking my back. I'm already on my way." Of course, the beds at the exclusive Vendue Inn in Charleston are expensive and therapeutic; I just need an excuse to return to the carriage house to be near Rachael and get some answers.

After parking my car away from some blooming trees that I recall tend to drop a sticky sap, I carry my meager belongings onto the portico at the front door near sundown. No lights are showing in the big house. I ring the bell three times. Remembering the hide-a-key location of years past, I go to the second azalea bush to the right of the steps and scratch the ground toward the base of the shrub. I locate the crusted fake rock that holds the key. The old key turns in the lock with a rusty click.

"Rachael, are you here? It's me, Bobby."

The foyer is dark, but through the center hallway with its two-story windows is a stunning panoramic view of the harbor and the lights of Fort Sumter. I walk to the kitchen and spot a note.

"Bobby, I've gone to Pawleys to close the sale on the beach house. I'm so excited! I'll return to Charleston Friday. Meanwhile, make yourself at home—oh, I forgot it is your home. ☺ Love you and so glad you're back! Love, Rachael."

the way home

Typical Rachael. She just assumed I would come here like a trained monkey. I grab a beer from her refrigerator and take a long pull on it and then discard my shoes in the shoe basket. In the stillness and quiet, the old house still snaps and pops with aging wood. It is a familiar, almost comforting sound as I stroll through the rooms in my bare feet. Rachael has changed little of the décor, and remnants of my mother's exquisite style still occupy some of the rooms. But in the garden room, the style is purely Rachael's and my father's. Chintz covers the cushions on my grandmother's white wicker sofa and chairs and cushions. The valences over the windows are covered in a complementary flamboyant fabric—pure Rachael. Beyond the garden room is the side portico with its nightly showing of the harbor and its scores of little Sunfish, the sailing club's racing boats.

The light over the harbor is beginning to fade, and I trudge up the stairs to a guest room. I stop in front of the bedroom my father and mother sometimes shared to open the door. Nothing much has changed. The wallpaper, paint, comforter, and drapes are still the same. After all these years, why would Rachael not redecorate this? As I leave the haunted room, I feel as if I'm opening a door on the past rather than closing it.

In the first of the two guest rooms, I see Rachael's touch. Sky blues and yellows in chintz, not unlike in the garden room, cover the bed and windows. The heart pine flooring still reflects a warm glow from the setting sun on the room. And Rachael has perfectly captured the natural light; the color of nature is reflected in everything in the room. This room appears comfortable and lived in. I open one of the two closets and see my father's wardrobe. His suits, shirts, and shoes occupy a large walk-in closet with a dressing bench and mirror. A poem called "Anyway" is taped to the mirror. I'm curious and read it. It is about forgiving, being kind, succeeding, being honest, happy, and doing good. I imagine that my father stood in front of this mirror getting dressed in the mornings and read this poem. I've never known my father to read poetry, and this poem seems out of character for him.

I open the second closet, and Rachael's clothes and shoes fill the large space more like they would a small department store than

judy norwood enter

a normal clothes closet. She seems to have moved little in this room since his death, and I assume it is as it was when she and my father lived here. This guest room, which I seldom ventured into as a child, seems to have been my father's bedroom with Rachael.

As I turn to leave, my eyes fall on the wall near the door. There hangs on either side an array of recent family photos of Trent and Trudy and their families as well as Brenda Grace and her children. And there's a photo of Jill, the girls, and I at a company picnic on Lake Michigan taken just last year. Jill and Rachael really were collaborating behind my back, I think, shaking my head.

Closing the door behind me, I decide to go to the attic. My small overnight bag in tow, I crawl up the stairs and enter the room, crossing it in the dark from memory to turn on the lamp beside our bunk beds. I've seldom seen anything more welcoming. I shuck down to my drawers and climb in the bottom bed, drawing the blanket up to my chin. Never having felt so alone or so much like a child in a long time, I drift into a troubled sleep.

seven

Louis calls early and wakes me to say he's delaying our meeting until after lunch. I call Jill and ask to speak to the girls. Jill has installed rules of engagement, and when I call she doesn't want to talk about us but immediately puts the girls on the phone. They think they're on vacation at grandma's house and tell me about going to the petting zoo and making peanut butter cookies. My girls weren't born when my mother died and will never know her as their grandmother. We throw kisses into the phone, and they're gone.

I have the morning to kill and am reluctant to poke around the house, but I wander back upstairs from the kitchen with a second cup of strong coffee. Rachael has put some cinnamon buns in the freezer, and I microwave two of them, trying to forgive myself the indulgence.

Out of curiosity I enter the second guest room on the pretext of discovering if Rachael has redecorated it. It's undisturbed but clean, some of the fabrics my mother chose a little sun-faded and dated. It's a mausoleum and seemingly hasn't seen guests in recent years.

To compound my snooping, I go to my old room on the same second floor, across the hall from Jeff's. It's been renovated into a study or office, but it's not my father's. His study is on the first floor. The room is slightly feminine and decorated with my mother's discriminating taste. An entire wall has been outfitted floor to ceiling with built-in bookcases. And they're filled with my mother's old

the way home

law books, books on religion, gardening books, sailing books, some works of fiction I don't recognize, and books on psychology and depression. They're methodically, obsessively organized, clearly the work of my mother, with each book cataloged according to subject and size and soldiered with the same indentation from the edge of the shelf. Perfectly positioned on the shelves of books are some beautiful, delicate pieces of pottery, some local seagrass baskets woven expertly by the hands of the Gullah Geechee women, and of course the indigenous snapshots that chronicle our lives. Some of the photographs are duplicates of the ones I saw in my father's office. Others I've never seen, but all are of the two families at some location or another. One very prominent photo is of my mother and father on the deck of a cruise ship many years ago.

At the very bottom of the shelf, near the large window behind her desk, are leather-bound books with no titles on their binders. Their appearance is worn from use and their covers faded by years of sunlight streaming through the window. These books are identifiable only by dates, and I'd often seen them in my mother's hands.

For now I sit at her desk and open first one drawer and then another. I find ordinary things like pencils and pens, notepads, and paper clips. One file drawer contains old bank records organized in three-ring binders. I run my fingers over some of these things and wonder if she was the last one to touch them so many years ago. A wayward son's guilt washes over me for having abandoned her in her last years. My God, I'm no better than my father. Her behavior grew more detached and darker in her last years. And her obesity was more shocking each time I came for a visit. The shameful truth is that I became embarrassed at her and for her. I tried to reason with her and begged her to see a doctor about her weight and the seemingly dark moods. I don't know which came first, the depression or the obesity. They seemed to compound each other. But she would only smile sadly and want to talk about the past, not the present. Eventually, my visits grew further and further apart.

There's a closet, the one where I used to stuff my boyhood belongings, and I find one lone coat in it. It's musty, nothing like how I remember she used to smell, and large and lightweight; it looks like

judy norwood enter

it might double as a raincoat. I have no recollection of seeing her in it. I search the pockets and draw, curiously, a written note out of one.

"Rachael, here is the list of groceries. Put them on the side porch, and I'll retrieve them. Leave me a receipt, and I'll mail you a check. I don't feel like company today."

Below is a long list of food, mostly sweets and high in fat and carbohydrates. I rub the writing with my thumb. If the list is in her pocket, Rachael never got it. Was it the last list she wrote for Rachael?

I turn back to the bookshelves and pull out a few sailing books to skim through. She had been an accomplished competitive sailor and had the good fortune of having long arms, a strong back, and the body of a mermaid. She and my father were members of the sailing club, and when we were young children, they would participate in some of the races. Many of the old photos, though, have only him with other racing team members, and so they must have been taken after she stopped sailing. I remember her as an avid reader. Even after she stopped practicing law with my father, she subscribed to periodicals and kept up with cases. I remember some conversations between them at the dinner table. They were friendly adversaries, then, debating points of law.

"Robert, please pass the mashed potatoes to Jeff. I heard today that the ADA is going for the death penalty in your case."

"Bullshit. Pure bullshit. I've already drafted a motion for the judge to dismiss. The prosecution has a ton of circumstantial but no hard evidence. The judge will dismiss, in my opinion. The prosecution is just sword-rattling, trying to scare us."

"Language, please. But, Robert, remember the case we tried together—the Mercers from Savannah? The husband and wife team whose crimes and lack of hard evidence parallel your client's. We lost because the jury was convinced, even in the light of only circumstantial evidence, they were guilty beyond a reasonable doubt."

"Not even remotely the same, Mother. Pass me some more of that pot roast."

I stand looking out the window, not wanting to indiscriminately plunder through anything personal, and inherently I know these dated leather-bound books are her most intimate thoughts. As

the way home

a teenager I would come into the kitchen for food and find her writing in one of these. She would close the book, put down her pen, and ask what I wanted to eat.

"Let me fix it for you. It's one of my greatest joys, cooking for you boys."

Threatening clouds have moved in over the harbor, and the room is darkening even at this morning hour. I switch on the lamp and pull a bound book from the early eighties off the bottom shelf. I lay it on her desk and rub it thoughtfully with my hand. I feel almost too invasive reading her scrawl on the grocery list and now in the journal. We all know that the truth is we don't want to know everything about our parents. There are things too unspeakable—too dark and absent—and too many secrets that we prefer stay hidden. The fact of growing up with these parents we did not choose and concocting our assumptions about them based on our childhood fantasies is easier than knowing the truth. Denial can be a comfortable place to live, but ultimately you're going to get evicted. I open the worn journal at a random page and read.

"January 15, 1983.

Bobby and Jeffrey have become the center of my life! At these tender ages of five and three, they are so full of naïveté and pureness and promise. They're fresh and unmarked by the regrettable humanness of adults. Coming from heaven, they have been with God more than with the scarred adults who care for them. I want to keep them that way, but I must live with the reality that I, among many offenders, will become their worst. The deplorable condition of their mother's mind and heart will, in their futures, mar their manhood, and I'm helpless to stop it. It's like I'm two people, one high and excited and able to juggle life with dexterity and the other dark and depressed and unable to function. I intentionally fill this house I love with color even though the sight of it repulses me at times. Keep the light and color and excitement for life before the boys. Maybe I can get away with hiding the darkness. Robert has said he will help me. I love him so for this."

"January 31, 1983.

judy norwood enter

When I was in law school, one of the greatest things I loved was the exactness of the law. It possesses no prejudice. There are precedents, order of law, the tried and tested law books, and the generations of law evolving but adhering to the same standards of moral and ethical conduct. I balanced my crazed self against this given order of things and fell in love with the law. It tells you how to conduct yourself, and if you don't, there are courtrooms to correct you. But I despise the jury. No admonishment or instructions by a judge could erase their prejudices. Twelve men and women usurp the authority of law and decide the fate of a man or a woman based on opinion. Order and rules are needed. Even judges are prejudiced and threaten to circumvent established law in the name of judgeship."

I restore the journal to its shelf, and my eyes fall on a photo of Uncle Jack in his Halloween costume of a giant, pink shrimp with feet, his head sticking out of the homemade suit and laughing.

Uncle Jack was fun. He played with us kids as though he were still a kid himself. My father was this larger-than-life, barrel-chested guy who could throw a football, teach us how to catch a fish, admonish us as to the ways of business, and seemingly know or at least think he knows every answer to all the questions of the universe. But he was no fun in the way of a child. I used to think my father must have been born an adult. Uncle Jack was short and slender, the very opposite of my father in every way. He could fry up a flounder on the bank of the creek we gigged him from and make an art form of it. He did everything with flourish. He was never a confidant for Jeff and I like Rachael was, and Trent would complain about him as every son complains about his father. But I must say again that Uncle Jack was fun.

He was the one who would rig the house in Myrtle Beach with all sorts of Halloween paraphernalia. I can't ever remember a Halloween spent in Charleston because you couldn't beat what Uncle Jack would do. My parents always drove us up for those special nights. Mother, Father, and Rachael would stay behind to pass out candy, but Uncle Jack, dressed in full costume, would accompany us to the neighborhoods to trick-or-treat for candy. Afterward, when

the way home

Trent, Trudy, Jeff, and I would sit on the floor comparing our hauls, he would always declare his was the largest.

A few years prior to my father's leaving us, Jack died in the boating accident. He and Trent took the Grady-White out near the entrance to Murrells Inlet north of Pawleys Island, like they'd done a hundred times. It was late autumn, and the temperatures and water were beginning to cool. When Trent and Uncle Jack navigated the boat into the inlet, the water piling up from the east on the outgoing tide produced a steep wave that broadsided the boat. They capsized in an instant. Jack had worn his fishing waders for the first time that season. As soon as the boat capsized, Trent was able to crawl onto the bottom of the overturned boat. He grabbed a gig that had fallen out when the boat rolled over, and held it out for his dad. But the weight of the water filling Uncle Jack's waders dragged him down. Trent clung to the bottom of the upturned boat for almost ten hours drifting with the outgoing tide, then slowly floated back in toward the inlet when the tide returned. The crew of a fishing boat coming out of the inlet spotted him just before he was ready to give up.

Jack's death seemed to be the first seismic shift in the quartet's relationship. Their perceived endurance had only been an illusion, and death could come at any moment and rob them. And it did. Jack's corpse was found three days later; he was still in his waders, sprawled on a bed of oysters near the mouth of the inlet. We had felt we were immortal teenagers, but death had reached out its cold, palpable hand and touched us. Trudy and Trent were inconsolable. We were unprepared and bereft of any explanation, and the adults were in even sorrier condition than we children.

Rachael poured herself into Trudy and Trent and eventually lost the restaurant in Myrtle Beach. She moved her fatherless family to Mt. Pleasant just across the bridge north of Charleston and went to work in a restaurant on Shem Creek as a waitress. She seemed a woman of great strength, but looking back now, much of it was clearly bravado for Trudy's and Trent's sakes. I've always suspected my father and mother aided her financially, but after my father left just short of two years later, I really didn't think about Rachael at all. The dependability of our families, which had started to shudder with Jack's death, began its final collapse.

My eyes move from the photograph of Jack and my mind from his memory to the clock on Mother's wall. I call Louis's office to see if we're on target for our meeting. We are, so I cut off the lamp in the shrouded room. One of Charleston's many churches is pealing its bells, announcing the noon hour.

eight

I'm impatiently sitting in Louis's office when he comes in and apologizes for being late.

"Bobby, I'm so sorry. Since your father died, we just can't keep up with all the work. Soon, I'll have to hire another attorney, and I'm sort of dreading that process."

"Louis, I'm sorry about your problem here at the office, but do you know my life has been turned upside down and that I don't want to be here?"

"Oh my, are we back there again? Bobby, there is so much we can get done even on a late start. Will you lay your opposition aside for now and let's deal with the children's home?"

"Louis, you said you were my advocate. Tell me about this man, my father, who uncharacteristically ventured into third world countries and gave his fortune away. He sounds like a stranger given to some very bizarre behavior to me. Who had he become?"

"Bobby, I'm working for not only your father but also you. I will do almost anything to educate you about your father's holdings, to facilitate your responsibility to his Will, and to answer your questions. But my role, actual and implied, is explaining the facets of his Will and his financial holdings; any personal observations of mine are subjective and have no place here. Your father and I were fantastic law partners, but we never tipped a glass after work, if you know what I mean. You can chalk it up to that old-school, southern male

the way home

character. Never let your peers know who you really are. Rachael was closest to him these last years. Talk to her."

"I don't want to talk to Rachael."

"Well, if you want answers, please consider that of the four people who could answer your personal questions about your father's character, only one of them is alive. Talk to Rachael."

I allow that to sink in, letting Louis off the hook. We pore over the children's home data, and I ask Louis if we can change the name so that it's not an honorarium to me but a memorial to my father. No, he says, my father would not have his name outwardly on anything. "Who are the children in Haiti for this home?" I ask.

"Many of them are street children that have been orphaned or just cast off by their parents because they can't afford to feed them. Rachael and your father had a big heart for them."

"An orphanage doesn't seem like the best option to me. International adoption is very popular right now. What are the chances of these children being adopted internationally or locally?"

"I don't know the answer, Bobby. I only know that the children's home is nearing completion and it seems the immediate answer to getting some of these kids off the street. That's what your father told me."

"How near completion is the construction of the building?"

"I don't know that either. You need to make an inspection for yourself. I think that eyeball-to-eyeball is the best way for you to decide what to do with the home. Your father's friend and boots-on-the-ground there is a man named Nicholas Trudeau. Your father trusted him, so I believe you can, too. I'll contact him after we've booked your flight and have him meet you at the airport. Your father told me you do some international travel with the pharmaceutical company you work for. You have your passport with you and your vaccinations up-to-date?"

"I have my passport, but I don't sell pharmaceuticals in third world countries. So I probably don't have the recommended vaccinations. And how did my father know about my travel?"

"Ask Rachael, Bobby. Ask Rachael."

...

I return to Rachael's house and call Jill. "I'm flying to Haiti tomorrow. Louis is arranging for me to visit the children's home as well as this medical clinic being built as a memorial to Jack. According to Louis there are some problems, and I should investigate on my own. There's a man by the name of Nicholas Trudeau there who will act as my guide and emissary. He worked with my father. I'm still adamant that I want nothing to do with the operation of any of these ventures. So Louis says he'll help me dispense the operations to a management company. And since I have no other place to be, I guess I'll go."

"I've seen on the news that Port-au-Prince can be dangerous. The UN soldiers maintain a heavily armed presence and patrol the streets. Please be careful."

"I didn't know you cared."

"Don't be sarcastic. Of course I care."

I speak with the girls, and they're giddy. They went to Six Flags Over Georgia and had pizza and a movie night. They have no worries and are in a grandchild's utopia.

nine

My connection takes me from Charleston through Charlotte to the Turks and Caicos. It's an overnight stay here, and I'm intoxicated by the crystal clear, aquamarine water. Jill and I traveled to some of the Caribbean islands on a cruise once, but I had forgotten the blinding sight of the sun on this shimmering, clear water. From my window seat at low altitude, I have a perfect panoramic view of the white sand and reefs just offshore. Provo might be the perfect place for a second honeymoon to smooth things over with Jill and convince her she'll have a better future with the new and improved Bobby. My hotel near the airport is plain vanilla, but the meal I indulge in at a waterside grill rivals any I've ever eaten. Conch fritters as an appetizer and fresh grouper that was probably swimming on the reef this morning was lightly seasoned and couched on a bed of steamed spinach. Homemade mango chutney tops the fish delicately and adds a little sweet and sour to the dish. Being a salesman and saddled by the necessary travel, I am accustomed to eating out alone. But here, tonight, in this place with its romantic vibe, I ache for Jill to be sitting across from me sharing this meal. Eating alone is sustenance; enjoying a superb meal and excellent wine on a small island set in turquoise waters with someone you love is a marvelous gift.

My flight into Port-au-Prince early the next morning is a short one, but the economic and geographic differences are a startling

the way home

contrast to the posh hotels, abundant restaurants, and tourist attractions of Provo. Even the water in the harbor is darker. As Jill warned, there are UN soldiers and guards manning the airport with guns, and I find the sight unsettling. Beggars, hawkers, and young children looking to pick pockets and crying for "one dollar" permeate the airport. The cacophony of shouts and haggling, the pushing and shoving, and the smells of filth are unconscionable. My emissary, Nicholas, whom Louis has arranged for, sees me right away. He is a short, thin man whose age is undeterminable. His face is deeply lined and very black and his mouth marked by a full set of yellow teeth he frequently flashes in a smile. As he accompanies me through Customs and Immigration, smiling and speaking the native Kreyol to the attendants, he instructs me to say nothing. Stepping outside the airport and into his waiting dilapidated bus, he remarks, "Mesye Chapin, I would know you anywhere. You look just like you father."

I look nothing like my father.

Two scruffy, stoic young men are waiting for us in the rusting bus, and they appear vigilant, their eyes roving the streets from either side of the bus. They say or do nothing to greet me, and as we navigate through the city, Nicholas talks to them only in their native Kreyol. Nicholas says to me they haven't had breakfast and stops the bus alongside a bustling open-air market. The three men quickly vacate the bus. I continue to sit.

Nicholas motions me from outside my window that it's all right to go with them. "Let us get food in our bellies. Come now. Much to choose from."

Now, I haven't believed myself to be cowardly, but that conviction has never really been tested. I haven't served in the military, so I haven't been in combat. And neither I nor anyone I love has ever been the victim of a crime. So I've never had to defend myself or my family against any violence. For the first time in my life, I am keenly aware that I may be unsafe and feel menaced by my inscrutable surroundings. The three men form a sort of triangle around me, with Nicholas in the lead. The uncommunicative, nameless men walk on each side of me, a little to my back. I'm wondering if they carry guns or would fight our way out if we're attacked by their own people, because a blind man could see that I am the sole white man in this sea of native Haitians.

I'm uncomfortable with these taciturn guards and ask Nicholas their names, primarily in case I need to call for help from one of them. "They don't want to talk to you, so names not important."

"Why don't they want to talk to me?"

Nicholas shrugs his bony shoulders and offers an explanation. "They don't like you."

"Great," I whisper. I don't know what to be more afraid of: the guards or whatever they're guarding me from. My doubts about my decision to come here continue to be confirmed. In this open-air market, the overwhelming putrid smell sets off my gag reflex, and I have to suppress vomiting. Raw sewage and garbage are being shoveled into a wheelbarrow by a man in rolled-up pants and with bare feet. I pull a few wadded-up tissues from my pocket and cover my mouth and nose. We continue to move through the long, narrow aisle of the market where wares of every kind are for sale. Open rice bags and beans as well as food being cooked on open fires are along the crowded path of the market. I watch as a large rat boldly scurries across my path into an open building with rice bags stacked to the ceiling. The men choose a bowl of rice and beans with a lightly fried egg plopped on top; they offer me some, but I see all this being cooked alongside the sewage and the rats in the unbearable heat and I decline. Nicholas buys a bottle of water for me, as I've exchanged no US currency for the Haitian money. It's not even noon, and the sun is scorching everything like the August sun during a heat wave in Charleston, the only difference being the smells cooked by the heat of the sun. The worst Charleston can smell in a heat wave is the diapered horse manure of the carriage horses touring Yankees around our history. But here in this beleaguered and bedraggled city, the nose is assaulted with the ubiquitous smells of human waste and need.

I'm elated when we board the ragged bus again for our hotel, the Hôtel Montana, where I'm told plumbing and electricity, comfortable rooms, American food, air conditioning, and even a bar are available. That evening we eat meat pastries—light on meat but

the way home

heavy on bread—and have a couple of beers together. I have been cautioned by Louis not to drink the water. In fact, the last thing Louis said to me at the airport was, "Remember, the water for Americans is inconsumable." It seems my father brought a colony of intestinal parasites back to the States from Haiti on one occasion, and Louis told me of his painful, protracted occupation of the restroom that could be heard in the hallowed halls of the elite law offices through the locked door. Louis swears he heard my father screaming for God to "just take me now!"

That evening Nicholas confirms the warning. "Haitians used to water…you Americans not. Give you parasites in your bowels. Last a long time. Much pain unless you take medicine." Also concerning me are the mosquitoes. I have no malaria pills but have brought mosquito repellant with DEET. So I bathe my body in this poison every morning and evening and swat away every living thing flying in close proximity to me. We have mosquitoes in the Low Country of South Carolina that after a warm winter and wet spring can be as large as small birds in the summer, but they bring only aggravating welts and don't carry the threat of disease and death.

The next morning, Nicholas picks me up at the hotel. "You sleep good in fancy hotel, huh? Americans like this place. Today, I take you to children's home on outskirts of town. Get in."

We board the same ragtag bus where the two men who don't like me are already onboard, appearing as stolid as the day before. This morning I am surprised and relieved to see four chattering Haitian women sitting at the back, and Nicholas explains he's just giving them a ride. Their dress is colorful and their heads bound in turbans on which they carry their goods like beasts of burden. I've observed that women like them ply these dusty roads on foot or by emaciated mules with their meager goods. Again, my companions stop for breakfast at a small grocery store, seemingly in a better part of town, on a filthy harbor with half-sunken boats. I slip off the bus behind them and find Diet Coke in the tiny convenience-style grocery. If there is one drink I love better than beer, it is Diet Coke. There are five cold Diet Cokes here, and I buy them all. I miss carbonation already, so I figure if I can hoard these five Cokes for the few days I

judy norwood enter

have left in this wilderness, I'll drink them warm if I have to. Returning to the bus, I happily pop the top on one of the Cokes and let almost half slide down my parched throat. I notice one of the women motioning to my Coke and then to the store. Nicholas has climbed back into the driver's seat of the bus eating another meat pastry. I asked him what the woman is saying.

"She say she want a Coke. Would you get her one from store? She probably have no money for it."

Knowing that I single-handedly cleaned out the inventory of Diet Cokes, I hesitate and then take one of my discovered treasures out of the brown bag and pass it to her. She smiles and bows her head to me. This small gift excites the women, and they smile and motion toward me. The first woman is sharing sips of Diet Coke with a woman seated beside her. So I take another can from the bag and pass it back. This woman is shy, but I smile and motion with my head and hand for her to take it. She merrily pops the top on this can and shares it with another woman. The four women are now giggling and chattering and sharing the two Diet Cokes with such gratitude and pleasure that it's like enjoying this small gift will be the best part their day.

I console myself with the knowledge that I have two cans left in the bag, and then I see Nicholas watching the women enjoying the cold carbonation and envying their little treasure. What the heck. I draw another Coke from the bag and hand it to him. Then our two stoic, nameless guards re-board the bus and look at us all enjoying Diet Coke. They slip into their watchful seats behind me, one on either side, and Nicholas flashes one of his yellow smiles at me. I pass the last cold Diet Coke in the brown paper bag back to them and immediately hear the *pop*. Maybe they might like me now. As the riders are enjoying their little Coke party and I'm savoring the last lingering swallows of my drink, I'm thinking of the irony of giving away Diet Coke with its zero calories to these thin, emaciated people who don't enjoy three squares a day.

We're underway on the bus but head back in the direction of the market. I'm praying this is where the women need to go and we won't have to traverse that insufferable cesspool again. Nicholas stops the bus, and the women exit, laughing and smiling. "Bonjou, Bonjou."

the way home

On the way to the children's home at the edge of town, I see men pushing their wheelbarrows filled with sugarcane, rice, beans, bread, bundles of charcoal, and anything else they might hope to sell. Wheelbarrows of every size and in every condition seem to be the vendor carts of choice. Nicholas steers the old bus down a narrow side street, where I see a contiguous string of thatch and fabric lean-tos with dirt floors positioned against an eroding block wall. These shanties are home to an assortment of withered adults and soiled children. Some are stirring a concoction in a pot over an open fire. The word *slum* does not do this squalor descriptive justice, and I look away.

I've eaten little since I've arrived, and the Diet Coke's carbonation nicely fills my stomach. Nicholas has noticed. "We stop at bakery, and you eat."

There is a currency exchange shop beside the bakery, and Nicholas instructs me to go and exchange my US Dollars. The Haitian currency, I observe, is as dirty and worn as the country. The limp, filthy currency with its ink long-ago worn off compares in stark contrast to the crisp, newly-printed US money I've just exchanged. And I think how sadly representative it is of the economic differences of the two countries.

I join Nicholas at the bakery and eat one of the meat pastries as well as a nice, big chunk of warm, delicious bread. It's so good and filling that I buy another piece to save for later. My mind wanders back to Rachael's homemade cinnamon buns another world away. I buy more water because I am now sufficiently frightened about providing parasites a free ride back to Charleston.

When we arrive at the children's home about fifteen miles outside Port-au-Prince, I find it is a modest, nondescript, two-story building. Workers are whitewashing the block walls outside and inside. I'm told there is electricity for a few hours a day and a generator for other times but frequently no fuel for it. A large trench has been dug at the back of the lot for a latrine. A drinking well has been dug near the latrine, and I'm wondering how long it will take for the leaching of the latrine waste to foul the water. This is crazy. If the kids aren't sick when they get here, they'll have this place to make them ill.

judy norwood enter

Cots with springs and thin mattresses line the walls of the two large sleeping rooms, attesting to the number of children with no one to care for them. There is a kitchen on the first floor with a propane gas stove, refrigeration, and a large, empty pantry. There are a half dozen boys and girls, squatters, filthy and emaciated but with bloated stomachs, wandering around. One of the boys has some marbles, and they sit on the concrete slab playing and laughing.

"Where have these children come from?" I ask Nicholas.

"Some of these kids orphans and live in street. They must beg for food during the day, sleep here at night. Others dropped here by parents with too many children to take care of. Your father know. He say let any who come stay while we are under construction. He bring money and buy food, but it goes quickly. Since he die, no one except Madam Rachael send money for food. Madam Rachael send some to bank account here says more when your father's death certificate come and estate closed. So we have a little but not enough."

"Did my father see the latrine trench and the well so near each other?"

"Yes, he blow up pretty big. Either well or latrine need to be moved."

"Have it done before someone gets sick."

Nicholas laughs and shakes his head. "You Americans expect we move like you. We have no big money after Mesye Robert die...I told you a little left in account he set up here but not enough to move well or ditch. I use that money to feed street kids here, and it run out regular. Most children come here already sick, and Haitians have pretty good stomach. Used to bad water."

"There will be no 'bad water' here. I'll see to the money when I return to the States. Who is in charge of finishing the building? Has anyone been hired to oversee the children, and who cooks for them?"

Before Nicholas can answer the questions I've peppered at him, a small child wearing only a dirty, once-white T-shirt and no underpants wanders in through the door near the kitchen. A woman, who I presume is his mother, follows him in timidly. In her native Kreyol language, she asks Nicholas for food. "Es'ke ou ka ede'm? M'gran

the way home

gou. (Can you help me? I am hungry.)" He speaks with her and turns to me.

"They hungry looking for food. Gabriel, little boy, not eaten since yesterday."

I'm shocked to see that one of his testicles is grossly large, hanging almost to his knee. His small hand supports the weight of it. The child's eyes are downcast; he seems unwilling to look up at us, like he's perpetually beaten down. I tell Nicholas to ask what's wrong with this child.

"He like this a year, but she have no money for doctor. It grows more every day."

"My God in heaven, help us!" I stare at the little boy helplessly.

I give Nicholas twenty dollars in Haitian currency and tell him to go back to the bakery and bring back all the food it can buy, and I pray he'll return and not run off with the money. In the meantime, I slam cabinet doors open in the small kitchen, looking for anything this child can eat and then remembering the extra piece of bread I bought that's still on the bus, now gone with Nicholas. In one cabinet I find a stale, half-eaten loaf of bread and a can of pork and beans. I find a rusty knife and no eating utensils. I thrust the knife into the can and get cut on one of the jagged edges. Tearing open the brown paper bag the moldy bread is in, I pour the beans out on it, using it as a makeshift plate. The mother, who seems no more than a teenager, tears off a piece of moldy bread and puts beans on top of it, using her fingers like a spoon. She stoops to little Gabriel and feeds him slowly. "Mesi, mesi!" she says over and over as she feeds her child from her hand. Then she begins to eat.

I want to speak to her to hear her story, but when I speak English she only smiles and shakes her head not understanding. Little Gabriel looks at me now while his mother feeds him. And I can only smile and nod my head and rub my stomach like the food is good. Food is an international language, I think. I step outside waiting on Nicholas motioning for Gabriel and his mother to remain inside in the shade of the building. Outside is hot and dusty and more children scamper around. A ball of gray road dust finally reveals the ragged bus and Nicholas. After he has set the brake on the bus, he

judy norwood enter

crawls out smiling extending two bags stuffed with bakery goods. We return to the kitchen and open the brown wrappers to Gabriel and his mother. They bite into the meat and pastry smiling at Nicholas.

I can't take my eyes off the enlarged testicle now bouncing loosely off Gabriel's knee. He has dropped it filling both of his little hands with bakery bread. "Nicholas, talk to Gabriel's mother and ask her if she will go to the doctor at the hospital in Port-au-Prince with little Gabriel if you will take her."

Before he can ask, two grieving women walk into the home. Nicholas translates for them so I understand their situation. They are sisters, and the one crying is looking for money to bury her dead child. Nicholas knows these women and attests that her young daughter has died. Nicholas tells me that forty dollars will adequately provide for a tiny wooden coffin and grave, so I hand her the money. The small, worn-looking woman overcome with grief takes my hand and bathes it with kisses and warm tears. "Mesi, mesi!"

Nicholas and Gabriel's mother, Micha, load little Gabriel on the old bus and leave for the hospital with the leftover bags of food and additional money. Alone in one of the long rooms with rows of empty cots, I sit heavily down on one. Deep within me, something has begun to shift, not unlike the great plates in the crust of the earth prior to an earthquake, and I fear I might not survive the sadness of this place intact. The enormity of palpable human need is invasive and assaults every sense. How can so many men, women, and children live in such dire poverty? And where to begin meeting those basic human needs of clean water, food, and roofs over their heads? I know inherently that having witnessed such a place will change me, that a slide show of filth, hunger, sickness, and orphaned children will forever play across my mind.

I whisper, "Dad, what have you done?"

• • •

On my third day in Haiti, I confess to Nicholas that this trip is a fact-finding mission for me and that my intention is to dispose of

71

the way home

my father's interests here. But in the meantime, I say, I can't possibly leave the children's home in limbo. I'm going to need someone I can trust here, someone who can manage the children's home and someone I can execute funds to—someone who can see that this place doesn't become another place of squalor. Nicholas is obviously not happy at this revelation but tells me that, for now, he can be that person because he has no job and was working for my father before his death. We agree on a temporary plan for money to be sent to the bank here that he can use for completion of the home, for movement of the well, and most importantly, to provide for food. A benevolence fund will be established as well for children like Gabriel.

"It is essential that we find a woman who will work with the children. You may manage the money and procurement of supplies, but we need a good woman to love and care for these children. There are cots for thirty-six children, so we'll need someone to hire other women, maybe as many as five, including her."

"I do this for you. My sister good with children and believe God. She good woman."

By late afternoon, Nicholas has gone for both his sisters and brings them to the home. I meet Monique and Marianne. Marianne is slender, her complexion a smooth brown, and florally dressed. She smells of rose water or some such scent. Monique is fuller, taller, very dark with a ruddy complexion, and plainly dressed. While Marianne seems shy and lowers her head when Nicholas introduces her, Monique's head is held high. Her eyes flash with laughter and her wide smile reveals the same yellowed teeth of Nicholas. She smells of grease and frying food. Neither of the sisters speak English, Nicholas explains.

In warm, rich, native Kreyol Monique begins to speak. Nicholas obviously slows her tale and asks me if I want to hear the story of the children on the mountain. I have no idea what this might be, but I'm already engaged with these two very different sisters, and want to hear their story. Nicholas begins to interpret for Monique.

"Families Haiti large. No birth control. Some families have ten children and no food to feed them. Even their mothers' breasts dry and shriveled when child is born. No milk. We climb mountains to poor villages to take food and blankets."

Monique is talking over Nicholas and Marianne has spoken as well, so to eliminate my confusion, he puts his finger to his lips signaling his sisters to be quiet. "Kompoze!" Nicholas takes over for them relating their stories of hiking as much as six hours and staying in the mountains for several days until all they've brought is distributed to the families. Without exception, he says, they bring a number of children back down the mountain whose families have to send them away because they cannot feed them. These women and others like them take these children into their already-large families, trusting God to feed them.

"These are the women I want. Will they work here?"

He asks them this in their native Kreyol, and they smile and nod their heads to me.

"Mesi, Mesi!" I say with humble gratitude. They laugh at my meager attempt to speak their language.

I notice that each woman had taken her shoes off while we'd been talking, and I see that their shoes have holes as big as their heels and soles as thin as paper. I make a note to myself that, on my next trip, I'll bring shoes.

I give them their first job and ask them to go to the hospital in Port-au-Prince to monitor Gabriel and his mother. I give them money for their own families as well as anything else Gabriel needs.

Monique speaks, "Mesi, ou tres genti."

Nicholas explains. "She say 'thank you, you very kind.'"

Nicholas leaves to drive them to the hospital, and I call Jill.

"Jill, you couldn't dream this place in your wildest imagination. I've never been so close to this much pervasive poverty. The need here is staggering". I relate to her the people and their needs I've encountered today here at the home. "Gabriel and Micha, his mother, are at the hospital in Port-au-Prince now. I'm hoping and praying that the doctors can help him." And when I tell her about the mother begging for money to bury her child, she cries. I tell her the story of Monique and Marianne and their trips into the mountains. I try to describe the city, the children's home, and the children wandering the streets but I don't have adequate words to portray the real-

the way home

ity that is Haiti. So I ask her, "How can just a few people and some money make a difference?"

"You can't help them all, Bobby, but you fed two, buried one, hospitalized one, and employed some others. It makes a difference to them. And it sounds like thirty-six other children will be fed and cared for. Good job! I'm proud of you."

Jill's approval washes pleasantly over me, and I realize how much I need it and how much I've missed it. She's right about me, about everything. And on the spot, I determine I will do whatever it takes to change. My girls are the best thing that has ever happened to me, and I'm in danger of losing them. Entering into marriage, I hadn't a clue about how to be a husband, and when the girls were born, I was totally bereft of any idea of how to be a good father. Rachael is right; no one gives you a book.

After talking with Jill, I take a walk outside and look at the dirty faces of little girls and boys with no one to love them or provide for them. The staggering truth that blindsides me is that these six and seven and eight-year-old children are living on their own not able to rely on any adult to take care of them. I watch them lazily playing marbles on the dusty ground and in the hot sun. One small girl is light brown with unusual blue eyes and matted grayish hair. She smiles at me and fluffs her filthy rag of a dress. As I watch these barefoot children, I imagine faceless, hungry children being brought down a mountain by Monique and Marianne and leaving the only home they have ever known for strangers.

Not for a minute do I believe I've solved all the present or future problems for this little children's home, but I am satisfied with these small steps. I'll have Louis check on Nicholas's trustworthiness and ability to manage the money sent here. But my gut tells me he can, and I recall that Louis said my father trusted him.

Nicholas returns late in the afternoon without his sisters and reports that Gabriel has a benign mass like a tumor that can be removed with surgery, and the cost would be two hundred dollars, half for the hospital and half for the doctor. And the hospital charges extra if the patient eats there. I decide not to wait until I return to Charleston to send money to the old account my father had set up at the bank in Port-au-Prince. Louis is contacted that very afternoon and will handle the initial deposit from which Nicholas will draw the necessary funds. As Nicholas drops me off at the hotel, I instruct him to keep a watchful eye on Gabriel and his mother and, if more money is needed, to provide it.

. . .

On my fourth and final day in Haiti, Nicholas picks me up once again in the bus, accompanied not with the men who don't like me but with two other men with GLOCK 9mm pistols carried in low-slung holsters on their right legs.

"Nicholas, what is this? Why do these men carry guns? And what happened to our two guards without guns? I think I liked them better."

These men obviously speak English because they're laughing at me and slapping their holsters. "We travel to different part of Port-au-Prince today, the Carrefour commune near Cité Soleil. Can be dangerous. Better to have them. They like you. He is Marcos and his brother Andre. Keep careful what you say 'bout them, Boss. They speak English." He laughs.

My protesting against this ride with armed guards finds no common ground with Nicholas, so he drives us into a section southwest of the city. Nicholas looks often at me in the broken rearview mirror, apparently assessing my cowardice. "Boss, you need to man up. Madam Rachael, she come with your father to this place and she not afraid. I take care of you."

This small plot of land my father has purchased in a particularly grave and wasted part of this city has no saving grace that I can see. "Nicholas, why was this site chosen? It's a ghetto and seems to be in one of the worst parts of the city."

"I tell Mesye Robert this, but he say he studied and this is where biggest need is. I try to get him to change his mind, but he no budge. He say AIDS and tuberculosis and malaria victims here and they no come to outskirts of town where safer for treatment, so he come to them."

the way home

Marcos and Andre seem to have lost their senses of humor, and their eyes search the landscape around us as we walk the dusty site. Each man has his right hand on his holstered gun. Nicholas reiterates that this small site my father has chosen for the clinic in the extremely volatile Carrefour commune is unsafe, with murder and rape common. Adding to my anxiety about this location, Nicholas explains that the Police Nationale d'Haiti is ineffective and has insufficient manpower to provide protection, so voilà, our armed accomplices.

I learn from Nicholas that AIDS is rampant in Haiti, which has the highest rate of infected people in the Caribbean. As many as one in twenty-five Haitians are infected with HIV, and it's the leading cause of death in women ages fifteen to fifty. Many of the street children are orphans of parents dead from the disease and are estimated at being in excess of one hundred thousand. Since the population of Port-au-Prince is estimated to be around 898,000, that is a staggering number of homeless orphaned children. Nicholas tells me that many of the children we will house at the children's home are these orphans whose parents have died of AIDS. Their families either cannot be located or else are afraid of taking the children in due to their belief that the HIV virus will be commuted to them. He adds to this dismal picture by saying malaria and tuberculosis are major problems in this insufferable country with an almost nonexistent health care system. Port-au-Prince contains half of the entire population of Haiti, the greater metropolitan population being estimated at 3.7 million people. So the high density of people living here with little infrastructure for water and sewage is a formula for disease and death.

Each day seems to expose me to a new horror of the human existence in Haiti, and this one follows suit. Squatters are milling around the site around whatever building materials are left and are eyeing us maliciously and suspiciously. Marcos and Andre menace them with their stares and guns.

"Mesye Chapin, your father build in worst place. Fast as we get materials here, they steal. They steal blocks, cement, lumber, tin for roof. I cannot stop it."

"What about security guards, like these we have with us?"

"We have Marcos and Andre when your father visit, but what they gonna do? Shoot people like soldiers do? No, I tell your father to stop building here. Put clinic outside town, but he no listen. Since he disappeared—died—no one here to direct work, so they steal most everything."

"Nicholas, here's what we're going to do. There have to be other medical clinics here in Port-au-Prince. Research all the clinics, their locations, the names of doctors, and their support groups. Maybe we can't stand on our own right now, but we may be able to stand together. Do this for me, and I'll wait for the report. Meanwhile, no more supplies for now. Just step back and let them take whatever is left. Don't endanger yourself or anyone else."

I'm anxious to go back to the relative safety of the bus and leave this doomed site, but Nicholas seems bent on delivering a speech. "Okay, 'Boss Man.' I call you 'Boss Man' now. I don't know 'bout you when you come four days ago. You uppity, you don't like Haitians or our country or our food. You not like your father either. You come with hatred in your heart. I see into some men's hearts, and you nothing like your father when you step off plane. You look like him, but your heart no like Mesye Robert's. But then I see you with little Gabriel and his mama…feed them and send them to hospital. Your heart have soft place for dead child and her mama, and I listen to you talk to Monique and Marianne 'bout these orphaned children. Some Americans who come have same money as you to spread around and make them feel good but have no heart to go with it. You grow a heart quick for us. Man don't change that quick, Boss Man, unless he is tired of hating. I work with you like I work with you daddy."

"Nicholas, I am not my father. I will not stand on his shoulders and call myself a giant. This is his work, not mine. I've been honest with you that I came here to gather information before disposing

the way home

of all this. But you are right when you say I came with hatred and bitterness. It's a long story, but I was not close to my father and still carry a great deal of resentment for him. I don't ask you to understand. I do ask for your patience with me as I'm trying to figure out why I'm here. Nothing in my life has prepared me for this, and I don't know what to do with my father's work."

"Nothing to figure, Boss Man. Your father dead, you alive. When you live in Haiti, you learn not to figure too much. You wake up, see the sun rise, and do best you can. Heart not afford to grow hard or bitter. You will die. Nicholas help you, Boss Man. That all to figure—you not alone. When you come back?"

ten

As my plane taxis to the gate in Charleston, I realize that half of my two promised weeks are gone and I'm still stumbling around confused. What I did in Haiti was a reaction to the blatant need right in front of me. There was no plan, no goal, no clear direction, and no order—just chaos. I don't do chaos well, never have. In a way, I guess I'm like my mother, whose love of order was compulsive.

I call Rachael to tell her my plane has landed, and she gives me a list of things to pick up. "Let's have a welcome home party for you tonight, just you and me. Pick up some filets, nice and thick, at the Fresh Market. Also, run by Total Wine and pick up a bottle of 14 Hands Merlot—better make it two bottles if you want some! On second thought, just get a case. I like to keep some in stock," she laughs. "And stop by that little bakery on East Bay for a praline cheesecake. You know Charleston can incorporate the south and New York into one fine dessert by putting pecans into it!" She's laughing again, giddy almost, sounding like a teenager. The Rachael of my memory could make a party of one, so I don't doubt her when she wants to make a party of two.

Louis sent a limo for me at the airport, and I will say it turned out to be convenient because Rachael solicited me as errand boy for a party. By the time my ride pulls into the gracious landscaped driveway and drops me and my groceries off, that amazing light

the way home

over Charleston Harbor that dazzles the senses has begun its evening sweep of the water, and boats with their white sails are bobbing in the wind and the current. I must confess that the savory salt air, the dependable tides, the white sand beaches, and this ethereal city with its bustling harbor and historical flavor are all still in my blood. I ran away from the Low Country of Charleston to the mountains of North Carolina, but I suppose if I hadn't had anything to flee, I wouldn't have left this magical place along the southern shore of South Carolina.

Rachael, in one of Mother's old aprons, too large for her, runs to help me with my bag and the groceries. Barefoot, the woman apparently still can't stand shoes. The lights in the old home are blazing, and the kitchen smells of warm bread baking in the oven. Rachael has been at the cutting board chopping up a variety of vegetables. As soon as I step into the kitchen, without thinking, I kick off my loafers and pull off my socks, tossing them into the shoe basket near the entrance to the kitchen. The cool pine floor is medicine to these dusty, tired soles. I exhale.

"Long travel day. Guess I need to get a shower."

"No rush. I'm going to marinate these steaks for an hour or so before we cook. And I have some sourdough bread in the oven that needs some time to finish baking and then rest before we slice it."

Rachael has torn open the case of wine and is opening one of the bottles. I finish uncorking the bottle as she pulls two of mother's impeccably designed antique crystal wine glasses—surely over a hundred years old—from the front glass cabinet.

"Here, rinse these out and pour us a glass. I never could wait long enough to let a good merlot breathe," she laughs.

"You seem about a decade younger to me than when I first arrived a few weeks ago. And I feel about a decade older." I pass her the precious crystal, and she turns the antique glass slowly in her hand, allowing the light to dance and fracture off its design. She fills them.

"You know, Bobby, what you put good wine into matters about as much as the wine. Makes it taste better and makes the experience a little stronger. Life is all about the details."

judy norwood enter

She raises her glass to mine, and we carefully clink the cherished crystal. "A toast—to the details."

She has blended soy sauce, honey, and sesame oil to make a marinade and then plops the thick steaks into the bowl to soak up the flavors. She resumes chopping the vegetables, sipping her wine between slicing and dicing. I walk to the bay window where the old table sits and drink in the last light of the day making a spectacle of itself over the harbor and its shore. I fondle Mother's crystal, which was her mother's and my great-grandmother's wedding crystal.

"How can such a fragile piece of glass live so long in the hands of so many and remain as beautiful and undamaged as the day it was forged?"

"Quality craftsmanship and careful handling," Rachael responds, "like a well-tended life."

Rachael has finished prepping the vegetables for roasting and is preparing the pan with extra virgin olive oil and crushed garlic. She ladles the green, red, and yellow peppers along with tiny fingerling potatoes and chopped sweet onion into the pan. She slices and dices yellow squash with zucchini and also adds it to the pan. As soon as she slides it into the hot oven, the smells of oil and garlic toasting in the pan around the vegetables blends with the smell of warm sourdough escaping from its own adjacent oven. My stomach emits a loud growl, and suddenly I'm back in Haiti watching its people forage for food: peas and rice, skinny little chicken legs fried to a crisp, fried plantains, and bread. There was water, too—dirty from a river or ditch or clean from a well, if you were lucky. Nicholas told me that fewer than half the people in Haiti have clean water.

Rachael stands beside me at the big window. "I never tire of watching that last light dance over the harbor. It's been a long time since you've seen it. Ever miss Charleston?"

" I guess I never really think about them. We have the mountains, you know."

She looks down at my bare feet. "I see. You go barefootn' up in those mountains?"

I peer down at my long, white-as-cotton toes, and we both laugh as I realize that I have mindlessly gone barefootn'. Every

the way home

house, not just the beach house at Pawleys, always had a large, natural wicker shoe basket sitting at every entrance door. Boats and yachts follow the same protocol. A basket for shoes is at the door to the saloon, and most doors have small lettering on them that reads "No shoes, please." At home we called it "barefootn" after a song of the same name recorded in the mid-sixties, and whether a resident or a guest, except at the adult's formal parties, barefootn' was duly encouraged. Even my prim and properly raised Charleston mother, who learned barefootn' from Rachael, taught us that shoes stop at the door and bare feet on old pine flooring is a cool way to grow up. Of course, we kids took the habit outdoors as well.

"It's so good to hear you laugh, Bobby. You sound like a boy again. What do you and Jill do for fun?"

"Not a great deal lately. I'm traveling more than I want, and I've told the company I don't like it. The international travel especially takes a toll on family life. They've promised to pull me back, so we'll see. If they don't follow through, I'll look for another job. A good salesman is always in demand."

Rachael has moved to refill her glass and mine, sets them both down, and stares at me incredulously. She begins with a chuckle, "You're kidding me, right?" Slowly her high-pitched, loud, wet-your-pants laughter with the characteristic tears streaming down her face begins. I can't help myself and begin to laugh at her laughing. I have no idea what she's laughing at, but soon I'm engaged and almost as hysterical as she. She grabs a dishcloth from the countertop to wipe the tears from her face and then tosses it to me.

"They say laughter adds years to your life…something about good chemicals the brain puts out lasting a long time and being good for the heart and brain. If I can live longer by laughing, then by golly, I will!"

My stomach muscles are already feeling the strain. "What are we laughing at?"

She stares at me, and for a moment, I think she's going to start the cycle of laughing all over again. "Bobby, you're a multimillionaire. Screw the company and the travel. You could probably buy that company if you wanted it. And you don't need another job! That's one of the greatest benefits of money, the freedom of having options."

That bit of forgotten news sobers me. I drag the dishcloth over my face again and think about blowing my nose. My mother would have a fit, but this is Rachael. I give a good, hard blow right into the dish towel. I move threateningly toward Rachael with the soiled dishcloth. "Yuck. Get that thing away from me. You're such a little boy!" I shake it at her, and she screams, backing away and laughing again. Feeling my sense of humor returning, I throw the snotty cloth in her direction. As I do, my hand hits the wine glass she refilled, and it crashes to the wood floor, spraying red wine like a fire hose. I felt like I saw it hanging in midair but was impotent to stop it from falling. We are both dumbstruck, staring at the glass shards and red wine. "I'm so sorry, Rachael. I'm so sorry. I'm a clumsy idiot!"

"Bobby, Bobby. Stop this talk. If you call yourself an idiot, you'll begin to believe it." We both get on our knees and pick up the larger pieces of shattered antique crystal and deposit them sort of reverently into a trash container Rachael has brought over.

"Mother's crystal. Grandmother's crystal. Great-grandmother's crystal!"

"Bobby, I don't know how to break this to you, but the dead don't need crystal. This crystal belongs to you now, and if you break it…well, you just reduced your inventory of crystal. Stop whining about it. It's unbecoming."

We finish mopping up red wine, and she draws another wine glass from a different cabinet. She fills it for me and extends it. "Now this lovely piece of faux crystal, as you can see, has the Palmetto State's emblem on it. Very fine stuff and readily available. You can buy it at the Piggly Wiggly for eight dollars. Since Jill might not want you to reduce the crystal inventory any further tonight, use it."

I laugh at this, and she smiles that big, warm smile I remember from boyhood. Rachael is one of those women full of forgiveness and redemption, no matter if the sin is big or small. Why can't I trust her again? I know innately that I'm desperate to openly love her again. But as she stands here in my mother's kitchen tonight, I still regard her as an intruder.

the way home

As though she can read my thoughts, she says, "You'll learn to trust me again, Bobby. If for no other reason than I'm all you've got now, you'll trust me. You may not believe me, but you and I are going to have some of the best times of our lives. You've been without a mother too long, and Mary Elizabeth would want us to be friends again. Tonight is a darn good start. Now do you still know how to grill a good filet?"

I carry the steaks out back to my father's grill, cleaning it and firing up the gas. As I do I hear the familiar strains of "I Love Beach Music" by the Embers drifting out the screen door. And I remember the four of them dancing barefoot on that scarred, sandy, wood floor at the old beach house in Pawleys. Rachael was the self-appointed teacher of this vintage dance.

"Okay, Bobby, you're fourteen-years-old. It's time you learned to shag from the best. Come over here and learn from the master! 'I Love Beach Music and I guess that I always will...'" Her voice was so bad it made dogs howl, but she sang along with the music and reached for my hand.

"Rachael, this is the early nineties, you know. There really is some new stuff out there. This music is old. Nobody my age dances to that stuff anymore."

"Hush your mouth, boy! There is no other music. And you're a beach boy and a Charleston brat. You've got to learn to shag. You won't ever be able to get a date as soon as all the girls know you don't know how to shag." She seemed genuinely troubled that I didn't want to learn the South Carolina state dance.

"Oh, please don't make me," I whined and objected, but she pulled me to her.

Mother walked into the room and dried her hands on a dish-cloth. "Bobby, it's part of your heritage. You've been blessed to have been born a Low Country boy, and you must learn to shag. First you learned to sit up, then you learned to crawl, then you walked, and now you learn to shag. That's the order of your life, so just get in there and do what Rachael tells you to do. And try to stay off her toes."

Mother and Rachael high-fived each other, and Mother started the music at the beginning.

84

judy norwood enter

The filets are the best I've ever eaten; you could cut them with a fork. And despite all the questions I have of Rachael, none are asked this evening. I am content to laugh, eat well, drink excellent wine from my Piggly Wiggly glass, and listen to her recount the memories of the good times we shared over the years. I notice that not once does she regale a story I wasn't included in. Sitting at the big, old pine table again with Rachael, I'm both mellow and sad. My mind involuntarily wanders back to Haiti as though the images are stuck there and I can't shake them loose.

eleven

The chartered plane in which Rachael and I are flying glides through the air just off the white, sandy shore of Grand Bahama Island. Tomorrow, Jill and the girls will fly into Marsh Harbour, Abaco, Bahamas. Don't ask me how Rachael did it. She calls my wife as if they were old friends and arranges for Jill and the girls to return to Asheville from Savannah aboard a charter plane for their passports and clothes. The same plane will bring them to Abaco to meet us. I care nothing about the Bahamas or my father's yacht, but I'm ecstatic over Jill's agreeing to meet us. Rachael is calling it a family reunion. I know it is for me.

"Bobby, look out the window at the color of the water. It's like jewels. There's Grand Bahama Island to the left. We took *Game On* to West End at the Old Bahama Bay Marina once. It's a beautiful place. There are hammocks strung between coconut trees on the beach, and they have the best cracked conch in the Bahamas. Your father loved their conch chowder!" That adventurous, child-like quality has entered her voice again.

"Oh, and by the way, I used my money for the planes." She put an emphasis on *my*. "Louis has your accounts set up, and you can begin to use your own money now. The next ones are on you," she laughs.

In all of the Little Bahama Bank, the water is shallow and aquamarine. *Bahama* actually means *shallow sea*. I can see the white,

the way home

sandy bottom even from this height in the plane. I'm mesmerized by the beauty and think about how the girls will love this place. Still peering out, I say, "Thank you, Rachael...for getting Jill and the girls here. I don't know if she would have come if I had asked."

"Sure she would've. She's just confused about the future. It's your job to unconfuse her." I'm thinking, I don't know how I'll do that when I'm confused as well. But I'm determined to try.

A large, black Bahamian man sharply dressed in beige boat shoes with no socks, creased khaki pants, and a white polo shirt with the emblem *Game On* stitched onto it in gold lettering meets us at the taxi to collect our luggage. "Mr. Chapin, so happy to meet you, sir. I'm so sorry about your father. I know this sounds strange coming from me, a stranger to you, but I loved your father. He's very good to me and my children, and I tried to be good to him. I will be as good to his son." The Bahamian lilt in his voice is like music.

"Captain Russell, I really don't require much, but you can be good to my family. That will make me happy."

"I will be good to your family. Miss Rachael says your wife and two girls arrive tomorrow. Can't tell you how good it is to have family aboard *Game On*. A boat just sitting at the dock is no good. She's meant to run and catch fish and have people on her having fun. She's just going to waste not doing what she's meant to do. This would make your father very happy."

My father's sports fishing yacht is large and well-outfitted and has all the comforts of home. Rachael had called ahead to have it washed down and provisioned with all the girls' favorite foods and drinks. There are kayaks on the dock, two Jet Skis tied to the yacht, a thirty-two-foot fishing boat alongside the dock with the lettering *T/T Game On*, and various floats and swim toys on the deck.

As the sun fades into the west, reflecting onto the Sea of Abaco, Rachael and I, requisite glasses of wine in hand, stroll the docks of Moon Harbour Marina in Marsh Harbour. My father's boat—well, my boat—is not the largest yacht in the marina, but it is certainly one of the finest. The marina is situated overlooking the Sea of Abaco toward Elbow Cay where Hope Town and its iconic red-and-white candy-stripe lighthouse are located. The settlement is a historical

judy norwood enter

village of pastel colonial-era houses that had been settled by Loyalist Carolinians fleeing the American Revolution and their detested, newly won democracy in 1863. Wyannie Malone, its founder, was straight out of the Carolinas. It must be a small world, I'm thinking, for these settlers and I to share the same terra firma roots. Captain Russell tells me that many of the settlers can be traced back to Charleston plantations. The captain joins us as we watch one of only three hand-wound, kerosene-burning lighthouses still operational in the world ignite the sea.

"We'll take *Game On* into Hope Town Harbour this week," the captain says. "Would you and the missus like to light the lighthouse while you're here? One of the lighthouse keepers will allow you. Would you like me to arrange it?"

"My wife is a school teacher, and she would absolutely revel in doing that. Arrange it for us. We'll make it a surprise for her."

We return to *Game On* in the fading light, and Rachael and I sit high on the bridge of the boat. "Rachael, I appreciate your not guilting me about refusing to come here when you invited us and my father was alive. I just…just couldn't…"

"That's in the past. Are you happy to be here now? Your family is coming, and we're going to have a big old time—a reunion. And I don't care if you like this or not, but your father instrumented this reunion even in his death. He loved this place, and he is here with us now. I can smell him in our stateroom. I can hear and see him laughing that deep barrel laugh with this rod in his hand and a big yellowfin tuna on his line, yelling at me, 'Rachael, get the wasabi out—we got sushi tonight!'" Rachael has strolled over to my father's fishing reel and is stroking the handle where his big hands once held the deep-sea fishing rod. "And I'm screaming back while he fights the fish, 'You know Captain Russell says Bahamians don't eat sushi, Robert!' To which he would say, 'Well, tell him to fire up the grill…we're grilling fresh tuna steaks tonight!' He was like a boy out here, playing and wringing every joyous moment out of every day. And he knew how to spread that joy around." She is sniffing back tears.

"Rachael, you and my father were pathologically happy."

the way home

"Yes, he was, and I am, and I hope there's no cure for it. It's a gift."

Captain Russell is chef as well, but Rachael keeps trying to interfere (she calls it "overseeing") with his preparation of the meal. He shoos her out of his galley. Fresh mahi-mahi—it's actually dolphin (not Flipper, but the fish dolphin)—coleslaw, and Bahamian peas and rice are on the menu tonight. I'm not sure what the difference between Bahamian peas and rice and Haitian peas and rice will be until Captain Russell invites me to taste from the pot on the stove. These are made with spicy rice, chicken stock, pigeon peas, and hot sauce. They're delicious, whereas the Haitian peas and rice were dry, lacked flavor, and didn't actually have many peas. But it was sustenance.

Captain Russell rings the dinner bell. We gather in the outdoor dining area in the cockpit of the boat. The warm teak deck glows from the lights; the large, lacquered table with an inlaid compass rose, the upholstered chairs in nautical stripe, and the china as well as the crystal setting all make for a scene that's like something out of a magazine. Rachael has cut hot-pink bougainvillea from one of the many tropical flowering bushes on the marina grounds and fashioned a centerpiece for our table. As if all of this didn't already make for a dreamy fantasy land, Captain Russell throws a switch before we sit down, and underwater lights that look like blue laser beams slice through the water. Rachael has asked him to join us and prays a blessing over our food. She surprises me by praying for those who don't have what we're enjoying tonight. Amen.

The delicate fish has been filleted and boned for us, and Captain Russell skillfully grills it. It's moist, and the texture is almost buttery to the palate. Being able to bring Jill and the girls here excites me, and I effusively thank both Rachael and Captain Russell for the plan they hatched to get us all here.

"Mr. Chapin, your girls are going to have a fine time. I'll teach them how to fish. They're big enough, with a little help, to reel in a yellowtail snapper or small mutton fish. I'll help them. And you and Miss Jill are going to ride these Jet Skis. I've got 'em all gassed up and ready for you. Of course Miss Rachael will love a ride, too!" He winks at Rachael good-naturedly.

We continue to enjoy the abundant, delicious meal. "Captain Russell, Louis Chandler, my father's partner and lawyer, tells me there's a large Haitian community here in Abaco. Tell me about it."

"Oh yes, Mr. Chandler came here with your father. He is a very kind man. Likes to fish as much as your father! What is your interest in the Haitian people here in Abaco?"

"I don't really know, to tell you the truth. You know, of course, that my father has charitable interests in Haiti, and Louis tells me it all started with his interest and inquiry into the Haitian population here. I guess I'm just curious. Trying to figure out my father's thinking and how all this business with Haiti started."

Captain Russell is removing our plates with Rachael's help and brings the key lime pie to the table with fresh coffee.

"I'll tell you from the Bahamian prospective what I know of the 'Haitian problem' here in Marsh Harbour. Then what you need to do is talk to Phillipe here at the marina. He works the grounds and maintenance. Been here 'bout twenty-five years. He will tell you from his view which is different because he is Haitian. He was a good friend with your father, you know."

I nod and bite into the tart and sweet key lime pie that was, according to Captain Russell, made in the back room at Vernon's Grocery over in Hope Town by Vernon himself. "Mr. Vernon made this fresh this very morning for us." The meringue is piled high and toasted atop this luscious, creamy delicacy. I'm thinking it must be at least one thousand calories, but I dig in, as does Rachael, and she's probably doing it without giving a thought to calories or her petite waistline. That woman must have the metabolism of a lumberjack.

We enjoy the pie and sip darkly roasted, steaming coffee while sitting around the table on this magical night. The temperature is seventy-five degrees, the stars are spectacularly brilliant, the Elbow Cay Lighthouse is searching the sparkling water with each rotation, and a gentle ocean breeze out of the east is cooling us.

Captain Russell is ready to speak. "You probably notice, Mr. Chapin, that I say 'Haitian problem.' Cause that's what it is to us

the way home

Bahamians. In Marsh Harbour there are two shantytowns, the Mud and Pigeon Peas. No one knows how many people are living there — guess two thousand to four thousand Haitians. Some are foreign-born in Haiti, but many second-generation children are born here to foreign parents, and this is the only home they ever know. These people live a ghetto life as squatters, and our government has just turned its head for over forty years. Bahamians resent them because they take jobs away from Bahamians, and we believe they bring crime and disease, smuggle drugs, and burden our schools with their children. They also send money back to Haiti, so it leaves our country for theirs and doesn't remain in our own economy. Fire is also a hazard in both ghettos. Houses are built very close together, and they run their own electric, stealing it sometimes. Fires happen from time to time, and people are killed. I know it is not a good thought, but as Bahamians, some say they just want the whole places to burn down."

"Why doesn't the government do something about it, either locally or on a national level?"

"Same reason your government does nothing about some things. Sometimes trying to fix the problem makes it worse. Local officials, from time to time, threaten and tear down some shacks. But it is like kicking an anthill. All the ants come running out of the ground and spread out because you've destroyed their home. Abaconians don't want Haitians moving in to their community. As is now we won't sell them land or rent to them. They sort of live in no-man's-land."

"But Haiti is worse," I say as a statement and not a question, remembering what I've seen during my trip.

"You talk to the foreign-born ones like Phillipe, and they still want to go home. Just nothing much there for them in the way of work."

"Yes, I know — I know."

"Oh, one more thing," Captain Russell says. "I don't remember how many years ago, but your father and I were out fishing the shelf off Hope Town near Tilloo Cut when we spotted a sailboat sitting very low in water. We looked through the binoculars and only counted three people on deck. Drug running is pretty cleaned up in these waters now, but some still get through, as well as human trafficking. One of the men on deck flagged us so we motored up our thirty-two-foot tender closer to them. The ocean swells were threatening to breach the sailboat. It was forty feet long. He asked us for a tow, so we hitched them up and pulled them through the inlet into the Sea of Abaco where the water was less turbulent. While I towed them, your father called the authorities for help, and when they arrived they found fifty-one Haitians aboard the boat. Forty-eight of them were hiding below, almost stacked on top of one another. They had sailed over five hundred miles from Haiti in that condition. Of course, the authorities took them into Marsh Harbour, where they were flown to Nassau for processing and their return to Haiti. It shook up your father quite a bit that they would risk their lives over that much open ocean in that small a boat with no engine. He said only if you were trying to escape hell itself would you board that little boat."

Captain Russell is shaking his head at the memory. "Not long after that, he made his first trip to Haiti."

Rachael has heard this story before, evidently, and has sat silently through its telling by Captain Russell. She clears her throat sensing we are ready to call it an evening. "Well, let's get to bed. We want to be well rested for Jill, Mary, and Elizabeth when they arrive tomorrow. I know they're going to drag Memaw Rachael's little butt all over the Sea of Abaco, swimming and snorkeling and kayaking!"

Captain Russell rises from his seat and says he is ready to retire to bed as well. "Thank you, Captain Russell for everything this evening. The meal was extraordinary, and the information on the Haitian community helpful. Good night."

"Phillipe will be around the marina tomorrow. Talk to him."

twelve

My best friend is Jill, but I'm not so sure she would say the same of me. I actually don't have many friends, and she reminds me of this infrequently, usually when I'm parasitically hanging onto her. "Bobby, to have friends, you have to be a good friend. Please go find someone to play with."

My retort is always defensive: "I have friends." Then I scroll down a litany of people I work with and people I sell to.

"Those are not friends; they're business associates. I promise you that if you died, not one of those people would come to your funeral out of friendship. They might feel compelled to come out of obligation, but out of friendship, I assure you not."

"Thanks. I feel so much better."

Jill is a good friend in that, as much as I don't want to hear it, she tells me the truth. Even though I may rail against it and question its veracity, her counsel motivates me to be a better man, husband, and father. She helped me tame my temper long before the girls were born. She flat-out told me if I didn't deal with my episodes of rage, she would not have children. While I was in college, I spent more than one night in jail after a drunken fight in a bar. I met Jill in our Junior year, and she witnessed the turbulent behavior. When I found I was in love with her, I stopped going to the bars and tried to purge the anger. It isn't easy to lay down a coping mechanism you've learned over a lifetime. One of the primary emotional drivers

the way home

in my repertoire has been anger; like one of the major food groups, it was at the top of my emotional pyramid. And as she's rightly pointed out, it's one of the reasons I don't make friends.

My dear wife and teacher has told me that another troublesome coping behavior I practice is isolation. As she has accurately pointed out, "Bobby, I've figured out that you don't like people. It seems incongruous to me when you're a top-producing salesman, but then I think about it and it makes sense. It's like you're a character in a play. You become what your client needs and wants and give it to them. You dazzle them with a performance and then pack up your tent and go on to the next performance and a new audience."

"And what is the problem here?" I would say back. "I don't have to like my clients; I simply have to sell to them." This was a mistake. And I was told in her most articulate teacher's voice what the problem was.

The truth is that I'm a prideful, cynical man made only a little softer at the core because of these three women. I don't want to live without them.

"Daddy, daddy! We got to ride on an airplane. Did you see us up high before we landed on the ground?"

Jill steps off the small plane looking like a desirable vision in a new, pale-blue sundress. Her long, dark hair falls softly to her bare, white shoulders. Her small, delicate feet with their perfect pedicure are wrapped in gold sandals. My heart flutters as I know that this extraordinary and incredulous beauty that one can observe with appreciative eyes meshes with the goodness of a kind soul. What you see on the outside is even more beautiful inside. I'm a fool for not tending this garden God has graciously given me with more care. I resolve to ask forgiveness and help in being the husband that she needs and deserves.

The girls have already run ahead and grabbed me in a leg lock as Jill slowly crosses the distance between us and the plane. "Hello, Bobby. You've kind of gone international on us! But it seems to agree with you. You look well." I drag the girls, still with their arms around my legs, the few steps it takes to get to her and kiss her.

"*Mesi Madam Chapin*. You look beautiful. I learned a few words of Kreyol when I was in Haiti, as you can see. *Bonswa*. That means *good afternoon or evening*, and it's used after eleven in the morning. It's 11:21, so I guess it's appropriate. Let's get your luggage and grab our ride, *souple*."

Jill is laughing at me, holding her big-brimmed, fashionable sun hat in her hand and slapping at her dress, which is blowing in the breeze off the nearby ocean. "I absolutely love this side of you, Bobby. You're so different somehow."

Oh my gosh, I think. I've made Jill laugh, and she "loves" the different Bobby!

"Come on, family. You can't believe the lunch Rachael has made for you. You'll need all that nutrition to keep up with the afternoon of water sports she has planned for you."

"Daddy, are you still mad at Memaw Rachael? Mommy says she thinks you might like her again. Do you, Daddy? Do you?"

"Well, yes, girls, I guess I sort of do. Come on and see Daddy's big, new boat that belonged to his daddy."

Jill is lagging behind, and when I turn to look, she's brushing away a tear streaking down her face and blows a kiss to me.

If there are days that are undeserved gifts from heaven, this is one of those in my life. My family in tow, we taxi back to Moon Harbour Marina and find Phillipe and Captain Russell waiting for our luggage. Introductions are quickly made, and the girls run squealing toward Rachael, who's racing up the dock with arms spread wide enough to embrace them both. I can't tell who is shrieking loudest—Rachael, the girls, or Jill, who's now running toward Rachael behind the girls. I watch the scene, tears barely in check, and remember Rachael's words: "We're going to have us a reunion, Bobby, and your father has instrumented it even in his death."

• • •

"Sunscreen, girls, sunscreen!" Rachael is running after the girls in their bathing suits trying to slather on a UV protector, but she seems to be losing in the chase. Eventually, she's able to catch them and smears on the concoction while their giggling turns into

the way home

screaming. "You're tickling me! You're tickling me!" Captain Russell launches the two seated kayaks, Rachael in one with Mary and Jill in the other with Elizabeth. They practice paddling around the protected harbor, and then I lose sight of them as they round the breakwater wall and slip into the placid, green Sea of Abaco.

Captain Russell, dressed appropriately in swim trunks for his shift watching the girls, leaves on one of the Jet Skis to tag along behind the kayaks. He is waving and grinning and looks like he's having as much fun as my family. When we arrived, I remembered his words about a boat being built for fishing and fun and how happy my father would be if he were here.

As I wave good-bye, Phillipe walks down the dock and calls to me. "Hey, Boss Man, you want to talk? Now good time?" Funny, I think, that was what Nicholas called me in Haiti.

"Sure, Phillipe. Step aboard. Can you have a beer with me, or are you working?"

"No, I off. I have one with you. You have Kalik?"

"Yes, we do. Captain Russell has us well stocked."

While getting us two Kaliks from the cockpit refrigerator, I look out toward the sea and catch sight of Captain Russell on his Jet Ski moving slowly into the lead, Rachael and Mary in their kayak following behind him, and Jill and Elizabeth paddling away right behind Rachael. The kayaks are yellow, and I amuse myself by thinking of how they look like little ducklings paddling away after the papa duck, Captain Russell on his Jet Ski in yellow swim trunks. I sit with Phillipe in the cockpit in the shade and remark on this beautiful place with its crystalline waters and clear, blue skies. He gazes out at the Sea of Abaco for a moment and frowns.

"I forget to look sometimes, Boss Man. I think it beautiful, but most times it is just a place to work. My country used to be beautiful." He says this wistfully with a certain faded sadness.

"Do you have family, Phillipe?"

"Yes, I have five children, three in Haiti and two born here. First wife in Haiti. Then I married here. Oldest is twenty-five years. Youngest is eight."

I want to know how he arrived here and why he left his family behind, but I hesitate to riddle him with personal questions.

"Big Boss Man, you father, he good man. Helped Phillipe. Give me money for my children. I still send money back to family in Haiti. I marry Haitian woman here and send money to her mama still in Haiti. You father never ask lot of questions. Just want to help."

"I'm glad, Phillipe, that he helped you. Did you do any work for him?"

"Sometimes, yes. Captain Russell use me on days off from marina to work on big boat, refinishing teakwood or waxing."

"Would you like to continue to do that until I decide what to do with all this?" I extend my arm toward the shiny white behemoth my father named *Game On*.

"Yes, I like to do that. You kind man like you father. You father go to my country, Haiti, to help people there."

I notice that Phillipe's English is very clipped and broken for a man who has lived in the Bahamas for twenty-five years. But during my brief time here, I've heard the marina workers, typically Haitian, speaking to one another only in their native Kreyol. It is fast and loud and an emotional language."Yes, I was in your country last week to see some of the work. I don't understand it all yet and don't know if I can be involved in it. But I can see your country very much needs help. Louis Chandler told me the Haitian community here triggered my father's interest in your country and that you were a big part of that. Can you tell me about the Haitians in Abaco?"

Phillipe takes a long drink of his Kalik. "Haitians first brought here 'bout fifty, sixty years ago to work in pulpwood mill 'round Snake Cay. Some work farm. Settlements built for them to live. My people be here long time. Plant close I don't know when, but Haitians have nowhere to go. Move toward Marsh Harbour to try to live and work. Good housing and work always a problem for us here. Pigeon Peas settlement 'bout five acres, and I don't know who land belong to. But they all squatters. Government try to move them out sometimes, but it no last. They say, 'I have to live somewhere, and I got nowhere else to go.' So they squat. Government do nothing for them. Can't move them. Afraid they'll move out into

the way home

Bahamian neighborhoods, and nobody wants them. Pigeon Peas developed with these shacks over thirty years. Nothing government can do with them they haven't already tried. The Mud another settlement near Pigeon Peas. I no live there. My boss let me and my family live in small house at back of property here. I'm lucky. I no want my family going there. No chance here for our children even when they born to us immigrants in Bahamas. They always treated as outsiders like they no belong here. Our children born here have Bahamian birth certificate but get no citizenship until they apply when eighteen years old. Then it expensive and complicated. And if they get citizenship, takes very long time to get passport. They are children without a country. Without citizenship, no travel, no buy land or house, no driver's license, no vote. No rights even for our children born here. Bahamas want our cheap labor but not us living here with them."

"Phillipe, did my father ever try to help the families in either of those settlements?"

"No, what he do? Can't drive down dirt roads throwing money out window of car. No way to get money to them like that, so he help one or two, like me, at a time. Sometimes I tell him who trying to do good, not do drugs, and work. So he send money by me and tell me not to say where it come from."

"Phillipe, I will tell Captain Russell to give you whatever work there is available to maintain the boat and equipment here. I would like to stay in touch with you and learn more about you and your family. I will leave money for you here, with Captain Russell, and he will pay you as the work is completed. Do you need anything right now?"

"Well, I need computer for my son. He going to sixth grade this year and need a computer."

"OK. I'll send or bring a computer for him. What's his name?"

"His name Benjamin."

"You tell Benjamin he'll have that computer. And bring him around to meet the family. I'll tell Captain Russell to take him and his friends out on the Jet Skis and kayaks."

"Thank you. You father a good friend and you one, too."

Papa duck and the ducklings have returned to the marina basin, and I capture them in several photographs before they get to the dock.

"Daddy, Daddy! Did you see us? Me and Memaw Rachael were the fastest." Mary is competitive, just like her dad.

"Mary, why do you always have to win?" Elizabeth says. "We all had the same fun, so what does it matter?" Elizabeth is my child of equanimity; she's like her mom.

Captain Russell and Rachael have conspired to provide Jill and me an evening of gastronomical dining pleasure alone in the restaurant at Moon Harbour. I don't know this for sure, but I believe they may have also arranged with God for a full moon we watch rise up out of the ocean together. Jill is wearing yet another new sundress, very floral and low-cut, with little straps hugging her now-pink shoulders. I'm thinking some of the new money is going toward sprucing up her schoolteacher's wardrobe. That would be good for both her and me. She's tied her straight, dark hair in a ponytail, and except for the shapeliness of her body, she looks like a little girl. I kiss her and cannot believe my good fortune. How a screwed-up, lonely, egotistical, angry maniac like me ever attracted artwork like her, I will never know.

We're seated on the deck of the restaurant overlooking the basin full of boats, and beyond the Sea of Abaco, the moon is draping its luminescent light over the water. Candles are lit, wine is in our glasses, and an appetizer of conch fritters is on the table. The fritters are tenderized pieces of conch pulled from the shell, blended with spices and peppers, and then bound with a batter of cornmeal and deep-fried. The Bahamians are a people after my heart, it seems, as they like to fry everything. Jill reminds me that when we return to reality, there will be no more fried food.

The conversation between us is light, and she says she wants to hear about Haiti but not tonight. Let's talk about our family, she says.

"Did you see the girls today, Bobby? Captain Russell took us on the smaller boat to Mermaid Reef and taught us how to snorkel. Rachael is an old pro at it and helped Mary. We saw an eagle ray,

the way home

clown fish, starfish, coral, and even a small shark. The colors of the reef are amazing, purple and brilliant orange and red and yellow. These reefs are so full of life. When we surfaced, Elizabeth asked us if we had seen Nemo. Isn't it great that the girls can have this experience? Tomorrow, the winds are predicted to be light again, so we're going out to Fowl Cay for more snorkeling. Do you want to go?"

"Me? Sure. Will you teach me how?"

"*Wi*—yes."

"Oh, Haitian, right?"

"*Wi*. Phillipe taught me a few words this afternoon so I could keep up with you."

Our entrées arrive. Mine is fresh-grilled Nassau grouper, found plentifully in these waters. It is accompanied with the native peas and rice and Bahamian macaroni and cheese, which is baked and cut in a square about three inches high. Jill's lobster tail is split and sautéed in butter and herbs and served with peas and rice and a small garden salad. These are spiny lobsters in the Bahamas without the claws the New England lobsters have. The meat is tender, and you can cut it with a fork. Jill reminds me I have two carbohydrates on my plate and says I maybe should have gone with the garden salad. My rebuttal is that we're only here for a few days and she may need to look the other way at mealtime. We're laughing, and I'm so grateful. It's not macho for a man to say this, but I feel my heart is so light it may float away.

We walk the docks, holding hands and enjoying each other and the view. She initiates some rather deep touching and tongue-kissing, and I feel like a college boy, only better—better because I know with humbleness and gratitude that this ethereal and exquisite woman loves me. And I know that my love for her has found tender new ground.

We return to our stateroom on *Game On*, slip out of our clothes, and fall onto the linen sheets of a king-size bed. Someone—Rachael, I suppose, or maybe Captain Russell—has put champagne in an ice bucket, two glasses by our bed, and chocolates on our pillows. While I'm in the bathroom, Jill pours us champagne and eats her chocolate. When I return I switch off the light and move into bed, whispering that I don't need any champagne—only her. Our love-making is deep and consuming, like we're two pieces of a puzzle that had been long separated and are finally being rejoined to make a whole. And did I mention the whole thing was highly sensual?

We lay close to each other in the big bed and look forward to a deep, restful sleep. The stars are brilliant through the large, open, glass hatch over our bed, and the water slaps lightly at the hull of the boat as we drift off to sleep. As I head down into that lovely REM sleep, I think, "This is the stuff of movies."

"Bobby, Bobby! What have you…done?"

The stars are gone and have been replaced by the bright morning light shining in through the open hatch overhead, and I try to pull out of what almost feels like a drugged sleep. I struggle to a sitting position in the bed and manage to get my eyes open and look at Jill. Her examining look is quizzical mixed with a little horror and speculation. Then the earsplitting laughter ensues.

"What? What is it? Have I grown a pair of horns overnight, or are boogers hanging out my nose? What is wrong with me?" The suave lover from last night is gone, having been replaced with a hysterical child.

Jill is pointing at my head and hair, so I rub the side of my face and come away with a suspicious, brown, sticky substance. "What in the heck is this? Oh my lord, what have I done?" Then I reluctantly put my hands to my nose and smell it. Jill is convulsing, all knotted up in the sheets, pulling her pillow over her head and desperately trying to stop laughing so she can breathe. The door to our stateroom bursts open, and Rachael, Captain Russell, and the girls are all startled and silently staring at us with their mouths hung open in disbelief at the commotion.

Rachael is the first to speak of the little audience our racket has garnered. "What in the hell is that brown stuff on your face and in your hair, Bobby?"

There's gasping and giggling, and then the whole ordeal begins for Jill again until she's finally able to say one word: "Chocolate!"

• • •

the way home

After I've showered and show up at the table in the cockpit for breakfast with my family, the laughter begins again. "OK, OK. I get it, family. You can't take me anywhere classy, right?" I try to change the subject. "What's on the agenda today?"

"First we'll head up to Fowl Cay Reef, and you can snorkel this morning," says Captain Russell. "Then, we'll continue north to Guana Cay to snorkel in the reef off the beach in front of Nippers, the world-famous beach bar and grill perched high atop dunes. We'll have a late lunch there and then head to Hope Town, where we'll stay for the night in Hope Town Marina at the base of the Elbow Cay Lighthouse. I've spoken with Sam McPhee, one of the lighthouse keepers, and he said to meet him at the top at half past seven so you and Miss Jill can light up the night sky tonight."

I seductively wink at Jill, recalling the sky we lit up last night. "Thank you, Captain Russell, for arranging the day. Somebody needs to teach old Dad how to snorkel."

The day on the reef is just as Jill described. All six of us don snorkel gear and view the world below with all its dazzling color and sea creatures. A giant green turtle swims just below us in a smooth, rhythmic motion, using its great flippers. I learn later from Captain Russell that turtles were one of the mainstays of the Bahamian diet many years ago but are now protected from fishermen. These reefs are life-sustaining, and nothing should be taken or disturbed, he tells me.

I let my guard down while I float in nature's aquarium and scrape my leg on a piece of coral. The fire that shoots through my thigh is instant and painful. My teeth lose their grasp on the mouthpiece of my snorkel mask and I inhale water which causes me to spit and gag seawater. I leave the group and swim as hard as I can to the boat moored off the reef. Jill is the first to see me leave and I hear her call. Captain Russell swims after me, but I reach the swim ladder first and can't get a hold on it. Frantically, I remove my swim fins and climb up to the deck of the boat.

Captain Russell is right behind me and sees the explosion of red blisters on my upper thigh. "Fire coral. You're gonna hurt like hell for a while. I'll get the vinegar."

Jill ascends the swim ladder on deck while Rachael has remained with the girls on the reef. "Oh my gosh. Bobby, your leg looks awful. Does it hurt?"

"Yes, it hurts. Did you tell the girls not to touch that stuff?"

"They know not to touch the reef."

Captain Russell dabs a cotton ball soaked in vinegar over the raging fire on my thigh. Jill takes over for him and sends him back to be with Rachael and the girls.

She strokes my thigh with cotton and vinegar. "Guess, tonight won't be as much fun as last night, huh?"

"Just try me!"

• • •

Nippers is a raucous, fun beach bar sitting high atop the dunes on Guana Cay and has the requisite gift shop, which all the girls enjoy. Captain Russell drinks water, but I indulge in a few frozen "Nippers," their famous rum drink. I explain to Jill that it is purely medicinal due to the pain of fire coral. I opt out of snorkeling the reef off Nippers on Guana Cay since Captain Russell says to keep my injury dry. So I capture my family in photos and move to the music blasting away, Barefoot Man's CDs, on the deck high above the beach at Nippers. I decide I know now where the phrase I see on T-shirts from the gift shop—"Gotta love Guana"—comes from. I love Guana!

With Captain Russell at the helm of *Game On*, we depart Guana Cay in time to catch high tide at the entrance to the harbor at Hope Town about twelve miles south. We need the extra depth to get the deep-draft boat into the harbor, Captain Russell explains. Rachael and Jill purchased a Barefoot Man CD on Guana and, with the CD player cranked up loud, are practically dancing on the decks of the boat all the way to Elbow Cay. I'm in love with this whole day. The frozen Nippers could have something to do with my elevated mood as well.

The narrow, shallow entrance to Hope Town Harbour leads into a natural basin filled with a variety of boats on mooring balls. Din-

the way home

ghies are the "family cars" of choice to get from one side of the harbor to another. The sign at the entrance to the harbor - "Slow Down, You're in Hope Town" — invites you to step back in time and decompress. Docked in the marina in Hope Town, we dine aboard on lobster and fresh hogfish, a delicately flavored white fish not unlike flounder. Captain Russell once again works his magic in the galley and on the grill. While Jill and I change clothes to begin our trek to the lighthouse to meet Sam, Rachael takes the girls for a swim in the pool at the marina.

Sam McPhee is a tall, dark Bahamian whose family members have been lighthouse keepers for generations, some in the southern Bahamas. His voice is lyrical and soft, and his smile is infectious. He's a big teddy bear of a man who I'm told seems to be in a perpetual good mood. Jill and I climb the 101 steps to the top of the eighty-nine-foot tall lighthouse, where visitors are allowed to go. We meet Sam at the top and find him unlocking the door to the area where the prisms are located. We follow Sam up a short ladder into the tight area, and I'm thinking I've got to lay off the conch fritters.

"Sam, thank you for allowing us to come and watch you light this magnificent lighthouse," Jill says.

"You not gonna watch, Miss Jill. You gonna light tonight. What do you know 'bout our Grand 'ol Lady? I tell you 'bout her."

While talking, Sam begins the prep work on the kerosene oil. As we sit on this circular ledge no bigger than about seven feet in diameter, the view out the prisms into the dimming daylight on the harbor, the Sea of Abaco, and the Atlantic Ocean is breathtaking. Jill is clicking photos so fast I think she might jam the camera.

"Correct name is 'Elbow Cay Lighthouse.' She was built in 1864 with imported red brick by the Imperial Lighthouse Service of London. She has five forty-five-inch diameter lenses called bull's-eyes and prisms that are a product of a French physicist, Augustin Fresnel. They are called Fresnel prisms. There is a spring mechanism that has to be cranked every several hours to maintain sequence of five white flashes every fifteen seconds. Fuel is old-fashioned kerosene oil with a wick and mantle. This lighthouse where you sit and light is one of three hand-wound lighthouses left in the whole world. This is a special place to be tonight."

The starter flame is strong and emits a sound of rushing wind as Sam prepares the lighting. Finally, he tells her the fuel is ready and hands Jill a simple box of matches. She strikes one, but the first attempt doesn't get the flame we need. The second try does the trick, and my inquisitive and adventurous wife has done what few people in the whole world have done. She looks like a little child at Christmas as the magnificent prisms reflect the kerosene light, projecting a warning to ships, as they have for 145 years, to stay clear of the dangerous reef.

As we climb down from our adventure in the darkness, I feel reverent toward the venerable things in life that still operate. Sam has told us the lighthouse is in constant need of repair and that the Bahamas Lighthouse Preservation Society and the Friends of Elbow Cay Lighthouse receive donations to maintain this unique and magnificent piece of history. I vow to write a check right on the spot.

. . .

I remove our lines from the dock, like Captain Russell has instructed me to do, as the sun rises over Hope Town. Two local charter boats head out to sea for their catch of the day; I notice one of the boats is named *Local Boy*. We'll travel north to Green Turtle Cay for one night, and from there we'll make the eighty mile trip over the Little Bahama Bank to West End, Grand Bahama. Last night we developed our end-trip itinerary to include a visit to Old Bahama Bay on the western tip of Grand Bahama Island. Rachael insisted that we should include it as our final destination. Our planes will meet us in Freeport to transport us back to the States.

We enter White Sound at Green Turtle Cay, again on high tide, to find another ideal harbor and a couple of marinas. Captain Russell maneuvers *Game On's* shiny hulk expertly into a designated slip at the fuel dock with help from experienced dockhands. The girls spot a small nurse shark and an eel that hides in the shadows of the dock.

the way home

Rachael jokes with me about my credit card limit while we gorge this guzzler of diesel fuel, and when I read the fuel consumption, I wonder seriously if VISA will allow it. Captain Russell laughs and says I'll get used to it. I don't think so.

The Green Turtle Club provides us with some of the finest Bahamian food we've enjoyed yet. The conch is fresh, expertly prepared, and served in generous portions. The bar is 1940's vintage "Hemingway" with lots of old wood, dark wicker couches, overstuffed chairs, and friendly staff. But the most striking characteristic is that the walls and ceiling are plastered by the signed dollar bills of past visitors - hundreds of them. The girls want to take a few of them and Jill is intent on reading the bills, many of which appear to be very old, wilted, and faded. Rachael and I are enjoying a rum punch when Jill screeches, "Oh my gosh - 'Tom Cruise' - his name is on this dollar bill near the door!" The girls are understandably confused about their mother's over-the-top reaction, when Rachael guides them to a worn bill near one of the windows: "Robert and Rachael - Charleston, SC - 2004". She tells them a story of their grandfather and how he loved this place. I produce a dollar bill and the girls write their names. They pin their autographed dollar bill beside their grandfather's.

"Will it still be there beside Granddaddy's when we come back, MeMaw Rachael?"

"Yes, my sweethearts, it will."

• • •

We have been underway for over three hours and speed across the calm, clear waters of the Little Bahama Bank when the boat abruptly stops and Captain Russell calls me to the bridge. "We've got trouble. The port engine vibrates and doesn't respond well. I'm shutting it down."

"What can I do to help?"

"Remain at the helm. The starboard engine is idling in neutral. If we drift on the current toward the rocks over there, move the lever like this." He inches it forward and backward to show me the movement of the boat as it responds to the rudder and the throttle. Jeff would be better at this, I think, as he was the one in love with boat engines.

Captain Russell disappears in the engine room below, and Rachael joins me in the adjacent bridge seat. "Does Captain Russell know what's wrong?"

"No, but he suspects we have something tangled in the propeller on that engine."

Captain Russell yells from the deck below, "I'm going in the water to check the prop. Remember, what I told you. No sudden moves while I'm in the water. Move us a little to the right away from the rocks before I go in, then put the engine in neutral. I don't want to lose a leg down there by the blade of the prop. I won't be down long."

I lean over the rail of the bridge to watch Captain Russell. He has donned swim goggles and fins. He sees me and gives me a "thumbs up". I must look worried because Rachael points out on the depth sounder that we are in only fourteen feet of water.

"If something terrible were to happen, can you operate this boat?"

"No. I've always depended on Captain Russell and your father. Don't worry. Captain Russell knows what he's doing."

Jill and the girls are outside, and she pacifies them by putting their two fishing rods in the water. She hands off the girl-size rods and tells them to look for fish.

Rachael and I scan the water around us in all directions. We see no other boats in sight. "What's that?"

"Where?" I say.

"Something protruding out of the water near that barren little cay. It looks like some sort of debris in the water around it."

Rachael scrambles in the helm station and produces a set of binoculars. "Oh mercy! It's the bow of a sunken boat sticking up out of the water. And the 'debris' - it looks like people!"

"Give me those!" It's exactly as Rachael described. The boat is capsized and the bow is exposed above the water line.

109

the way home

"Go down and splash the water to get Captain Russell's attention."

"We've got some rigging from a sailboat wrapped around our propeller. The son of a bitch is bound tight." Captain Russell has surfaced and sounds aggravated.

"There's a sunken boat up ahead and I think there are people in the water." Rachael tells him.

Captain Russell quickly climbs aboard *Game On* and runs up the ladder to the bridge. He peers through the binoculars and identifies the scene we've described to him.

"May Day, May Day, May Day. This is sixty-one foot recreational fishing vessel, *Game On,* location coordinates N 26 56.190' W 77 41.660 We are in route to an overturned vessel of undetermined size and what appear to be survivors in the water." Captain Russell uses our one operable engine and accelerates our speed in the direction of the upturned boat while he sends out "May Day" on the radio. He repeats the same message, since there is no response. I know from my boating days on the harbor that "May Day" is the extreme distress call for mariners who are in danger.

We see a few bodies as we approach the wreckage. "Jill", I scream, "take the girls inside and stay with them. Now!" I hear Elizabeth crying that Mommy has made her drop her fishing rod over the side of the boat. Jill, uncharacteristically, screams at the girls to get inside.

Captain Russell idles the boat and scrambles down the ladder. He instructs Rachael to continue to repeat the distress call until someone responds. I follow him. He grabs a grappling hook from its cradle as well as a boat hook and thrusts it at me. We are about fifty yards from the overturned boat, and drift into the debris field. I count three male bodies floating near us and a few more near the sunken boat. Their heads and shoulders bob above the water line and their bodies are draped below the surface in a bizarre position.

We hear over the radio someone responding to Rachael's distress call. "Who are you? You have trouble?"

judy norwood enter

"Yes! This is *Game On* and we are sitting off Center of the World Rock. There is a sunken boat and people in the water!" Rachael has identified our location on the chartplotter.

"You 'bout five miles from Parrot Village on tip of Little Abaco Island. I call Bahamas Defence Force."

Captain Russell assesses the gravity of this scene and yells up to Rachael to get back on the radio and ask for any boat in the area to relay a message to the Bahamas Air and Sea Rescue as well as the United States Coast Guard. Captain Russell leans over the side of the boat with the grappling hook and gently moves a body as he looks for any sign of life. He motions for me to do the same. I poke one of the bloated bodies, a young man, with the boat hook, and neither he nor I can find any sign of life. As we drift closer to the overturned boat, Captain Russell returns to the bridge to steer us away from the wreckage. I see a small black hand that grabs hold and clings to the overturned bow.

"Captain Russell! At the bow of the wreckage. I see movement!"

He steers us a little closer.

"There, see?"

I run to the bow deck of *Game On* and from there I can see the boy's wild eyes as he loses his grip on the wreckage. "I'm going in the water!" I jump as far out and away from our boat as possible and swim for the child. When I reach him, he grabs me and pulls me under the water. I strong-arm him and turn him away to get a grip and float him on his back. He speaks the gibberish I've come to recognize as the Haitian language."Ede'm! Ede'm!" (Help! Help!) I swim with him to the ladder of our boat and push him toward Rachael who waits on the deck.

From the bridge Captain Russell yells, "Anyone else out there alive?"

"I didn't see or hear anyone else."

Rachael dries the boy and soothes him in the Kreyol she has learned. "Ki gen'w rele?" (What's your name?) The boy shakes uncontrollably and does not respond. Rachael speaks to him again, "Mwen se ameriken." (I'm American.) Still no response from the

111

the way home

boy in her arms. "Pa enkie te'w." (Don't worry.) She rocks him in her arms.

Jill brings Rachael a pair of girl's shorts and a T-shirt as well as a bottle of water and a blanket. She gives the bottle of water to the boy and he gulps the cold, clean water. Captain Russell continues his radio transmission and BASRA, the Bahamas Air and Sea Rescue, finally responds. They have a boat in route to our location, and he is directed to secure the scene until they arrive. He also tells them of the boy. Jill takes the frightened child inside away from the gruesome scene.

Rachael is the bravest woman I know. She helps me gingerly pull the few bodies we can reach alongside our boat and secure them with spare lines. Captain Russell drops an anchor to secure our position and helps us. We count six bodies we've lashed to the side of *Game On*, two women and four men. Rachael, as we tie off another body, says, "How could they bring a boy? He's only a boy."

Captain Russell says, "He's just a small man to them. His plight is the same as a man's in Haiti. He was leaving for a better life. His father or mother may be among the dead." He points to the bodies tethered to us like objects. "Or he may have been an orphan who stowed away on the boat leaving Haiti after dark. This boat is about a thirty-eight foot sailboat by the size of its bow. It was headed for the United States through these waters. It is quite common for these renegade boats overfilled with refugees to traverse these waters. May have been as many as forty people on this boat. When the boats founder in storms, the Haitians who survive swim for shore and live here as immigrants. Sometimes they beg their way aboard recreational boats bound for the United States. They will do anything not to return to Haiti."

The sun is setting and I fear we will be forced to stay the night alone with the corpses of these men and women lying at our side, when a siren and flashing lights burst through the solemn scene. It is a Coast Guard-style, high-speed inflatable BASRA boat with a larger steel-gray Bahamas Defence cruiser following at full speed. I confess that I'm glad we will be relieved of this morbid duty, and wonder what will happen to the boy.

• • •

  Captain Russell frees the tangled rigging from our prop the next morning and determines we have no damage to either the shaft or the prop. He confirms that it was a rigging line from a sailboat, and most probably from the wreckage of the doomed refugee boat. If we had not tangled with the debris, we would most likely have passed in the distance and never have seen the overturned boat or the small boy. The United States Coast Guard arrives out of Miami with two helicopters and searches for survivors. We have slept little during the night at this anchorage of such great loss and are anxious to depart. As we cautiously leave the surreal scene, we wave goodbye to the nameless boy, who wears my daughter's clothing, as he stands alone on the deck of the Defence boat. I'm told he'll be flown to Nassau and returned to Haiti. I question to whom will he be returned, and will I see him one day in the children's home or on one of the dusty roads as he forages for food.

thirteen

I accompany Jill and the girls back to Asheville on the fancy plane, which I pay for along with Rachael's ride back to Charleston. Spending large chunks of cash on luxury items must be an acquired skill because it feels awkward to me. Our mood is somber and reflective as we remember the events that ended our cruise. Old Bahama Bay was beautiful and the girls loved the beach and waterfall pool, but compared to the Haitian boat and its tragic end, the opulence seemed unfitting.

School begins soon, but I need to return to Charleston to continue to meet with Louis. On the ride home aboard a luxurious King Air, on which we behave like celebrities, Jill and I agree to tackle one life change at a time and keep the girls as grounded as possible—but this is said while the steward on the plane is catering to their every whim. My job is the first obstacle to overcome, since I will either have to return to work immediately or resign. It's an easy decision for us both because we inherently know, without discussion, that my time in the foreseeable future is required in Charleston. There's simply too much hanging over my head I need to deal with and too many people waiting for decisions.

So after one glorious night in my own bed, this same plane flies me to my home office in Chicago, where I submit my resignation. The fact that my father left me so much money has yet to fully sink in, and I feel insecure and anxious as I talk to my

the way home

superior. He says the news of my newly acquired wealth traveled fast and they expected my resignation. I transfer my active accounts to another salesman, who's happy for the opportunity for extra sales and income. I walk out of this former life, board my plane, and fly to Charleston.

Jill and I agree to wait until the end of the school term to make another big change in our lives and move to Charleston for the summer. It's like we've been involuntarily shoved onto a merry-go-round and can't get off.

As the plane approaches the airport in Charleston, I remember that day not so long ago, the dread building in me like a dam about to burst. Today, fresh off the time in the Bahamas with my family, there is supreme thankfulness but, at the same time, the enormous weight of the job I have ahead. And the encounter with the wreckage of the Haitian boat and its doomed refugees, especially the little boy, make the responsibility more personal.

"I have a new career," I think to myself. "OK, Bobby, you have a new career. Approach it with energy and passion, not unlike your sales career. Treat this like a career change you're trying out. Be resolute and committed, and if you find you don't love it, then pass the work on to someone who does. If you can't perform this work with even greater interest and pride than you did sales, then you'll find someone who can. These poor, forgotten people in Haiti deserve that."

Louis sends the driver and car for me. I'd already spoken to Rachael. At her direction I shop the same Fresh Market for the same menu items as I did last time, opting to forego the praline cheesecake because the scales in my bathroom in Asheville confirm that I smuggled three pounds through American customs from the Bahamas.

"Oh, Bobby, you didn't bring the cheesecake." Her disappointment registers.

"Rachael, what is it with your metabolism? You ate and drank like a small horse in Abaco, and you look like you shrank. What are you, thirty years older than I am? I gained three pounds…my decision if you want me to be your errand boy. No praline cheesecake."

judy norwood enter

She smiles. "Well, how about some chocolate? And I am not thirty years older than you, but it's none of your business how old I am."

"Very funny. Let's don't play 'embarrass Bobby' tonight, OK?" She was obviously alluding to my messy encounter with chocolate in the Bahamas.

The halls of the house on Waterview are lined with Rachael's moving boxes. She purchased the beach house at Pawleys fully furnished and is only taking her personal effects. As I negotiate the halls, I notice that many of the boxes are marked "Photographs." This family loves its photographs. I'm remembering all the photographs of the girls on our home computer and feel like an anachronism when I realize I like the old photographs printed on paper and placed in albums better. I vow to myself to organize my computer files and begin to print them out when I have time. Jill, the girls, and I can begin our own tradition of old-fashioned photo albums to chronicle the history of our family.

Tonight is a replica of our party for two that was only a few weeks ago but seems a short lifetime ago. As I watch Rachael prepare dinner, I analyze the epiphany I formulated on the plane back to Charleston today: I have never known relationship with Rachael as an adult; I've only known her from a boy's perspective. I overheard a conversation between her and Jill at Old Bahama Bay that stirred a desire in me to know her, really know her. I had returned from a walk and gone to the bridge of the boat to be alone, when I heard Rachael and Jill come outside to the cockpit deck below me:

"Are the girls finally asleep?" Jill asks.

"Yes. It took two Dora the Explorer stories."

"Thanks, Rachael. It's been hard to answer their questions about the boy and what happened back there. Elizabeth keeps asking where his mommy and daddy are."

"Try not to worry about them, honey. Their memories will fade."

"We let that little boy slip through our fingers and there wasn't anything we could do. Did you see his little eyes? He was scared to death standing on the deck of that Defence boat."

117

the way home

"Jill, I feel helpless every time I go to Haiti. A clean cup of water and some food is all I can offer. The work we do in Haiti is all short-term. We tend to be long-term investors in this country. We put our money and time in projects that bring us mature returns. But where the poorest of the poor live, short-term benefits are what the majority need and want. Most Haitians we serve don't see themselves as moving much beyond where they are now. There's a man, Dennis, a Haitian, on a small cay near here. Each day he brings his oversize cooler to the beach and uses it as a float to swim out on the Bank where he free-dives to gather lobster and conch. He puts his catch in the cooler and swims back to shore where he cleans and sells the fish, conch, and lobster. Robert asked him about the cooler, and he said it was his boat, his seafood storage, and his storefront. Robert offered to buy him a small fishing boat but he refused. The cooler was all he needed to do his work, and a boat brought with it responsibility. The next year when Robert visited him, he took him a new cooler from *Game On*. He thanked Robert and told him he would save it for when his old one wore out."

"So Robert met his short-term needs, he didn't try to change him or give him something he didn't want or need?" Jill says.

"Yes. Robert said that *he* needed to give Dennis a boat, but Dennis didn't want it or need it, and that a wise man knows the difference. Dennis has accepted his life where good weather, fish and conch for the day, and a cooler is enough."

"Why, exactly, did you tell me this story?"

"Mary Elizabeth had a saying, 'water seeks its own level'. People rise to the level where they are comfortable, and they won't move much beyond that place. They want our respect and our support at their level, not to be moved to ours. That little boy was born in Haiti. You can't overcome that level to which he was born, no more than you can switch out your girls' lives by placing them in Haiti. He must find his way, and I pray to God his people will help him."

• • •

judy norwood enter

Some beach music by the Dominoes haunts the old house as Rachael and I eat our steaks. "This *is* the twenty-first century. Some very fine music has been recorded since the sixties. Ever think of buying it?"

"There is no other music. Who taught you the shag? Jill told me one time she married you because you could shag so well." She laughs.

As we finish our dinner, she grows somber and asks me a loaded question. "Since you've been back here in this house, have you been to your mother's study?"

"Yes, I was rambling around that first night I returned and you were in Pawleys. I wandered into the study. It is a little disconcerting for me, like she just got up from her desk and went to get a glass of tea and she's coming back. Why have you kept that room intact all these years? Actually, why haven't you gutted the entire house and put your stamp on it? The garden room looks like you, but most of the house is unchanged. Why?"

While I've been talking, Rachael has been clearing the table and refilling our wine glasses. She opens the pantry and pulls out a bag of chocolate Oreos. She sits down in my father's chair at the table again, drawing a cookie out of the bag. She separates the cookie so the filling is exposed and begins to lick it, sipping wine between licks.

"Yum, chocolate Oreos and wine. Glad you didn't bring the cheesecake. Want one?"

I contemplate the cookie bag and snatch it toward me. "Of course, and if you tell Jill, I will know."

She smiles, chocolate cookie crumbs dotting the sides of her mouth. "Aw, I can still tempt you over to the dark side. 'Dark side' — chocolate. Get it?"

"Yes, Rachael, you don't have to be so obvious with your double meanings. You're changing the subject. Talk to me about the house."

She brushes away the cookie crumbs and leans back in her chair, swirling the wine in its glass. "Nice legs — the wine, I mean."

119

the way home

"You're doing it again. I went to college and actually have a degree and all—I can figure out your double meanings. And you're stalling."

"Let's take our glasses to the portico, Bobby. And I'll tell you most everything."

"Most?"

We sit in my grandmother's ancient Charleston green wicker chairs that have recently been painted and splashed with Rachael's favorite floral chintz across their upholstered cushions. It's late, and we both blankly stare into the depleted light on the harbor.

"Yes, most things I will tell you. But I told you early on that some things from the past you need to search out for yourself. My job is to put you in a position to make these discoveries on your treasure hunt, and if you need a little more 'north' on your compass to give you direction, I'll help you. But you have to do the hard work yourself. You know the story about the cocoon and the emerging butterfly? If you try to help the butterfly by opening its cocoon, which he constructed as a caterpillar, he will die. The divine design is that he struggles to free himself in order to strengthen his wings so he can fly and live. Well, that's how I see you. If I rush in and destroy that shell you've built around your life, you'll be worse off than you were before. You need to struggle your way out so you can be stronger."

"That's overly dramatic and a little corny."

"Maybe, but it's the truth. Besides, I thought it was beautiful, and a little drama is expected from a southern girl."

"Rachael, you use being a 'southern girl' to excuse an awful lot of your behavior."

"I know. It's a gift."

Following this light banter, she fixes her gaze out across the darkness of the harbor again. I discern that something deep is coming out and it's easier for her to talk into the black harbor than directly at me.

"Bobby, this was always your father and mother's home. I agreed to move back in here after her death because I made her a promise. She didn't know when she would die, of course, but she

judy norwood enter

made me promise that if something happened to her, Robert and I would move in and tend the family home until you boys were ready for it. She loved this place and wanted you to have it. You know me, Bobby. I'm an old Myrtle Beach girl; I like new things, not this old stuff you people in Charleston cling righteously to. Anyway, I made the promise frankly because I didn't think I would have to do it, and then she up and dies on me. So I kept my promise, and that's why your father and I wound up here. Now, to you, it probably looks like I took your mother's husband and then her house. But neither is true. It's one of those lies you believe that became one of the many roots of your bitterness. So you see, I never loved this place. I loved your mother, and I did it for her. And the way things developed with everyone else dying, well, I saved it for you. She would like that.

Bobby, your mother's family lost most of their money near the end of their lives. Some embezzling asshole of an accountant drained about everything they had. Your mother's trust was breached by that thieving evildoer, and she had little money to keep this albatross up in the last years. Copious amounts of money are required to maintain one of these relics. You'll find out. Your father supported your mother and maintained the house for her until the day she died."

"Well, that explains a lot. Jeff and I wondered why she left us no inheritance—not that we were greedy, but we were just wondering."

"What are you going to do with this old place, Bobby? It's worth millions, you know."

"And what would I do with more millions, Rachael? I don't know what to do with the excessive money I already have."

"You and Jill talk about moving the girls here? Not a bad place to grow up, this big, old piece of Confederate history. Jill's an old southern Savannah girl. She would fit right in here and raise your girls like proper southern women."

"Rachael, I resigned my job in Chicago before I flew back here. It was the only big decision we were able to manage at the time."

"Well, there's plenty of time. Might I make a suggestion?"

"Can I stop you?"

the way home

"School will be out for the summer in a few weeks. Why not move in for the summer and see how Jill and the girls take to it? I still see it in you, Bobby. You'll adapt just fine."

"See what in me?"

Rachael turns to examine me now. "I see salt air and moon tides, oysters and shrimp and flounder, bare feet on cool, wood floors, sailboats on the harbor, sipping a little libation on this grand portico in the evening light with your family and friends, and the respect you garner from people here who know you and your family. So you've been gone for a few years on a little mountain sabbatical. You're home, and you know it. And I'll tell you a little secret I probably shouldn't. Jill knows it, too."

I walk around the portico, still in earshot of Rachael. "I don't know, Rachael. So much change. I'm a lot like Mother in that I don't like change. All that's happening to me and my family is not what I planned. I like knowing the beginning and the end of something. I like my books lined up on the shelf, the dirty dishes washed and put away at night, and pictures hung straight on the wall. That's how I planned my life. Not what I had as a child where everything seemed off-center and off-balance to me. Mother could obsessively line up the cans of food in the pantry, label and stack meat in the freezer, organize our closets by the colors of our shirts with the seasons, and line up the damn books on the shelves, but she couldn't straighten up our lives here. I plan, and if it's not in my plan, I don't do it."

Rachael's eyes glisten in the dim light and hold the faraway look of an old sage. "Only God knows the beginning and the end. Life is fragile, and we who live it forfeit control the day we're born. Control is an illusion. Anything and everything happens. We have choices, and our choices are critical, but we don't control an outcome. Jack drowned when he went out fishing like he always did. Trent clung to the bottom of that overturned boat and almost died that day, except a boat happened by and he lived. Mary Elizabeth's desperate attempt to control her life and change the past ate her alive, and your father was helpless to stop it. Jeff's demons chased him finally into his grave. And then Robert vanished into thin air. You couldn't control any of that, and they couldn't either. You, because of Robert's death, are cast into a new role that you didn't ask for simply because you were born the son of Robert and Mary Elizabeth. You're alive, your father is dead, and you have some new choices to make. It's just that simple." She stands and hugs me firmly from behind. "Heck, if I had any control, they would all be alive, and we would be living back at the beach house in the eighties."

I turn into her and embrace her. We stand like that for a minute. When we part she takes my face in her hand and speaks softly, almost in a whisper. "Bobby, your mother wants to talk to you."

It takes me a second or two to realize she's not referring to herself. "What?"

"Her journals, Bobby. She left them for you and Jeff."

I spin around and take a few steps down the stairs, holding onto the banister. "Rachael, I did go to her study, and I randomly read a few pages. I'm bewildered about my mother's life and frankly would rather remain in that state of confusion. Compared to my father, she was a saint. And I guess I'm afraid if she falls from sainthood, I will have lost both my parents. I need my good memories of one of them to be intact."

I detect the tone of Rachael's voice has changed from consoling to parentally authoritative and the purpose of her words to giving orders. "I'm sympathetic to what you're saying, but that's a childish view and not a particularly healthy one. And I cannot put a Band-Aid on this wound of yours like I used to do when you were a little boy. Take your pain to your mother and allow her to tend it. It may hurt more for a while, but allowing the truth to make you well is the kindest thing you can do for you and for your family."

"I wouldn't know where to start, Rachael. She has over two decades of journals in there. I don't know what I'm looking for or if I would recognize it when I find it."

"Eventually, most of her writing is going to be important to you. In the last years, as the depression worsened, she didn't write as much. She told me one time it made her feel worse to see her 'sickness,' as she called it on paper. So I told her not to write the damn things anymore. I think she wrote until she died but not with

the way home

the same consistency as in the earlier years. I haven't read them all myself. If I were you, I would start with the very early ones."

Rachael had put my bags in the carriage house earlier. But I retrieve them and take them to the attic room. On my way there, passing down the hall past mother's study, I linger a moment and enter. Following Rachael's instructions, I choose one of her earlier journals and take it with me to my bed in the attic.

fourteen

Rachael's Christmas lights in the attic room creep me out, so I crawl into my boyhood bed in the dark and turn on the old floor lamp. The bulb seems weak, so I clean about ten years' worth of dust off it with my dirty T-shirt and open Mother's journal. I don't know where to start, so I figure my birthday would be a safe and happy place to begin.

"July 8, 1988.

Bobby is ten years old today. He is tall and slender, skinny even. I keep trying to fatten him up. His personality is like his father's. He can talk everybody into anything and make it seem like it was their idea. He is brilliant and an A student in school in all courses except math. His teachers absolutely love him but tell me he doesn't have many friends. I worry about this, but I don't need a lot of people around me, either, so maybe in this way he is like me. But I recall, before the great darkness invaded me, I had lots of friends. I pray to God that I am not leaving Bobby a legacy of isolation and fear.

Happy birthday, my treasured second son."

"Second son?" I say aloud to the vintage light bulb.

Mother recognized math was never one of my strong suits, but I know Jeff was born two years after me. I was born in 1978, and he, the unwanted brother to me, came to us in 1980. Maybe she had grouped us and was just calling me "second son" after Jeff came along.

the way home

I'm tired after what has been a long, arduous day, and I turn out the light. But restlessness keeps waking me, so I give in to it and switch on the old lamp. Picking up the journal, I begin thumbing through it, looking for nothing in particular. My eyes pick up on various lines of her writing, and I find some of it is rambling, like she was drunk or on drugs. Reading it is like watching someone you love trying to sober up and make sense. It hurts me to try to decipher it, so I push the journal to the floor beside my bed. I cut off the light again. I turn it on.

I slip quietly down the attic stairs and return to Mother's study. She has carefully catalogued the journals with date labels like "January 15, 1981–October 26, 1981." I search a couple of journals that would include entries she wrote on Jeff's birthday, if there are any, and read one.

"December 4, 1989.

Jeffrey is nine years old today! He and I completed his science project last night, and I've observed he possesses a quiet, introspective way of thinking. He is quite analytical and is happiest solving problems on his own. The day he was born, he didn't cry when they took him from me. I was frightened until I heard his noise, a quiet whimper. The pediatrician brought him to me and said he was a quiet one...Nothing wrong with him, he said. He just didn't have the need to cry. And so even today Jeffrey is more likely to suffer alone. I love you, my third son. Happy birthday."

My heart is racing as I read and reread her entry on Jeff's ninth birthday. What is she saying? I can explain away *second son*, but not *third son*. What are you saying, Mother? Looking for an answer, I grab another journal inclusive of one of Jeff's birthdays.

"December 4, 1992.

Number twelve. My third son is a milestone twelve years old today. His brothers are fourteen and seventeen. Jeffrey is my third and final son. There will be no more children for Robert and me. We are blessed with these two sons to share our lives with and desire no more children. Jeffrey is strong, athletic, and proud but quiet. He doesn't adore school but loves athletics. I wish his father could value the strength of his body as much as he relishes a strong mind. Happy birthday, my third son. Your family loves you."

Mother was obviously living under some delusion that she had three children. She even switches from *third* to *two*, but why would she give some contrived third son an age of seventeen? That would make him born in 1976, the year after my parents were married.

There is no recognizable order to what Mother is writing, although she has meticulously catalogued and labeled dates, and someone, maybe Rachael, has organized them. I have an idea and begin to go back down the line of journals until I come to a few books with the year *1976* on them. I pull out one and leaf through it hurriedly, not seeing anything that jumps out at me. The door to Mother's study opens, and Rachael floats in, barefooted and wearing a white, flowing house robe, which makes her look like an apparition. She looks at the year I'm trying to search and issues an edict: "June 2, 1976."

"I don't think I want to."

My hands feel like sandpaper and shake as I try to locate this date in the journals. My eyes are dry and tired, and my mouth feels like cotton. The clock on Mother's wall strikes three.

"June 2, 1976.

On this morning in June at 3:00 a.m., my womb dislodged the child I secretly carried for nine months. And suddenly I am desperately empty. I saw him only briefly and heard his loud cries. A sympathetic nurse told me I had a son and whisked him away for the pediatric evaluation. Then he was taken away to his adoptive parents' waiting arms. I don't know their names and will never know his. My breasts are throbbing with milk that my child will never taste. How can a seed sown in such acute violence by a stranger bent on power and destruction become such a part of my soul? I've loved this child since I first felt him flutter in my belly, though Rachael warned me to bear no feelings for him. How can a mother prevent her love for her own flesh? Unless she is evil like his father, she cannot and she will not. The father of this child will not know him or even want him. And this son will not know the evil his father engaged in that resulted in his life, the great darkness that invaded

the way home

his mother's body. If he knows anything, it will be that his mother gave him life disengaged from the one who planted the seed and that I bear him only love. Will he be loved, will he be secure, and what will my son become without his true mother to guide him? And for me, will this sadness have an ending, or will it follow me forever? I believe I would rather mourn the loss of a dead child rather than this living child for a lifetime. Will I meet him on the street one day and not know he is my child? Will he pack my groceries or wash my car and I will not know he is my teenage son? And in the wisdom of God, if Robert and I have children, how will I tell them they have a beloved brother?"

"She was raped." I state this as a matter of fact. "My mother was raped." I look to Rachael for confirmation.

"Yes, shortly after opening their first law practice above that bakery."

I deposit the journal on my mother's desk, wanting to leave this baffling place that has intruded on my life with its bitter renderings. I vow to myself, Rachael, and God to never enter this room again. I hear one short, shattering sentence as I walk from this chamber of horrors.

"He's alive and living in Virginia."

fifteen

Almost a week has passed since I discovered my mother's dark secret. Louis and I have worked together every day, with Rachael joining us in some of our business meetings. Rachael, like my father, has a keen interest in Haiti and its people. She made a few trips there with my father, and her primary interest is in the orphaned children. She lays out her plan for me one morning over coffee on the portico at Waterview.

"Children's Home is an orphanage camouflaged with a better-sounding name. These children need to be in homes, preferably with their blood families—you know, aunts, uncles, cousins. Blood family isn't always the answer if they're derelict or drugged-up or whatever, but we need a resource to help us find these children's families and interview them to see if they can love and care for these children."

"If their blood families wanted these children, why don't they have them?"

"Not enough money to feed them is my guess. A monthly allotment of money can be set aside and administered to these families. It should be enough for living expenses, like adequate housing, food, and education, but not exorbitant so some families aren't tempted to take the children only for the money. Someone once said, 'Give children enough to do something, but not enough to do nothing.'"

the way home

"And if we can't locate the children's families, then what?" I ask.

"We need to set up foster families on the same basis, like Monique and Marianne have in a random way for the children they bring down the mountain. Now, I've discovered online a resource I believe we can begin with just by asking some questions. If you agree, I'll contact North Shore Haiti Mission and begin some research. Although its focus is in the rural area well outside Cap-Haïtien, if we like what they're doing with the foster care plan, we can simply emulate it in Port-au-Prince. What do you think?"

"I think it's a fine idea. Why don't you pursue it? And keep up your communication with Nicholas as to what you're investigating. He may have some suggestions for resources right there in Port-au-Prince."

"OK, but I think I need to go to Haiti soon. Not only for research on the foster program but also because the Children's Home needs some oversight. It'll still need to be operational as well because we won't be able to find homes for all the children. I want some time with Monique and Marianne. Someone needs to set up some rules of conduct and establish an inventory of stocks for the kids. They need medical exams and clothing."

"You are not going to Haiti alone."

"Now, Bobby, don't be telling Rachael what she can and can't do. Although I do agree with you that I shouldn't go alone. So you go with me. It's about time you went back as well. You and Louis and the investment group have got a handle on the trusts. Robert left us in good hands with all of the complicated details. What we need now is a whole lot of heart and a few good feet on the ground."

"We'll return to Haiti soon. Can't give you a date right now, so work through the internet and phones to contact these resources."

"I also want you to think about Brenda Grace and Jill becoming administrators of not only the monies we'll be transferring to Haiti but also researchers for new projects. This is a family business. The more, the better."

In such a short time, it has been decided that my father has left us all a "family business." I no longer threaten to dispose of it, although it hasn't been concretely determined by anyone that I will lead. Right now I'm leading by assumption.

Rachael and I haven't spoken of what I read in Mother's journal. Instinctively, she knows I need time to process these new facts that my mother was raped by an unknown assailant she calls "the great darkness that invaded my body" and that I have a half brother living somewhere in Virginia. This new knowledge rolls around in my head every day and keeps me awake at night. But I haven't been ready to talk about it with Rachael. I know she can fill in some details, but my brain needs time to assimilate this horrific piece of knowledge and other details I don't know how to handle at this point. I've immersed myself in this "new career" my father has designed for me and am actually enjoying Louis's guidance and Rachael's sharp business acumen. Exploring the avenues to new business has always both stimulated and distracted me.

The knowledge Rachael and I share about my mother's son has produced an unspoken bond between us; each of us know we will make an inevitable journey to Virginia to see my mother's face in his, even if from afar. We will be quietly driven to see Mary Elizabeth's son, this woman we both love unendingly, this woman and mother who suffered and grieved so much loss. I can't wrap my mind around the fact that my mother has another son, that I have a living brother. I wonder how he would react to knowing he has a family here.

I break my vow and return to Mother's study on some of these sleepless nights. Her later writings are of a sad and vulnerable woman struggling with a husband who loves her and is patient with her but who wants his wife back. But in her own words, she cannot surrender herself to him and believes every day she fails him. She mourns the loss of her first son and isolates herself into dispassionate loneliness. Mother became like one of those great sea turtles that have for centuries come ashore in the dark, following the light of the moon along our coast in South Carolina. She covertly laid her eggs in a nest of dug-out sand, a nursery, which she fashioned with her great flippers. When her body expelled the last egg, she covered the nest with sand while tears streamed down her reptilian

the way home

face, and then she returned to the sea. She would never know her children, and perhaps she possessed the instinctual knowledge that few of them would survive as they hatched and made their journey across the sand into the sea. This all may seem unreasonable and a bit dramatic, but who, besides her creator, really knows why she was crying?

My mother writes repeatedly that her greatest joys are Jeff and I and her greatest sadness the loss of her first son. But, she writes, the happiness she found in us is not enough to overcome her grief of the lost son. In one of her writings, she quotes from the Bible a parable in which Jesus taught that a good shepherd should leave the ninety-nine sheep secure in the pasture and go out to look for the one that was lost. And yet there is no mention of a passion or effort to locate him. She writes halfheartedly and with little expectation of my father's search: "Poor Robert believes if he finds my child, I can be made well." And so my mother, desperately sad, surrendered to depression, pills, and food because, in her words, "On the night of the 'great darkness,' I lost control of my life, all my dreams, and the right to be happy."

I'm not a mother, so I cannot understand the profound loss of a child you've carried for nine months. But I am forgiving Mother her grief more and more each day. I believe that my mother's sadness affected Jeff and I in an enigmatic way and we didn't even know it was happening. She writes frequently in the annals of her life about her love of my father. He was defeated in that he lost the woman he loved on the night of the great darkness. That thief raped my father as well. He invaded this husband's life, stealing the body, heart, and soul of his greatest love. Mother writes of my father's impotence to save her and how she eventually sent him away.

"August 21, 1997.

I asked Robert once again to leave. I cannot bear to look at the pain in his eyes any longer, nor can I bear the way he looks at me. I fail him every day. And he says he has failed me. What is left in a marriage when both have failed? Failed to love enough, or to forgive enough, or to accept without condemnation. Failure is a miserable obstacle to wake up to every morning. I have failed my sons, failed

judy norwood enter

Robert, and failed Rachael. So I asked him again, and this time he agreed to go. I will ask Rachael to look after him."

Everything I've believed to be true about these two people who gave me life is being shattered. It's as though I'm living in a dark fairy-tale. "Humpty Dumpty sat on a wall. Humpty Dumpty had a great fall. And all the king's horses and all the king's men couldn't put Humpty together again." I don't know how to share this with my best friend. When I fly back to Asheville for a visit or call Jill, she senses the sadness and confusion and asks about it. I tell her I can't put words to it right now but that I don't want this to be a barrier between us as we're healing. And she listens, and we speak of the girls and the summer. Rachael and I have decided to wait until summer for my father's memorial service, and I've asked Jill to come to Charleston to help us.

• • •

Rachael decides it's time for us to visit the wing at the Medical University of South Carolina and then head up to Charlotte to the drug rehabilitation center dedicated to Jeff's memory as well as stop by for a visit with Brenda Grace. This morning, we tour the Mary Elizabeth Hargrave Treatment Center for Depression and Obesity at MUSC in Charleston. The director is Dr. Mack Longworth, a jovial, slimmer version of Santa Claus with white hair and beard and, evidently, a love of bright-red ties.

"Bobby Chapin!" He takes my extended hand in a tight grip of a handshake and pumps it until I pull it back. "I can't tell you how good it is to see you."

I look at Rachael, querying her with my eyes. Am I supposed to know this man?

"Bobby, I see your mother in your facial features as well as your height, but I see elements of your father in you as well. I'm so sorry about your father's death. He was a fine man and very good to us here at the clinic."

"You knew my mother?"

133

the way home

"Yes, I'm a longtime friend of both your parents. It was for that reason, I believe, that Mary Elizabeth and your father trusted me with her treatment. We've all known one another since our early college years at USC."

He turns his attention to Rachael, and they exchange hugs and cheek kisses. "Hello, my old friend. How are you holding up?"

"Better now that Bobby is here. Mack, you should see his two girls. They're absolutely beautiful, and Memaw Rachael got to play with them in the Bahamas two weeks ago."

"Excellent. I guess you were in the Abacos aboard *Game On* and playing with all Robert's toys," he says, laughing. "Don't forget old Mack here. Those fishing trips with Robert were fabulous. I never could out-fish him, but I loved trying. Is Captain Russell still onboard?"

"Yes, he is," I answer.

"What are you going to do with that big, old boat, Bobby? I know you and your family didn't show any interest in it in the past, so I just assumed it's not your cup of tea."

"Well, my family certainly enjoyed it, so I haven't decided. It seems like a pretty vulgar use of money to use it as little as it is now."

"Funny, I never heard 'vulgar' and 'money' used in the same sentence before. I kind of like it and all that it can do. Your father enjoyed his toys, but he always shared them. And he spread his money around in some of the best places, like this wing. Are you ready for a tour?"

What I really want to do is escort this man to the cafeteria for coffee and ask him to tell me everything he knows about my mother. I especially want him to tell me why, if he was treating her, he couldn't save her.

The wing is a warm, state-of-the-art residential facility for women suffering depression and obesity. A staff of twelve therapists and six dieticians are on staff under Dr. Longworth's professional direction. There are seventy-five well-equipped rooms that can house two patients each. Mack explains that these women are suffering self-imposed isolation, and sharing a room with another patient forces them to relate, for better or worse, with another woman. In each large room, there is a half bath and a full bath as well as a retractable screen in the center. The furnishings look like something my mother would have chosen: high-end reproduction four-poster beds, mahogany dressers, mirrors in several locations, and beautifully quilted, colorful comforters. A small table with two chairs sits in a large window area, an oriental rug is placed on the hardwood floor, and a couple of comfortable reading chairs are upholstered in gay fabric like you might find in a very fine living room. The lighting is cut glass, brass, and expensive.

The room we tour is vacant, but I see women with dark eyes and blank stares navigate their large bodies down the halls. Mack Longworth hugs several of them and asks in a genuine tone of voice how they're doing. They all respond to him warmly. He appears to be a well-liked man. We visit the cafeteria, which could be a nice bistro on the streets of Charleston sans the bar. We're greeted everywhere on the wing with enthusiasm and warmth. There is nothing medicinal or clinical about this place. I sense it is a place of healing, if maybe a last resort for these women.

It is one o'clock, and Mack has arranged lunch for us at a small table near the back of the cafeteria. We're served a tasty, healthy meal of generous proportions. My mind again travels back to my mother, and I wonder whether if she had this place to flee to she would have been able to disconnect with the past and its damage while finding hope in the restorative love of her family.

"Mack, were there facilities like this when my mother was alive?"

"Yes. There was one in Colorado, but she wouldn't even visit it with me. She said it was too far from home and you boys. Then I located a small facility in North Carolina, but she refused to go to that one as well. Robert and I tried to convince her to just go and observe the work there. She wouldn't go."

"I remember those two facilities. You brought brochures and other information on the residential facilities. I told her we'd go and make a girl's trip out of it." Rachael says.

the way home

"She didn't want to leave Charleston and there was no facility for her here. That's why Robert, after her death, wanted to launch a program here. So many women, a lot of them local from South Carolina, come here for treatment and benefit from their families living close enough for frequent visits."

"Mother loved her home."

"And she loved her family," Rachael says.

We finish our meal, and more coffee is poured. Rachael stands and says she has a friend hospitalized downstairs and wants to visit. I'm to remain with Mack. Her setups are transparent.

Alone now that everyone has eaten and returned to their rooms, the library, or the media room, Mack leans back into his chair, sipping coffee.

"Bobby, you've been quiet. What's on your mind?"

"What do you know about my mother?"

"Well, Bobby, that's complicated. As a doctor I can't reveal to you what I know about her treatment. But if you ask me as her friend, I'll tell you all I can." Mack Longworth is one of those men who even in deep sadness can wear a smile that comforts his audience.

"How many people know about my mother's rape?"

"Rachael called me to tell me you discovered this in your mother's journals. Just as you read, your father, Rachael, Jack, and me. No one else I know of, unless she told someone else."

"What about the police?"

"Negative. Your father found her in the alley behind the bakery. They both were working late that night, and he left to go to one of the restaurants to pick up dinner. He said he stopped at the cigar shop as well and chatted with a couple of friends as they were choosing a smoke. When he returned through the front door and up the stairs, she wasn't at her desk. There were signs of a scuffle, and he ran downstairs from the little office they shared, calling for her. He saw the back door to the alley open and heard her crying. She was injured and bleeding and half naked. She was traumatized and begging him to get her inside because she was so fearful her attacker would return. Robert took her inside and locked the door,

judy norwood enter

and she began to clean up. He asked her not to wash because the police would need to collect evidence from her. But she refused to allow him to call the police. Later she told me she couldn't bear the public disgrace. Against Robert's better judgment, he took her home, where she showered and felt safer. He called me right away, because I'm a doctor as well as a trusted friend. Mary Elizabeth had been beaten, and her nose was broken. She was bruised and torn where her attacker forced himself on her. She fought him pretty hard. I tended her wounds and sat with her that night alongside your father and pleaded with her to call the police. We gave her a sedative, and she slept. The next day Robert returned to the alley and cleaned up her blood. Your father was trying to be strong for her, but his emotions ran the gamut from anger to guilt for having left her alone. He believed that, had he not stopped at the cigar shop for a smoke with friends, he could have intervened. He had no idea how the rapist knew your mother was alone unless he had been watching them working late at night and knew Robert went out to pick up their dinner around the same time each evening. He was usually out for forty-five minutes or so, and that was time for the rapist to get to her. Also, Charleston in 1975 was a pretty safe city, so he left the front door unlocked. He blamed himself."

"What about the pregnancy?"

"When she suspected she was pregnant, she didn't want to go to her own gynecologist and came to me. I examined her and found she was seven weeks into the pregnancy. She told me that she and your father had been working nights establishing their new practice and were tired and had not engaged in intercourse over two weeks prior to the rape. We determined the pregnancy was a result of the rape."

"And my father—how did he learn about the pregnancy?"

"I went to the house that same night, and together we broke the news to your father. He was devastated, wanting to find the bastard and kill him with his bare hands. Your mother wanted Jack and Rachael there as well because she needed their support and help. Jack agreed that he and your father should kill him. Mary Elizabeth very calmly told Robert and Jack that they were never to speak of this man again and that we all were to help her conceal the preg-

137

the way home

nancy and then put the child up for adoption. Your father wanted to talk about keeping the child as his own, but Mary Elizabeth grew hysterical and Rachael had to put her to bed with a mild sedative again.

"After your mother was asleep, we agreed to meet again the next evening to concoct a plan. Those four were so inseparable—connected at the belly button. I declare, I've never had a friend like the four of them were friends. I believe any one of them would have died for the other. Anyway, it was a heart-wrenching evening. And I believe we made an unrecoverable mistake. We determined that because Mary Elizabeth was almost six feet tall, she would probably carry the child well and could conceal it with allover weight gain and loose clothing toward the end of her pregnancy. In her final term, Rachael and Mary Elizabeth would fabricate a "girls' trip" to New England, where they were apt to visit on occasion. Some little cabin in upstate Maine where they would meet some old fraternity friends. Anyway, I would handle setting up delivery as well as the adoption at a remote location well outside the prying eyes of Charleston."

Outside the cafeteria, a huge woman in excess of three hundred pounds is wobbling down the hall with the help of a walker. The sadness she bears is penetrating. Mack is quiet until she has passed.

"The five of us conspired to conceal the child, and I knew from the beginning it was an egregious plan. But we believed we had no other choice. Your mother simply couldn't vanish for four months in order to complete her term, and she was adamant about not keeping the child and assuming the pregnancy as Robert's. What I did not foresee was that the weight gain became a safety crutch for Mary Elizabeth. The more she ate and the more weight she gained, the safer she felt with her dark secret. She hid in large dresses and kept to the house and office, only writing briefs for your father and other legal work a paralegal could do. When your father was in court and until they could afford a different location for the law practice, she worked from home. She was terrified at being in that little office above the bakery alone."

I shudder at the image of my mother being so terrified. "I've heard of women who didn't know they were pregnant until they gave birth because they were so large, but I never believed it. Mother was pregnant, but to all outward view, she was simply gaining weight. The *Roe v. Wade* decision was in early 1973, as I remember, so abortion was available to her."

"You didn't know your mother very well if you think abortion was an option, even if it was legal. This was her first pregnancy, and she was in awe of the life building inside her. That baby deserved a chance, she told me, no matter the depravity of its father. She grew to love that child she was carrying, and giving him up almost killed her. In a way I guess it did, emotionally."

"What about my father and the marriage?"

"After the child was born, I counseled her to change her eating habits, and she took off some of the weight. She wanted a 'normal' life and children with Robert. And it seemed to work for a while. If this child had died, maybe Mary Elizabeth could have done the work she needed to do to get well, but it was in the front of her mind all the time that she had given her son away. And she never reconciled it. Your father came to believe that the key to your mother getting well was locating her child, and he became obsessed with it; but she never told him the truth about the birth. She intentionally misled him every step of the way. So everything he did to try to find the child he did on his own. Tried to solicit my help, but I refused. Your mother continued to slip further and further away. The best she ever became was during her pregnancies and when you and Jeff were young boys. Finally, one day when you and Jeff were older teenagers, Robert came to me crying. By then Mary Elizabeth was obese, deeply depressed, and hardly left the house. He told me she asked him to leave her because she couldn't bear his disappointment in her any longer and because he kept trying to make her well. He said she told him she wanted to see you and Jeff into college and then she wanted to die. I tried to talk to her, I adjusted her meds, but by that time too much sorrow had dug its claws into her, and she had grown accustomed to it. She confessed that she only saw embarrassment and shame of her in all your faces, and she just couldn't bear it

the way home

any longer. Jack had drowned a few years prior to this time, and his death seemed to compound her sense of loss and spiral her deeper into this abyss."

"I remember well Uncle Jack's death, but the adults and the children seem to go to different corners to come to terms with it. I don't recall a lot of interaction between the adults during this time."

"Jack was as good a friend to your mother as Rachael. He was a brother to her and shouldered some of the responsibility for her care after the rape. Some women are better friends with men than women, and your mother was one of those. When he died I swear it was like another assault on her. Like everything she tried to hold on to kept getting ripped away." Mack shudders and shakes his head. "And then there was Rachael's grief and her children to care for. It was insurmountable to her. There was no way she could climb over it. So she just continued to lay down and let it all roll over her."

"How can so much bad happen to a person so good like my mother? She kept getting knocked down every time she tried to stand up."

"That's an apt description, my boy."

"Thank you, Mack, for being her friend." We rise to leave, and as we're walking out the door, a thought occurs to the good doctor.

"Bobby, Rachael was privy to every detail of the birth, including that your mother insisted that her altered name as 'Elizabeth Mary Hargrave' be put on the birth certificate with no father listed. The baby was delivered in Carteret County, North Carolina."

"Rachael's located him as living in Virginia. So you never told my father the details of the delivery?"

"No, I told you that while he was searching, he tried to solicit my help, but I refused. Your mother asked me not to ever reveal the actual details of the delivery to him."

"Well, in that time period, the technology wasn't what it is today for searching for missing persons, so how could he possibly find a child with no information?"

"Oh, he had information, but it was incorrect. She lied to him, telling him she delivered a daughter in Maine."

"Then she didn't really want him to find her son?"

judy norwood enter

"No, and it put Rachael in a difficult position, forcing her to perpetuate your mother's lies, since she accompanied her to North Carolina where I arranged the delivery with an old medical school pal of mine. She confided in me that the dynamics of all their relationships had changed, and she hated the lying. This one heinous act by a stranger infected all their lives and relationships."

Mack looks much sadder than when I arrived, and I suspect I do as well. I shuffle to the elevator where an enormous woman and her smaller companion join me in the ride.

Rachael and I had agreed to meet in the parking garage. She is sitting in the car reading a magazine.

"Have you been waiting long?"

"Not really."

"You didn't have a sick friend downstairs in the hospital, did you?"

"Not really."

I lean on Rachael's car door with its window rolled down. "That's a hell of a story. You can't write fiction like that. And I hate it! I despise that some bastard raped my mother and cut away her soul leaving her incapable of ever being whole again. He took her from us before we were ever born - Jeff and me. We never had a chance." I slam my fists on the roof of the car.

Rachael pushes on the car door but my weight against it blocks her getting out. "Bobby, let me out. You get in the passenger side and I'll drive. We'll talk." But I continue to lean on the side of the car for support.

"What did you think when you brought me here - that I could hear firsthand my mother's story over a nice meal in a nice facility by Mack Longworth and Bobby would be nice? Don't tell me anything else. I don't want to hear it." I hit the roof again.

Rachael has crawled over the console and out the driver's side of the car and is standing beside me. "Step back a little and let me open the car door for you. Let's get in and drive away from here."

I yield and collapse into the passenger's seat. "Get me out of here."

sixteen

The pace of the unraveling of my life seems to increase in direct proportion to the amount my parents' past is pulled up. It's like pulling a loose thread on the sleeve of your favorite sweater: the thread looks harmless enough, but the more you tug at it, the greater the damage to the fabric. Leaving the hospital in Charleston, I can't seem to recover my ability to focus on the simplest things, like buckling my seatbelt. Rachael leans over before exiting the garage and pops the clip into the buckle. We speed toward another footprint of my father's in Charlotte where this drug rehabilitation clinic has been built in Jeff's memory. We're to stay overnight with Brenda Grace and the kids. This is another chapter on the past I'd rather not read. We don't speak until Rachael is barreling down I-26 toward Columbia.

"Talk to me, Rachael. And please slow down. The speed limit is seventy miles per hour. I feel like I'm on a scavenger hunt and you've given me a list and a ride but that's all you'll give me. I can barely absorb the face time with Mack where I picked up some important pieces of the past, and now you're dragging me to Charlotte to this clinic and to Brenda Grace's."

"I'm not dragging you, you agreed. It's a large part of the business of the Will that you see the facility and know how it's operating - who it's helping. We'll turn around and return to Charleston any time you say the word. I don't want to be an interloper in your life."

the way home

A car horn blares at us as Rachael cuts into the left lane in front of an irate driver. "Don't you ever feel like you just want to be a petulant child and kick, scream, and knock the slats out of your surroundings?"

"Heck, yes. Can I do that?"

"Not while you're driving." We smile.

"I mean it, about going back, you know. Tell me and I'll turn around now. It's your decision."

"No, I just need the option. Thank you."

"Let's deal with the overnight stay at Jeff's house. What are you afraid of by going there? Brenda Grace is thoughtful and sensitive and one of the kindest people I know. That woman is providing Jeff's children with a secure and loving childhood. Robert supported them and continues to support them through his gift. They've remained connected to this family all these years and enjoyed our visits to Charlotte as well as the times when they visited us. These are your brother's children. I believe you're afraid to see them because they'll remind you of Jeff."

"I remember the little girl as a baby, but I've never seen Jeff's son. Does he look like my brother?"

"A little...you'll see. I'm sorry you have to face all this, Bobby. I am well-acquainted with grief, and it's an ominous companion. I wake up some nights from horrible nightmares crying out for all of them - Jack, Mary Elizabeth, and Robert. Some nights it's Jack and the water that swallows him. Other nights I dream I'm being raped by Mary Elizabeth's attacker. It causes me to question my sanity. And it's all born out of fear of loss. I believe that your fear stems from having to reach back into the past and struggle with what you lost and how you lost it. Whether it is the boyhood you believe you were robbed of, the paradigm you built around who you believed your mother and father to be, the brother you couldn't save, or me, the friend you taught yourself to hate. And I believe you're afraid of facing some mistaken judgments of others you've made or perhaps regrets you can't go back and recover. But know this truth: this family you dispossessed in order to run away from the past—we have been waiting in the wings for you to come home. Your father

judy norwood enter

couldn't bring you home in life, but he has brought you back to us in death."

"A man is not supposed to be afraid, Rachael. All you good southern women taught us to stand up straight, not to let it hurt, and not to cry. Strength and responsibility and never let 'em see you sweat was what our fathers taught us. So, you tell me, how am I supposed to tear down the walls I've built to deal with this veritable collection of human suffering? My mother was raped, my father and mother are both dead, my brother died at his own hand, and I have a half brother living in Virginia, and oh, I almost forgot, my wife doesn't like me. The whole damn mess just makes me angry, and I want to hit something!" I slap the dashboard in front of me. Rachael sits very erect and looks a little tense.

"You've given my car a couple of good punches this afternoon, and if you keep up the assault on my dash I'm afraid the air bag will blow up in your face. I should stop at Walmart and buy you a punching bag."

"That wouldn't be near as much fun as seeing the look on your face when I pelt your car."

We stop at a rest stop and use the facilities. "Get me a Diet Coke out of that machine. I need caffeine," Rachael declares.

I offer to drive but she tactfully declines. "Bobby, you're not only going to survive all this but you're also going to be an asset to this family. No one wants to strip away the man you've become, that big heart and smile—when you remember to use them—the integrity and honesty that are inherently parts of your personality and character. We love you, and we respect you. This bitterness and resentfulness and the hatred you've developed out of fear and anger are liabilities. That's what busting out of that cocoon is all about. You see, when that butterfly emerges, he has successfully torn through the shell he doesn't need any more. He leaves it because it served its purpose for a time, but now it's useless. Your response to your hurt, this shell you built, held you together all these years, and maybe it even served a purpose. I don't know. But what I know now is you've cracked the shell and begun to emerge. It's too late to go back. All you can do is move forward."

the way home

"I'm tired of that damn cocoon story. I'll pay you not to bring it up again."

• • •

Rachael and I stand at the door of Brenda Grace's attractive home on the east side of Charlotte, co-conspirators in this quest for the truth, myself the reluctant partner. *Ding-dong*.

"Memaw Rachael!" Hardy looks like a reduction of my brother. I almost audibly gasp. Brenda Grace was pregnant with the little boy when Jeff died of an overdose on prescription and illegal drugs. He never saw his son. Hardy's big sister, Sarah Sinclair, comes to the door as well with her mother. She is a blond miniature of Brenda Grace and Jeff.

"Hey you two, you made good time from Charleston. Come on in. You're just in time for drinks and appetizers. We'll eat dinner in about an hour."

Brenda Grace hails from Beaufort, South Carolina, another one of the South's fine historical cities. Her family still resides there, and she visits them often, Rachael has told me. So, Brenda Grace has learned well in the order of "Girls Raised In the South" (or GRITS) the attention and focus that should be put on cooking for guests and offering up impeccable hospitality.

I take our overnight bags upstairs to the two guest rooms and notice that the home, while large and attractive, is not ostentatious. Evidence of young children is everywhere in the large country kitchen with its adjoining den. Brenda Grace is serving a hot crab dip and gourmet crackers on the large, granite-top kitchen island. She has opened Rachael's favorite merlot to let it breathe. She pulls three antique crystal glasses from a glass-front cabinet that she explains were her grandmother's.

"Better get Bobby one of the Piggly Wiggly glasses for his wine if you want to keep a full inventory of your grandmamma's crystal, Brenda Grace." Rachael elbows me in the ribs.

Brenda Grace looks suspiciously at the two of us. "What are you two up to?"

"I think I can be trusted with your crystal, Brenda Grace. I'm not a child." I stare Rachael down.

The aroma of the steaming crab dip is tantalizing, and I can hear my stomach juices at work, preparing for the receipt of this dish of fresh lump crabmeat, artichoke hearts, mayo for binding, parmesan cheese, and Old Bay spice cooked to bubbling. While I'm munching on crackers and crab, I fight the impulse to pick up a nearby spoon and eat gobs of it right from the casserole dish.

The wine and crab has our full attention as Brenda Grace speculates. "I suppose I should have served a white wine with the crab, but I know how Rachael likes the Fourteen Hands Merlot."

"Not to worry, my dear. This wine pairs nicely with my love of drinking it." Rachael winks.

"How was your visit at the center? Did you see Mack Longworth? He is a teddy bear of a man, and I just love him. Robert and he built an amazing tribute to Mary Elizabeth."

Rachael looks to me for a response, and I stand there like I'm deaf and mute.

"The center looks good. Mack says they have over one hundred residents currently. And Mack gave us a first-rate tour that even included lunch. He and Bobby spent some time together, as well."

I don't want to think or talk about the center and the load of unsolicited and unwanted information I trucked away from that place, so I change the subject.

"Brenda Grace, why have you remained in Charlotte instead of returning to Beaufort after Jeff's death? Looks like your parents would want you all closer to them."

The three of us continue to devour the crab dip. "A couple of reasons, really, some obvious and some not so. I was pregnant with Hardy when Jeff died, and Sarah Sinclair was only two. We did go to my parents until after Hardy was born, but I had a real desire to return to Charlotte and raise our kids here. I'm of the opinion that living close enough to conveniently visit your parents is a good thing but living on top of them not so good. Anyway, Robert offered me the opportunity to return here and sell the small house we were living in when Jeff passed. He bought this house for us, let me choose

the way home

it, and offered me the generous stipend so that I could remain home and raise my kids. But what really sealed the deal was his proposal of the drug rehab center in Jeff's memory. He and I wanted to honor Jeff's life and allow his kids to see that there's no shame in what happened to their father, that addiction is a sickness and that help is available to so many young men like Jeff. Instead of kicking his memory under the rug, so to speak, because of the way he died, we wanted something good to come of his death and to make that possible in his name."

Brenda Grace stops to monitor the lasagna baking in the oven. When she returns to the island, she comes with a salad out of the refrigerator and tosses it with balsamic vinegar and olive oil. "The children love my lasagna." Two places with bar stools are set for the children at the counter.

With my hand still in the crab dip dish, I profess to love lasagna. And Rachael, who eats everything and anything, is ecstatic. "Brenda Grace makes the best lasagna in the world!" She scoops up three place settings and heads toward what I believe to be the dining room. "We big people should eat in this stylish dining room tonight. I helped decorate it, so you know it's colorful and beautiful." She winks at me.

Hardy and Sarah Sinclair move from where they're watching *Nemo* to their settings, where they can still see the movie. Brenda Grace serves them small portions of the lasagna and salad with a piece of garlic French bread she removes from the oven. Since our being there, Brenda Grace has explained to the kids that I am their father's brother and have been "away" for a while.

A blessing over the food and the children is prayed. Hardy asks, "Uncle Bobby, did you know my daddy was dead when I was born?"

I swallow hard. "Yes, Hardy, I did. And I am so sorry. I know he would be sorry, too."

"You look like a picture my mommy shows me of my daddy."

"Eat your dinner, children. The adults will be in the dining room if you need us."

At dinner Brenda Grace tells the story of how she and my father found a piece of property with existing buildings and renovated them together to make them suitable for residency. Evidently, the zoning restrictions and inspections in this county were difficult to work with and the taxes high, but they were finally able to pull it all together in about two years' time. The center was only operational a year before the plane crash and my father's disappearance.

"I volunteer at the center two days a week while the children are in school. Sometimes I work in the office, but what I really love doing is teaching reading in an adult literacy course offered to the men. We find that a large number of them were school dropouts and consequently remedial readers."

It seems both Jeff and I had an attraction to teachers, as Brenda Grace was teaching grade school when they married. Maybe subconsciously we were both attracted to the qualities of these women who patiently teach and guide immature children.

"Tomorrow, we'll take a little tour of the center, and then there's someone I want you to meet, Bobby," Brenda Grace says.

The morning traffic in Charlotte is heinous, and Rachael drives again, following Brenda Grace to the center. There's no need to tell her to slow down, though, as we're moving at a snail's pace on the six-lane interstate connector.

The residence and its adjacent treatment center are filled with large windows overlooking the flow of unending traffic. But on the far side where the connecting buildings form an L, a well-tended garden has been designed with groupings of tables and chairs for visiting.

As with the wing at MUSC, the facility is staffed with doctors, attendants, and office staff. I can't even imagine the money invested in this place and what regular payroll must be. The facility has a gym with instructors, two upscale cafés, one of which is a coffee shop like Starbucks, group rooms, a music room, a library, and two classrooms, as well as a small auditorium.

We stop at the coffee shop and indulge in flavored coffees. Brenda Grace chats up a pale young man sitting at the next table. She brings him over to the table where Rachael and I are drinking coffee and reading a brochure that touts the facility's benefits.

the way home

He smiles broadly and affectionately at Rachael and embraces her. "Hey, Miss Rachael, how are you doing?"

"I'm good, Trevor. Thank you for asking, and thanks for the card. It was beautiful and gave me a lot of comfort."

"I keep looking for Mr. Robert to come around the corner to check on all us. I really miss him. And this must be Robert Jr. You look just like your father. I'm Trevor Lewis." He thrusts his thin, pale hand forward for a handshake. "Your father told me all about you."

Brenda Grace interrupts. "Excuse me. Some of the residents help care for the garden, and Rachael and I are going to talk to them about some extra care it needs here in early summer. Do you and Trevor want to go with us. The garden is magnificent."

"Sure. I'll go with you." I clearly didn't want to be stuck here in the coffee shop with this stranger.

The garden is beautiful, professionally landscaped with indigenous plants to Charlotte with a little of Charleston thrown in for good measure. Rachael and Jill pluck dead blooms off plants and give instructions to two men. Trevor motions me to a painted bench next to a small table where he sets his coffee down. "I drink too much of this stuff. But I switch to decaffeinated in the afternoons."

I sip my own coffee and try to think of small talk I can make. Then Trevor helps me as he laughs. "Man, you look as nervous as a long-tailed cat in a room full of rocking chairs. I'm a drug addict, not a serial killer. You don't have to be afraid of me, man. I take regular showers, I'm in class for remedial reading and math, I attend group therapy and individual counseling sessions, I work in the bakery in the café, and I even have a few family members who are warming up to me again."

It's hard not to like him. "I'm sorry for being nervous, Trevor. It's not you. It's just that, well, I had my own problems with drugs a lifetime ago, and my brother Jeff, you know, he died of an overdose. I'm more comfortable not confronting all that, even here with a stranger."

"Man, I don't want to get you into therapy. I just want to tell you that if it weren't for your father and this place and Miss Brenda

judy norwood enter

Grace, I would have joined your brother. I started smoking dope when I was fourteen, me and my brother. We gradually added alcohol and some pills, and the race was on. We ran away from our crazy, alcoholic parents before we finished high school and never looked back. Our father had a thing for putting his fist through walls and through our heads when he was drunk and mad at either our mother or us. Just thought if we could get out and stay high, we wouldn't have to think about the shitty life we were dealt. But, you know, it didn't turn out so good for us." He removes the plastic lid from his coffee and stares at the dark concoction in the cup. "I don't like lids."

I don't want to know any more about this tactless stranger's life, but he goes on, a little sarcastically. "Since you didn't ask, I'll tell you anyway. The way it didn't turn out so good is that we both got into gangs here in Charlotte. My brother was killed after we were into it about two years by rival gang members. I was scared and ran off to Richmond, Virginia. But there are gangs there, too, and I was right back into it. The stupidity of it is they make you feel like they care about you, that you matter to them, sort of like family is supposed to. But it's all just a lie. Nobody cares about you until you care about yourself. I come back to Charlotte and see this place being built, wasn't even finished. I was hitchhiking and just walked up to this big, old man standing there telling people what to do. It was your daddy. I asked him if he could help me get into this place he was building, and he told me it wasn't ready and wouldn't be for a while. Miss Rachael and Miss Brenda Grace were with him that day, and the sympathy they all had in their eyes for me, you know, not judging me or criticizing me, well, I knew I was home." Trevor is visibly emotional. "I know he was your real daddy, but he was like mine, too. I most cry every time I think of him dying like that and never coming back."

This broken man wipes away his tears and continues. "Anyway, they took me to lunch, and I told them everything. By now I'm almost twenty-five years old. I've been in jail in Maryland, Virginia, and North Carolina. And after I told him my whole story, he said he had two sons that he let slip away and that if he could help me, he

151

the way home

would. But he got hard on me and told me I had to do my part. He took me to another resident drug rehab place here in Charlotte for addicts that he had investigated before he built Jeff's. I checked in that very day, and he paid for all of it until, six months later, I moved in here. He spent a lot of time with me and told me about you boys. I don't think he ever made peace with Jeff's death, and I hate to tell you this, but his heart was purely broke because you wouldn't see him. He poured not only his money into me and others like me but his big, old heart, too. You know your daddy had a big, old heart? Well, he did. He became the father to us that most of us never had. He visited us a lot and stayed here in one of the rooms, didn't go to a big hotel or nothing. Ate with us, slept with us, went to the gym, and even sat in on some of the classes and the group sessions. Finally, he offered me a permanent job here working with new residents and in the bakery at the café. There's no doubt in my mind that your daddy saved my life. And since he done it for me, I'm trying to do it for a few more just like he taught me."

I see Rachael and Brenda Grace stroll the brick-paved path back to our bench. And I'm so grateful because I can hardly breathe, much less speak to Trevor. I jump to my feet.

"So did you two get everybody straightened out and their work assigned?"

Trevor is still seated and smiles knowingly at me as I avoid making any comment on his story about my father. He and Rachael make discreet eye contact, and he nods toward her as if to convey he has done his job.

"Good-bye, Trevor, and good luck to you." I shake his hand.

"Well, Mr. Bobby, don't be a stranger to us. Come this way and check in on us like your father did. That would make him happy, and it would sure look good to see his son in these empty halls. You look just like him."

seventeen

Before Rachael's contrived road show of a swing through Charleston and Charlotte, I agreed to go only if we could drive on to Asheville for a visit with the girls. And, of course, she was eager to see Mary and Elizabeth, so she agreed. In the two hours it takes to get to my house from Charlotte, we speak little. I had insisted on doing the driving of the gargantuan silver Lexus to distract myself from thinking about Trevor's story and also to keep my life from being on the line again, what with Rachael's penchant for speed. Crossing Black Mountain between Charlotte and Asheville is tedious because of its steep grade, curves, and 18-wheelers hogging the lanes.

Jill stands in the door to greet us in the early evening, and the girls are playing on their swing set in the backyard in the fading light. No matter how little or how long a parent is away, it seems that a young child expresses the same excitement at seeing him. It is an expectant, unconditional, faithful kind of love that says "I knew you would come home." This not yet knowing how parents can hurt and disappoint you strikes me as pure naïveté, and I'm silently grateful that my girls do not yet know that deceitful and untrustworthy parental behavior. I pray they never will.

My thoroughly southern wife is frying chicken, boiling potatoes for mashing with globs of Irish butter, and cooking green beans until one bean couldn't stand alone without crutches. The term *al*

the way home

dente is not in the glossary of real southern cooks. And, of course, homemade bread is one of the major food groups of the South, and no meal worth its salt would be served without it. This and coconut cream pie for dessert can partially explain why my size thirty-four waist is expanding. I'm not complaining…It all smells of home and love and my girls. I'm thinking about getting down on my knees and kissing the floor of our little home. Instead, I'm slathering kisses on jubilant Mary and Elizabeth and engaging in a bit of deep tongue-kissing with their mother.

"Memaw Rachael! Where have you and Daddy been?"

"Well, children, we are on an adventure. We put Memaw's big, old car on the road, raised our sails on fair winds, and caught following seas on our tail."

"Memaw, cars don't have sails. You tell stories." Elizabeth has always been vigilant for the truth and bent on exposing any deception the adults around her insist on. I also think how perceptive she is: "Memaw" does indeed tell stories.

"Well, maybe I did embellish our trip a little, but we have been on an adventure. Right, 'Daddy'?"

"Go wash your hands for dinner, my little princesses." Jill inspects dirty hands.

In our modest home, the girls dine on their children's table and chairs while we three fill our plates from Jill's stove and sit at places at the table out of earshot of the children. Jill asks Rachael to say grace. She includes Trevor in her blessing, and in my mind's eye, I see the frail yet strong-hearted young man who believes my father saved his life and that now his calling is to pass his own help on to others drowning in addiction.

"Bobby, we've missed you. We're wrapping up the school year soon, and the girls are so excited. When can we come to Charleston?"

"I'm still indecisive about a summer move to Charleston and the old house. What about your friends and the girls' playmates? It's a big step."

Rachael has her mouth wrapped firmly around a crunchy piece of breaded, deep-fried chicken breast and is indelicately gnawing her way toward the bone. She appears uninterested in our conversation and in fact in everything else in the room besides her work on the breast.

"Bobby, change has never been your forte. You carry your resistance to change to a boring level sometimes. Let's add some excitement to our lives and give the girls an experience in that old Confederate city that they wouldn't have otherwise. Think of it. We'll be living in a house where their father grew up on that wonderful, old harbor. We can get them sailing lessons!"

Rachael completes the greasy job of the chicken and wipes crumbs away with her napkin. She seems to reengage with what we're saying.

"I agree with Jill. Take the summer, live in the old house, have some fun, and see what happens."

"You women lack order. You neither formulate a plan nor ever consider obstacles or the results of your serendipitous decisions. You see, and you do. In other words, your collective motto is 'ready, fire, aim.'"

Jill and Rachael smile at each other in that knowing way that you can tell means you aren't in their circle of knowledge.

Jill goes into the kitchen to check on the girls and to serve up slices of coconut cream pie. Rachael uses her absence to broach the subject of the journal I've brought - Mother's journal dated June 1976. "Take all the time you need. I'll go play with the girls and help them get their baths."

"I've been dreading it. I thought I would ask her to read that one entry tonight, she can read the other entries I've marked later." Jill returns with our dessert and fresh forks.

"I've got decaf coffee brewing. We'll settle plans for the summer later. I don't want you to stress over a move, however temporary. Just think about it."

The coffeemaker beeps. Jill leaves for our coffee and then returns quickly.

The sweet coconut pie has begun to taste bitter, and I lay down my fork. "Jill, I need to talk to you tonight. I can't get my head wrapped around all the new information about my parents I'm learn-

155

the way home

ing. Everything I thought I had figured out and what I believed I had gotten right side up is now upside down. What I want is to be shed of all of it and to come home. But I can't right now. I have to make another trip with Rachael tomorrow to Arlington, Virginia. We'll be gone for a couple of days."

Rachael stands diplomatically and says she's going for more coffee. She will not return soon, and I know this because she's taking her pie with her.

Her pie uneaten, Jill lays her fork down. "Why are you going to Arlington?"

"Jill, I have a brother - a half brother living in Arlington."

"Half brother? That would mean your father or mother had a child with another person. Who is it?"

"My mother. She gave the boy up for adoption. His name is Mitchell Cummins."

"Whoa...your parents were married in 1974. Mary Elizabeth had a child with another man? I don't believe it."

"Come with me to my study. I want you to read what I've brought. Rachael will watch the girls."

We move into my study, my favorite room in the house with its dark green walls, stained walnut wood, and plaid draperies. I shut the heavy door and we sit together on the leather couch.

"Jill, my mother was raped outside her office in Charleston 1975."

"Oh my God, no!"

The rest of the story, including Mack's personal rendition of the events, is told by me as though it had happened to someone else's family. I explain the facts to Jill matter-of-factly, as if I were telling her an idea I had for writing a novel and wait on her reaction.

"How can this be? He would be thirty-four years old. How could you not know?"

I place Mother's journal in her lap and open it to the day of Mitchell's birth. I sit back and just let her read. I watch her tears begin to fall as she reads Mother's pain of letting her child go. When she has read it and re-read it, she closes the book and returns it to me.

judy norwood enter

"I'm so sorry, Bobby." She slides closer to me on the couch and lifts my arm putting it around her as she lays her head on my shoulder. I want to tell her about my mother's son. "His wife is Betsy, and they have two boys, twelve and nine. They live in Arlington, Virginia, where he and his partner operate a security business. They customize their services to some high-profile people in Washington. He's a former special ops man who was wounded in an operation and then left the military. He's a good family man, and he tells Rachael he'll meet with us."

She listens and asks no questions about Mitchell. "What this must have done to your mother and to your father - their marriage. They couldn't survive it."

" I've brought a few more of Mother's journals and marked some entries that may help you understand what happened to my mother and their marriage. I'll leave them with you, and we'll talk about all of it, if you like, when I return. But tonight I need to be with my family - hear my girls laugh - all of you. I'll clean up the kitchen and Rachael is helping the girls with their baths. Come watch me work my magic in the kitchen. Sit at the table and drink a cup of coffee or have a glass of wine. Tonight I really need my family."

eighteen

Rachael speaks to Mitchell, and he agrees to meet us at his office, where we'll have some privacy. I think to myself that I would be far more comfortable in a public setting, but maybe Rachael has acquainted him with my short fuse.

I again insist on driving the luxury behemoth, and the traffic on I-66 and I-81 near Washington makes Charlotte's look like that of a rural country road. Rachael is uncharacteristically nervous, and I don't think it's my driving or the indigenous DC traffic.

"What's up, Rachael? Spit it out before we get to Arlington."

"You know that I was with your mother at her delivery in North Carolina? And I saw the baby before they took him away. Mary Elizabeth and I got one quick glance at him, and then he was gone. He was healthy, large, and bawling his eyes out. Would you like for me to tell you more about him? I'll tell you anything and everything you want to know."

"Gee, you mean you're going to break open a piece of the cocoon for me? I don't think so. I don't want to hear a blow-by-blow description of my mother's delivery of her first son before me and Jeff. It's damn painful to even imagine it without having an eyewitness play out the scene before you in living color."

"It may make it easier when you meet him if I describe him to you."

the way home

"What, that he looks more like our mother than Jeff and me? I'll look him in the face and decide that for myself."

Rachael's patience with me appears to run thin. "You're stubborn like your father, Robert Jr. Have it your way. Before noon we pull in to the parking lot of this boutique security service. It's a small building, very discreet, and the name on the sign out front reads *CUMMINS and GOINS Custom Protective Services*. Hysterical... the guy is a comic.

Rachael's nervousness has been replaced with that old, familiar panache. Her dress today is over-the-top expensive, like she mistakenly thought she was attending a White House luncheon. I ignore her trendsetting garb and go with the old, reliable uniform of creased khakis and a blue button-down shirt with a navy blazer. My shoes are standard southern boy loafers sans socks.

We disembark the circus-mobile and walk smartly to the office door of Cummins and Goins like we're in the market for a bodyguard. Rachael turns the knob and trots in with me on her heels like a good, little puppy. The reception office is military utilitarian in a modern but tasteful way. A framed picture of a Black Hawk helicopter dominates the room. The door to the office on our right opens, and a large man in a gray suit walks out, appearing surprised to find us there. He introduces himself as Benny Goins and excuses himself, saying he's on his way out and is sure Mitchell will be with us shortly. We stand stiffly and silently for door number two to open. It opens suddenly and briskly, and standing in it with a warm smile is a big bear of a man well over six feet tall with hands the size of my head. At his appearance, I confess I hoped there was a door number three. Mitchell Cummins engulfs Rachael's tiny hand and then mine in handshakes before escorting us into his office. My mother's first son is an African-American.

Mitchell takes his seat behind his desk, and we sit in front of it. I recognize the move as establishing right away who's in charge of this meeting. Mitchell speaks first.

"Rachael, I received the photo album you mailed a few weeks ago. I have to tell you that my family and I have enjoyed the pictures. It has been a bit unsettling for me to see my mother's features in me and even in my children. I have told them basically the truth about the adoption but not about my mother's rape. My wife knows, but the boys are just too young."

I'm about to blow a gasket, and Rachael sees it coming. "Bobby, take it easy. I offered to make this easier for you."

I ignore her. "Mr. Cummins—Mitchell, supposedly you're my half brother, meaning that my father is not your father but my mother is your mother. Somehow all these years your existence was hidden from our family. And the first reason is that you are the product of rape, and—let's face it—the second reason is that you are African-American and my mother was white. In 1975, a black man in southern Charleston, South Carolina, brutally raped and beat my mother, and you were the result."

"You make the fact that I was born sound very clinical, but I will agree that you're right on all counts. And that is reason enough for my existence to have remained hidden from your family. My adoptive parents told me the circumstances of my birth when I was thirteen years old. For years after that, I struggled to look for any traces in my character that would link me to such a despicable man. I feared that some latent seed in me would erupt and I wouldn't have control of the outcome. So I joined the military for its discipline and training and went on the offensive to crack the skulls of men like him. The knowledge of my origin set the course for my life of strict adherence to rules and law and fighting the bad guys so I wouldn't become one of them. I am not my father, Bobby, as you are not yours. We are two men shaped by the parents who raised us and the environment we found ourselves living in. From what I understand, you took a pill, and I became Rambo. We are two different men with the same mother who chose two different methods of dealing with what ailed us."

Silence fills the room. "You shoot straight, Mitchell."

He grins at the play on words. "Yes, I do. Out of the twelve men in my company, only my superior shot straighter than me."

This man is clearly confident, disciplined, and unafraid of anything, even meeting his half brother. "Mitchell, I see my mother in your face. It's a little disconcerting."

the way home

"Unless you ever imagined your mother black, I guess it is. So where do you want to take this, Bobby? If you want to leave it right here in this room, it's fine with me. I've never looked for my mother or her family. You all found me. I will not subject my family to racial prejudice from yours or the smirks of uppity people who disgrace my biological mother for something she had no control over."

"Thank you for wanting to defend my mother…our mother. I like you, damn it, and I was prepared to hate you."

Mitchell laughs loudly. "Bobby, you poor, little, rich white boy, you don't have it all figured out either. Tell you what. You want to see me again—me, not my family, yet—then you call me, and I'll meet you somewhere for a beer. But it will be you that calls. If I don't hear from you, you'll never see me again. Just go back to pretending that I don't exist."

"Do you have a card?"

Mitchell pauses and then slides a business card across his desk to me. He turns to Rachael. "Miss Rachael, I guess you're the one who hired the agency to find me."

"Yes, and can I say that I see my friend in you - physical features like your eyes and chin and even some of Mary Elizabeth's mannerisms. I observed you as you spoke to Bobby and you possess a certain directness with humor that Mary Elizabeth had in her earlier years. You would have liked her."

• • •

Back in the car heading to Charleston, the dread of having to face the unknown is gone. The pieces of the puzzle of my parents' lives are fitting together, pieces I would have rather not seen but that are out of the box now. I need to put them together for a full picture.

"What Mack Longworth said about Mother becoming hysterical when my father wanted to raise the child as his own and then misleading him about the child's birthplace and identity—it was because he never knew that her rapist was black. Did anyone except you ever know?"

"She told Mack Longworth because he was arranging the delivery and adoption for the child by African-American parents. But she didn't tell me, and I didn't know until I saw the child briefly along with her just after his birth. Your mother and I could talk about most anything and everything, so I hit her headlong with it. And her response was what I should have guessed. Prejudice in the South was still thriving in the mid-seventies. The sixties were violent, and an atmosphere of volatility between the races still persisted in Charleston. Your mother believed her family would disown her and that your father would never touch her again if they knew she bore the child of a black man. It was the same reason she wouldn't allow your father to contact the police. Your mother carried the shame of the rape, the fact that her child was black, the lies she told to hide it from your father, and the guilt of giving away her son. When you and Jeff were born, I was hoping and praying that all that garbage would be flushed away, but she couldn't let it go. That one vile act by a hellish villain in an alley in Charleston changed all our lives. I hope he's rotting in hell as we speak."

nineteen

Our first night back in Charleston, Rachael and I sit on the familiar portico overlooking the harbor, again watching the sailboats plumping their sails with the last winds and light of the day.

"Bobby, let's go sailing tomorrow."

My mind races backward in time to a Saturday afternoon when Jeff and I fled the house while our parents were arguing and headed out on the water in our little homemade sailboat. It was late July, and Charleston was steaming hot with its usual summer heat and humidity. In that atmospheric environment, the Low Country was ripe for a thunderstorm.

"Bobby, let's head out toward the mouth of the harbor." Jeff said.

"I don't want to go out that far. We're likely to have a thunderstorm this afternoon."

"You're such a chicken. You're the oldest, and if it weren't for me, you would never go on any adventures or have any fun. Let's sail out past Fort Sumter and watch the big ships come into the harbor. Let's see how close we can get to them without getting sucked into their wake."

"Nope. If I wind up listening to you, we'll get into trouble, and because I'm the oldest, I'll have to get us out of it. Did you ever

the way home

think it's not that I'm chicken but just that I'm responsible for you." I asked.

"Bullshit. You are not responsible for me. Nobody but me is responsible for me."

That afternoon we were caught too far out in a hellish thunderstorm. The little, homemade skiff turned out to be formidable in the high winds and waves. We were able to tie it up at a stranger's dock in Mt. Pleasant and wait out the storm.

"Hey, Bobby," Jeff said as lightning cracked all around us. "You ever think about dying?"

"Hell no. I'm sixteen, Jeff. I'm just starting to think about living. Why are you talking about dying?"

Jeff stood up on the stranger's dock with his arms thrust skyward where thunder boomed and lightning flashed. "You know something? I think I'm gonna die young and it doesn't scare me."

"Get your ass back down here with me." I'm huddled low and wrapped in a sail in the bottom of the boat.

"Dumb brother of mine. If lightning hits here, it don't matter if you're on the dock or in the boat. You're gonna die."

After the storm we bailed the boat, raised the sail, and raced toward home. "Jeff, don't you ever tell Mother or Dad that you think you're going to die young. And if you don't stop doing stupid things, you're gonna."

"Bobby, did you hear me? Want to go sailing with me tomorrow? Let's get a Sunfish and head out on the harbor. Weather is supposed to be beautiful."

"I can't, Rachael. I have an eleven o'clock meeting with Louis. I'm sick of these meetings. Just when I think we have one thing solved, another problem needs our attention. Management from inside a corporate office makes me restless. Never was one of my greatest strengths. I do my best work on-site, seeing and hearing what needs to be done. I'm eager to get on the ground again in Haiti. You're going back with me, right?"

"Yes. I'd like to meet with Monique and Marianne and see the progress on the children's home. Are you moving the girls from Asheville here before we go?"

judy norwood enter

"Yes. I've decided to go for them right after school is out. I just hate to move them in and take off for Haiti for a month."

"Oh, stop worrying. That wife of yours doesn't need you to babysit her. She'll do fine."

Rachael doesn't treat me as a guest in this grand house of mine any longer. She makes frequent trips to her beloved beach house in Pawleys, but when I'm here, she makes it a point of returning to the old house often. Once a mother, always a mother, and I guess she thinks I need one. She laughs at my preferring my old bed in the attic but accepts it. I've had all of Jeff's sports equipment as well as his plaques and trophies and some of the photo albums shipped to Brenda Grace in Charlotte. The attic is being dismantled of some of its past but it still feels homey and safe for me. And on these evenings, I frequently stop by Mother's study and choose another journal for my nighttime reading.

"January 2, 1976.

The holidays have been depressing, and I haven't been able to journal much. Robert has been helpful and kind and carried the load of buying Christmas gifts. Thanksgiving was a disaster as I experienced not only morning sickness but also sickness in the afternoon. Trying to pull off the holidays with our family was the hardest thing I've ever done. I've been carrying this child for four months now and not showing at all. Since I have never been pregnant before, I don't know how large I'll get with this child, but I've got to start eating to disguise its growth. The nausea seems to be passing, so I'll try to eat more.

Robert and I haven't slept together since early December. I've moved in to one of the guest rooms. I feel so guilty and ugly that I don't want him to have to lie with me. We haven't made love since before the rape. I don't know if he will ever want to touch me again. Will I ever have his child, I wonder? This horrific act by this villainous man has distorted life as we knew it, and I imagine it will never be the same again.

I have loved Robert since my eyes first met his in our freshman year at USC. He was funny and loud and always attracted an audience. It was enough for me to just be in the group he always seemed

167

to have around him. But then he singled me out, and we just knew that life would be grand for us. A big law practice together, lots of children, fabulous family holidays, and travel. We would raise our children to have good hearts and teach them that life is not about what we accumulate but how we use it to do good. How could one moment in time change our dreams?

I wish I were stronger and could accept this thing that has happened to us, to return after the birth and pick up where we left off. But who am I kidding? It will never be the same."

There is a light knock on the study door, and Rachael enters, finding me hunched over Mother's journal at her desk in the dim lamplight. "Hey there, I brought you some hot chocolate. It will help you sleep."

"Thanks. I need the help."

"Bobby, you don't have to read all those journals. In fact, I don't believe it's a good idea."

" I'm reading them for Mitchell. I'm methodically marking the entries of her pregnancy, his birth and birthdays, and any other references she has made about him. He needs to know how much she loved him. And before you think what a benevolent thing it is I'm doing, the fact is I don't want him to read all of what she wrote. The parts that she wrote about us are none of his business."

Rachael blows and sips at her hot chocolate. "I promise you that your name and the word 'benevolent' does not appear in my mind in the same sentence. Changing the subject, I want to ask you to help me plan Robert's memorial service. I want to have it on July 10, one year after his disappearance. And I want it to be happy! I've talked to Jill and Brenda Grace. They'll help me with the service and the party afterward. It's what Robert would have wanted. Are you OK with having a big, old Charleston party here at your house? We girls will have most of it catered with our own little personal touches, of course."

"Sure, we can do that. What do you have in mind for a memorial service?"

"We'll have it at the church, of course. But you know Robert wouldn't want a bunch of empty eulogies for him. I don't really know how to honor him without making him out to be a saint. And as we both know, he wasn't!" We share a laugh, and she asks, "You have any ideas?"

"I think we should just invite people whose lives he touched and leave up to them what they want to say. Say Trevor Lewis, Mack Longworth, Nicholas if we can get him a visa to come from Haiti, Louis Chandler, Captain Russell from Abaco, and any others you can think of. Let's just consider these are his friends and he would want them there. He loved them."

"You're right, Bobby. We'll just invite his friends and give them the freedom to tell their stories of Robert. I like it. Let's get Jill and the girls moved in here, and we'll start planning."

"Sounds like a plan. I'm ready."

"Can I just say that after you met Mitchell, some things seemed to shift in you? You don't seem angry or afraid of the truth and are a mellower, happier version of your former self."

"You were right, Rachael..."

"Well, don't I just love hearing those sweet words come out of your mouth?"

"Do you want to be quiet and hear what I have to say?" We both laugh. "I can't encapsulate it and make a neat package out of it all, but the paradigm I had constructed about my parents was all wrong. I built it little by little as a boy and carried it on my back into adulthood. But truthfully, I don't know how else it could have happened for me or Jeff. Both my parents were damaged by this vile individual's criminal act, and there was no way they could explain that to their children. We all sort of went to our separate corners and developed the unhealthy coping skills of depression, food, drugs, work, money, and isolation. It resulted in a family so divided that anger, bitterness, resentfulness, and fear were the natural outcomes. On top of that, we buried Uncle Jack, Mother, Jeff, and now my father. Just pondering it all, the sadness is overwhelming. And now you and I are left to come to terms with what's left of our lives."

Rachael is uncharacteristically quiet, so I continue. "You might want to sit down for what I'm about to say now." She sits with eyes wide. "I know now why you married my father. It was the kindest thing you could have done for them both, my father and my mother.

the way home

I've read in some of Mother's later journals that she gave her blessing to you both and wanted you to find happiness and take care of each other. And I know that you guys never left her behind but continued to care for her financially and in every other way until the day she died. She loved you both with all her heart. And I'm happy that my father wasn't alone when Mother and Jeff died. The man had enough sorrow in his life for six people, and you were his anchor."

I stand and take a deep breath. "And then there's the grief I, the angry rebel son, caused him. I hear Trevor claim him as his 'father,' and I'm a little jealous. I wish I could do it over. I wish he could forgive me for blaming him and snatching away the last son he had."

Rachael stands and throws her arms around me. "He forgives you, Bobby. Now you forgive yourself. Robert loved you with all of his heart, and he knew you didn't understand the circumstances. He never blamed you. Now, that bighearted father of yours has left you the resources to continue the legacy he left you to do good, not in his name but in your own. He's happy, I guarantee you. And he's proud of you for being brave enough to look for and act on the truth."

I'm crying openly now, heaving into this petite mother's breast while she consoles me. "Let it all out, honey. It's been hung up inside you for a long time. Let it all out."

Rachael and I stand that way for I don't know how long, although I eventually notice the front of her robe is soaked with my tears and the hot chocolate is cold. I go to wash my face and meet her in the kitchen to heat up some more chocolate. Sitting in my father's place at the old pine table sipping hot chocolate with this woman I trust again, I confess. "I love you, Rachael."

And that night I sleep.

twenty

"Daddy, we like living close to the water. Can we ride in one of those sailboats this summer? Mommy says we can take lessons." Mary, one of my mother's namesakes, is eager in her new surroundings.

"Daddy, are those things safe? Can we fall in the water?" Elizabeth, my mother's other namesake, is so conservative and rational and very different from her twin sister. But I know that they'll mesh well with this new city this summer. And that we will never leave.

Jill and Rachael have been busy with hiring contractors and choosing paint colors and new fabric. My old room, Mother's study, and Jeff's boyhood room are being redecorated for the girls. I've given them carte blanche for every room in the house except two: my father's study, which I've taken as my own, and the attic room. In time I'll allow Jill to convert the attic room into a play room, but right now I still like to return there for a little meditation on the past as well as the future.

The women have also been planning my father's memorial service and the party afterward. I like that they're making both informal affairs with lots of friends and family. Some of my father's oldest and dearest friends from Charleston will speak as well as his newest ones, like Trevor and Nicholas, for whose brief visit we were able to procure a visa. And Rachael has convinced me to speak as well.

the way home

    The party is being catered by a restaurant in Mt. Pleasant with great pots of Frogmore stew, or Low Country boil, as most prefer to call it. Frogmore is a small South Carolina community on Lady's Island for which many believe the stew was named. But it was christened with another name because that one implied to the novice that there were frogs in it. The stew is layered in great steam pots with potatoes, Vidalia onion, sweet silver queen corn, kielbasa sausage, and loads of creek shrimp. Each layer is generously sprinkled with Old Bay seasoning and steamed until the shrimps layered last in the pot turn a soft pink. Great vats of coleslaw, hot hush puppies, and dipping sauces such as horseradish cocktail sauce and melted butter are served with this hearty main course.

    Giant white tents, a portable dance floor, a DJ stand, tables, and a bar will be set up on the grounds. All of Charleston would probably like to come, but we limited the guest list to 250 and received 250 acceptances. Jill, Rachael, and Brenda Grace have done all the planning and all the work and, of course, have chosen all the music. My father would have loved the celebration. And speaking of Brenda Grace, Jill and I have had two spare rooms decorated for her and the girls for their regular visits. We want Jeff's family to feel at home here where he grew up.

    Sitting in my study trying to write my speech for the memorial service, I hear the sounds of my four girls agreeing and disagreeing, squealing and laughing. Decorators are finishing up the final work on the rooms. Jill has taken Mother and Father's former master bedroom for us and won't let me see what she's doing until the renovation is complete. She says she has big plans for us in there. I like that!

    As I sit in front of the blank document on my computer screen, the only sentence in my head is "I wish my father were here to enjoy this." I seem to cry easily these days and wonder how I'll get through the service without succumbing to tears. When I shared with Rachael how much trouble I was having writing this memorial speech to my father, she said, "Don't worry about correctness or protocol. Just open up your heart and let it flow." This isn't generally my style, as we all know, but I decided to give it a chance. I begin to type.

judy norwood enter

I am Robert J. Chapin Sr.'s first and only living son. To all of you, he was a business partner, a nationally known trial lawyer, the man who married the beautiful Charleston debutante Mary Elizabeth Hargrave, the deacon in his church, and the civic-minded activist in this great city he loved. These descriptions of Robert Chapin can be observed by anyone, whether they knew him well or not. They don't reveal the heart of the man who was my father.

You have already heard from his friends from Charlotte to the Bahamas to Haiti that the real man they knew possessed the heart of a giant. Unmatched generosity, genuine love for his fellow man, contagious joy, selfless sacrifice, and enviable devotion to the "least of the least" made Robert J. Chapin Sr. a Goliath of a man with the heart of David.

From a son's perspective, I have observed that sometimes the strongest and most committed men are known better by their true friends than by their closest family members, especially their sons. I believe my father was such a man. Strong, responsible men are commissioned with holding their families together in the event of devastating circumstances, even at the expense of their own reputations in the eyes of the ones they love most. I believe my father was such a man. Strong, reliable men become vulnerable and sacrificial for the sakes of their families. I believe my father was such a man. Strong and wise men know how to laugh at themselves and live in a way that shows others life is fragile and a gift that is to be lived to the fullest. I believe my father was such a man.

This spring, in my father's dressing closet, I found taped to a mirror Mother Teresa's "Anyway" poem. It meant nothing to me the day I read it, but it explains everything now. Thank you, Dad, for protecting your family and for showing me the right way to live.

ANYWAY

People are often unreasonable, illogical, and self-centered. Forgive them anyway.

If you are kind, people may accuse you of selfish, ulterior motives. Be kind anyway.

If you are successful, you will win some false friends and true enemies. Succeed anyway.

the way home

If you are honest and frank, people may cheat you. Be honest and frank anyway.

What you spend years building, someone could destroy overnight. Build anyway.

If you find serenity and happiness, they may be jealous. Be happy anyway.

The good you do today, people will often forget tomorrow. Do good anyway.

Give the world the best you have, and it may never be enough. Give the world the best you have anyway.

In the final analysis, it is between you and your God. It was never between you and them anyway.

• • •

The sounds of decorators and contractors have ceased, and the whole house is silent as I ponder what I've written to my father. But the growl of my stomach and the smells from Jill's kitchen remind me of dinner. I close my computer and think I'll review the speech tomorrow, but I know in my heart I won't change it.

I swing open my study door and run dashing barefoot down the big hallway on the freshly refinished pine floors toward the kitchen. "Where are my girls? I'm in a tickling mood and need to make somebody laugh! Girls, where are you?" Pots are on the stove, but the kitchen is empty. I hear laughter coming from outside.

On the green lawn overlooking the harbor, Rachael has set up a croquet set and is teaching the girls to play. These proper Charleston women of mine are all barefoot and have grass stains on their feet. Elizabeth sees me coming toward them in my current uniform of Bermuda shorts and bare feet. "Daddy, come play with us. Can you hit this ball through that wicket? Memaw Rachael says this stick is a 'mallet.' Do you know how to play?"

"Yes, my dear, your daddy knows how to play. Your uncle Jeff and I used to play in this very spot. In fact, this looks like our old croquet set. Rachael, where did you find this?"

judy norwood enter

"It was in the old carriage house when we remodeled it. I put it away and saved it for today." She winks and smiles.

I pick up my old mallet and then Jeff's, examining the old scars and chipped wood.

"Hey, dork! Let's go play croquet. I'll beat the pants off of you."

"No way, little brother. Your puny shots lack direction. You couldn't hit that ball through a wicket if I stuck it at the end of your nose."

"Bullshit. I'm an ace."

"Boys, boys. Language. You sound like your father." Mother was sitting on the portico steps with some sewing. She watched our antics and laughed at us. We could tell she was in one of her playful moods and decided to take advantage of it.

"Excuse us, Mother deah," Jeff teases her. "We truly do not want your proper southern sons to offend you." He gave me a knowing look.

"Your proper southern sons are coming to tickle you till you wet in your pants, Mother deah. Whatever will the aristocratic neighbors think?" I said.

And we chased her across the lawn while she ran from us. When we caught her, she began her inevitable descent to the ground in a heap of giggles and laughter. When all three of us had fallen into a human mound in the cool summer grass, she looked longingly at us and elicited a promise.

"Will you boys promise me that you'll bring your children here one day to play on this lawn just like this? It would make me the happiest grandmother in the world."

Smiling, I gaze out at the croquet group now dangerously smacking balls in all directions. I whisper into the wind, "I brought them here, Mother, and I hope you know and are happy."

And as I dodge a wild, menacing croquet ball belted by Elizabeth, I say, "I do wish you were here to help me tame your namesakes into proper southern ladies."

twenty-one

Beach music is blasting away, and dancers are shoulder to shoulder showing off their best shag moves on the portable dance floor on our lawn. The smell of steamed shrimp permeates the air until even tourists slow down to watch the jubilant dancers and hungrily smell what's cooking in the big pots. Children are running wildly all over the lawn and porticoes playing tag and hide-and-seek. The croquet set has been moved to the side yard where the teenagers are playing. The day is July 10, 2009, the anniversary of my father's disappearance, and we have finished celebrating his life at a memorial service in town. At least 1,500 people attended that service, and there are over 250 people now on the big house's plush lawn. The weather has cooperated in that temperatures are in the high eighties with the humidity at a tolerable level.

I see Trevor Lewis has Louis Chandler's ear about something. He's probably trying to convince him to come to Charlotte to the residence for a visit with the men. Poor Louis is mostly business and doesn't like to get too close or too personal. Rachael is on the dance floor with Nicholas and trying to teach him how to shag. I question how useful knowing how to shag will be in Haiti. Jill and Brenda Grace are overseeing the caterers, and I stroll over to my dazzling wife, who's wearing a brilliantly floral sundress, the white in its background showing off her tan.

the way home

"Hey, sweet thing. How'd you like a date and a dance with an old Charleston boy?" Brenda Grace giggles and pushes Jill to dance with me, saying she has food service under control.

The DJ pops on "Sixty Minute Man," and I grab my sweetheart and lead her to the floor. We begin that slow shuffle, moving nothing above the waist except our arms. "It's all in what's below the waist, how you can use it and how you can lose it." Can you imagine Rachael teaching that to a fourteen-year-old boy? The other dancers appreciate our moves and part the dance floor to watch and cheer us. I had forgotten how to be happy or else I never really knew it because this moment, watching my wife slide her feet in rhythm to the music, her delicate hand in mine, is sheer bliss. I hear the girls screaming, "Look at Mommy and Daddy. They're dancing!" All is right with my world.

The party begins closing down around nine, and the satiated guests are shuttled back to their parked cars. I walk toward the harbor and experience a real desire to speak to my father. If he could hear me, I think, what would I want to say? There's no one on the walk overlooking the harbor at this time of evening, so I say it softly aloud. "Dad, if you could see this, it was for you. The memorial service at church, the party here in this home you and Mother loved and left us—we thought it would be a happy way to remember you today. I hope you know we're rebounding from your death and we'll remember your life and describe it to your grandchildren. Jill, the girls, and I are living in the big house, and it still feels like it doesn't fit, but these women in my life will make sure I stick it out until it does. And, Dad, please forgive me for blaming you all these years. I know the truth now, and I respect you for trying to protect us. What I said today at the church was not for those people gathered; it was for you. I love you, Dad."

Strolling back toward the house, I see my family of so many girls and long for another man in this happy group. My mind strays to Mitchell. It's time for him to read the journals of Mother's that I have marked. I'll take them to Virginia after I return from Haiti this summer.

twenty-two

I'm embarrassed to let Mitchell know that I've chartered a small plane to return to Arlington, but I'm lazy about making the long drive from Charleston alone. I rent a car at the airport and meet him again at his office. All of Mother's journals that I marked as pertinent to his life are with me.

"Good to see you again, Mitchell. How is your family?"

"My family's good."

"I'm curious to know if you've talked to Betsy about a meeting, so I can get to know your family a little better. Jill would make the trip to Virginia for a visit."

"We're talking and I think it's a possibility at some date, but we're still a little cautious. You understand?"

"I do understand. Take your time and just let me know."

Mitchell says, " I didn't expect to see you this soon. Your e-mails have been coming out of Haiti. I like reading about the work you're doing there. How many children you got there now?"

"We're full at the home but Marianne and Monique seem to be able to find room for one more. Some of the kids coming from the streets are in homes now. We've been able to locate some of their family members who will take them in. That's Rachael's specialty. She likes getting these kids into real homes."

"Why didn't you bring Rachael? That is one sweet, pretty lady."

the way home

"I left her in Haiti. You know that she and I went in late July after my father's memorial service. She's completely absorbed with Monique and Marianne in the children's home and the small adjacent children's clinic we were able to erect pretty quickly. She stayed to provision medical supplies and personnel to the clinic. In fact, Louis Chandler, my father's law partner and administrator of his estate, is preparing the legal documents to change the honorarium on the home so that my name is taken off. It's going to be called the Rachael Crawford Chapin Children's Home and Clinic. The woman is a consummate mother, and it's only appropriate that the children's home should be named in her honor."

"Where is she staying, and who's with her?" Mitchell's demeanor has shifted from interested friend to professional, authoritative, protective mode.

"She's at the Hotel Montana in the Pétionville suburb, where we usually stay, and Nicholas Trudeau is looking after her. Nicholas was my father's right-hand man and our emissary there. Why?"

He leans across his desk toward me. "I don't think you should leave her there alone, that's why."

I lean back. "Well, I don't think it's any of your business. At the risk of sounding defensive, I would never leave Rachael in harm's way, and anyway, I would fear for the life of anyone who tried to mess with her." I laugh, but he doesn't.

"Look, Bobby. Offense is my business. Defense is a weaker position, and sometimes you have to use it, too, but offensive prevention of crime is always better than defensive when it comes to protecting you or your loved ones from it. I'm sympathetic to the work your family is doing there following up on what your father began. But that volatile country is prone to rebellion and violence, and you need to be on the offensive while you're working there. Couple the political instability and volatility with a hungry population, drugs, rape, prostitution, and child-slave trade, and it all adds up to an unsafe environment for even the savviest outsiders. That area you're in, Port-au-Prince, is the worst. I know through the e-mails we exchanged that you went into the Carrefour area of the city. You saw with your own eyes the hopeless condition of the people and their desperation. You need to stay out of that area, man, and Rachael needs to return to Charleston."

"Rachael is on the outskirts of town dealing with the children's home, and the Hotel Montana is in a better area of the city. We use that hotel on every visit and have never had a problem. I don't think she's in any danger."

"Bobby, you're a nice guy but a little naïve. Haiti is a volatile political scene with a violent history. It's politics have always focused on retaining personal power. It is racially unstable, and a majority of its people live in abject poverty. Violence has always been the only effective route to change for Haitians. In my memory, 2004 was the most recent time there was civil strife in that country. It could break out again without warning. I think it's heroic what you and your family are doing to help these people, especially the children, but you're not on some fantasy island. And my fear is that you take it all too lightly. People like you with a lot of money—I see it every day—you think it insulates you. Well, it doesn't, and the truth is that sometimes it makes you more vulnerable. Some unscrupulous, destitute men in Port-au-Prince would just as soon slit your throat for a dollar in your pocket. I read last week that a UN soldier was killed by a member of a group fighting over food in the street. If some of these starving, hapless people will kill for food, what do you think they would do for some real money and the escape route it could provide out of that hellhole?"

"Look, I know these people are desperately poor and a lot of them try to leave the country. But the ones who want to leave usually buy their way aboard a small boat headed for the Bahamas or the United States. I've not heard of anyone's throat being cut for money to leave Haiti."

He leans back and his desk chair squeaks and complains at his bulk. He apparently thinks of one more scare tactic. "Haiti has always been prone to natural disasters that frequently sweep over it—floods, hurricanes, earthquakes, and fires. We're in hurricane season, and you don't want to be there when one crosses that country. The mountains—you've seen them—have been denuded for making charcoal. Even if they don't take a direct hit, the accom-

the way home

panying ten to twenty inches of rain in a big storm will create mud slides and flooding that will kill and destroy everyone and everything in its path."

I sit dumbfounded. "Have you ever been to Haiti?"

"Can't say."

"I see. Evasive. Look, Mitchell, thank you for the history lesson, and your concern is touching. I personally think you've seen too much action in your special ops days, and maybe that Rambo persona of yours is getting in the way of reality. We are safe, or else I wouldn't be there, especially with Rachael. My father never experienced an incident. There are definitely some really scary parts of the city in Port-au-Prince where I've been, and we have security guards that carry GLOCK 9mm pistols. They were my father's security guards as well."

"Your father hired armed security guards to accompany him and you think he wasn't aware of the danger? Look, it's your decision, but if it was my mother or my wife or my sister, I wouldn't leave her there alone even with guards. You're too far away in Charleston to get to Rachael quickly if she gets in trouble. Better to stick with her while she does her work. Then leave together."

"Mitchell, I respect your opinion - especially about international governments and the safety of travel in foreign countries. I still think you're overly concerned, but I'll bring her back a little early because of what you've told me. She's due back to Charleston in two weeks anyway. I'll send a plane for her tomorrow, but she's going to be fighting mad at me."

Mitchell and I leave his office for a little neighborhood bar and grill for a beer and dinner, as we had planned. I follow him in my rental car and transfer Mother's journals to his car when we arrive. "That a rental car? You fly here?"

"Um…yes, I flew."

"I see." And he smiles knowingly. "Well, get your rich ass back on your little plane and go get Miss Rachael."

182

twenty-three

Rachael's cell phone has sporadic service when she's outside the city at the children's home, but when she's back in her room at the hotel, it tends to be better. When I can't reach her, I try Nicholas.

"Nicholas, I'm on my way back to Charleston from Arlington, Virginia. I can't reach Rachael on her phone. Do you know where she is? I need to reach her right away."

"Boss Man, she tell me she need to go to the wharf to pick up supplies for the children's clinic. I send Andre and Marcos in bus to take her early this morning."

"Shit, Nicholas. Why did you let her go down to the wharfs? She's a white woman and stands out like a neon sign."

"She very convincing. Need medicine for the sick kids and want to see to it herself. Say she been waiting on it since you two arrive late July. Been over a month now."

"Well, it's after two o'clock. Find her and have her call me. If you can't locate her, contact the Police Nationale d'Haiti, whatever good that will do. And contact that mayor she had her picture made with last week for the newspaper in Port-au-Prince that covered the dedication of the clinic. Ask him for help. He seemed to like her. Find her, now!"

the way home

"Boss Man, you get all excited. You know roads are bad and she may stop for other supplies. Miss Rachael big talker, too. Talk to everybody."

"Go now, Nicholas, and call me right away when you find her or, better yet, tell her to call me."

My heart is pounding as I board the plane, and I want to divert to Port-au-Prince, but this little plane can't carry enough fuel. Mitchell has scared the hell out of me and probably for no good reason. I feel like a child who's been told a horror story before bedtime and can't stop thinking about it. It may not be reality, but it sure is mine at the moment.

We touch down in Charleston, and I'm off the plane in an instant. I haven't gotten a message from Nicholas. I call him, and there's no answer. Damn cell phones. He may not have a signal. I text him so the message will be there for him as soon as he picks up his phone and has a signal.

Next, I call Jill and tell her the situation as rationally as I can, but Mitchell's fears have invaded my thinking, and I'm not making sense to her. I try to pass off my irrational fears to Jill as paranoia.

"What are you saying, Bobby? Is Rachael hurt or missing?"

"No, we just can't locate her as fast as I would like. And it's making me nervous. Get on the phone with the charter company and ask for a larger plane to take me to Haiti. Find out how soon I can leave and tell them I have no concrete return date yet. Do it now!"

"Well, hang up the phone so I can call!"

Next, I make a dreaded phone call to Trent. "Trent, I don't want to alarm you, but I can't locate Rachael in Haiti. Nicholas said she asked him to send the bus and guards this morning to the hotel so she could go to the wharfs and pick up some supplies and medicine for the children's clinic that had come in by ship. It's now almost five o'clock, and I haven't spoken with her. I don't know if her cell is out of range or if the battery is dead or what. It could just be something that simple, so I just don't want to alarm you."

judy norwood enter

"My mother hasn't been heard from since early this morning in that godforsaken country, and you don't want me to be alarmed? Well, consider me on high alarm! What are you doing about it?"

"I spoke to Nicholas around one o'clock just as I was leaving a business meeting in Arlington. He told me the bus was sent for her at the hotel early this morning, and he hasn't heard from Marcos or Andre, the guards, or Rachael since. He thinks there's a simple explanation, but now I can't even reach him."

"I'm heading out the door to your house, Bobby. I'll be there within half an hour."

"Jill is chartering a flight, and I'm flying to Haiti as soon as it can get me in the air."

"I'll call Gladys and have her pack me a bag and bring my passport to your place. I'm going with you."

I try to call Nicholas again, but there's still no answer. I call Mitchell; he doesn't pick up either, and I leave him a message.

"Mitchell, this is Bobby Chapin. I'm back in Charleston, and I can't locate Rachael in Haiti. I think I'm probably overreacting because of what you told me today; on the other hand, she hasn't been seen since early morning when the bus took her to the wharfs. Please call me. I need your help. Thanks."

When I pull in to my driveway, the house is ablaze with lights, and there are cars parked in front of the carriage house. Jill steps onto the portico along with Trudy. Then Trent pulls his car in behind mine. This is not going to be good.

Trudy runs down the steps and, crying, beats me on the chest with her fists. "Where is my mother?"

"I don't know, Trudy. I'm trying to find answers right now. Try to be calm. If she wasn't OK, I think we would have heard. So that's good news. Let's all go inside."

Gladys, Trent's wife, is now in the parking lot of my lawn carrying a packed bag for Trent.

"Before I tell you what I know, let me speak with Jill about the plane and try Nicholas again."

Jill has a pot of coffee brewing, and the trio drifts anxiously to the kitchen for cups.

185

the way home

Jill whispers, "Bobby, what is going on? Rachael is never out of communication for this long. Is she in trouble?"

"I honestly don't know. Mitchell Cummins scared the shit out of me with his horror stories today about how dangerous a place Port-au-Prince is for vulnerable, rich white people, especially women, and I think I've invented a worst-case scenario. Let's all try to stay calm."

My cell rings, and I frantically dig for it from my pocket. The caller ID shows that it's Mitchell.

"Mitchell, thanks for calling. I've got a situation here." I explain the scant details, as I know them, to Mitchell.

"You've got a potentially dangerous situation there; if she's been abducted you're going to need help. I'm standing by here for you if you learn anything else. Call me no matter the time. Do you know when you're flying out?"

"No, checking on that after we hang up."

"Call me or, if you can't, have Jill keep me posted. And, Bobby, I know this woman is like your mother. If you need me, I'm there."

I swallow hard. "Thanks, Mitchell." The plane, I find out, can't be ready until six o'clock the next morning. Jill packs my bag, and she and Trudy entertain the girls, trying not to convey our borderline hysteria to them. Trudy leaves to go home to her children and husband, admonishing Trent and I to stay in contact. Gladys leaves with her, too.

Jill, Trent, and I barely sleep that night and keep meeting one another in the hallway at odd times of the night. At four o'clock, Trent and I give up and head for the airport. I still have no word from Nicholas.

• • •

Both Trent and I manage to get some sleep on the flight out of exhaustion, and the trip seems brief when we're awakened with coffee from a steward. Port-au-Prince is another one hundred miles, and we'll be in Customs and Immigration for clearance within the hour.

Trent speaks over coffee. "Bobby, I'm not blaming you for this. I was just a bit hysterical yesterday, and shit, I may be again today, depending on what we find. This isn't easy for a son to say, but I know you have a special bond with my mother. I've never been jealous of that—I've been respectful, actually. We'll find her, and she's going to be all right. She has to…or else we'll have lost them all." Trent buries his head in his hands and cries softly.

As soon as we touch down, I try to call Nicholas again, but his phone goes directly to voice mail. I don't know how to reach Monique and Marianne except to drive to the children's home, and we have no bus, so I'm left to consider whether we should find a Haitian driver or use one of the "tap taps." These wildly colored pickup trucks are basically shared taxis where all the riders jump on the back of a beat-up truck and tap the top of the cab when they're ready to get off. I chastise myself for becoming so dependent on one man here, Nicholas. It may be time to go to the American embassy.

We clear through Customs and Immigration, giving them an open-ended departure date, which they don't like. Once outside Trent and I find a piece of shade, and I call Mitchell. He answers immediately.

"Mitchell, we're at the Port-au-Prince airport, and I still can't reach Nicholas. How in the hell could he just disappear after we spoke yesterday afternoon around one? I don't have a driver, but I'm going to get to the Hotel Montana and to the children's home. They're the only starting places I have. And I'm thinking about going to the American embassy."

"The embassy is not your first line of information or defense. Don't go there and show them your cards."

"Cards! I don't have any cards to show. I need answers." The late summer heat is broiling us even in the shade.

"Bobby, I shouldn't have sent you there alone. This is my gig. This is what I do. You're a salesman. No offense. Go check in at the Hotel Montana. Discreetly ask a few questions around the hotel about Rachael and then go and stay in your rooms. I'll stay in your

187

the way home

room with you. I don't want my name on a reservation or to show up anywhere at the hotel."

"Call Jill. Tell her to charter you a plane out of Arlington or DC for as early as you can leave. Let me know when you'll arrive."

Trent and I locate a car and driver to deliver us to the Hotel Montana for an exorbitant price. We each get rooms. We question the hotel clerk about Rachael, and he says he knows her but hasn't seen her since yesterday on his shift. I ask if I might check her room, and he exchanges the key for my fifty-dollar bill. Trent and I enter Rachael's room, trying not to disturb anything but looking for any clue as to her whereabouts. Everything is meticulously in its place, with all her clothes and toiletries as well as her empty luggage untouched. The bed is made and her window locked. There are no clues here.

I disobey Mitchell and ask the hotel clerk if he can arrange a car and driver to take us to the children's clinic outside town about fifteen miles from the hotel. We leave a message for Mitchell at the front desk in a sealed envelope. I figure if he arrives before we return, it will be better for him to read we are gone than for me to call and tell him. It's that old "better to ask forgiveness than permission" reasoning.

As we drive to the children's home, Trent is aghast at our surroundings, and I realize I'd forgotten how the senses reel at this filthy foreign place the first time you see it. That coupled with his borderline hysteria from knowing his mother is lost in this inferno makes him just about useless. I suddenly remember that Mitchell instructed me not to leave his name on anything at the hotel, and the envelope I've left with the desk clerk clearly has his name on it. I'm no good at this covert thing.

At the children's home, our driver pulls into the lot we've managed to cover in gravel to keep the dust down. It seems quiet except for a few boys and girls playing nearby in the grassless yard, playing like there's no tomorrow, and that might be true for them. I wave to them and offer a smile and a few return the wave. I call out for Monique and Marianne, and only Marianne comes running out. She is hysterically crying and runs to us exclaiming her brother's name.

judy norwood enter

I can't understand another word she's saying. She thrusts a dirty, crumpled-up piece of paper with writing in Kreyol into my hand. She screams, "Nicholas, Nicholas!"

"Please, Marianne, what is this note saying? Note. Find someone who can read the note to me." A volunteer doctor from the little clinic next door has heard the commotion and comes out into the yard. He sounds British.

"What is the problem? Who is hurt?"

"Can you read Kreyol?" I ask him.

"I can speak it but not fluently. And I read a little."

"What does this say?"

He drops the reading glasses from the top of his bald head to the bridge of his nose and squints. Trent and I wait.

"This says we have a white woman - a rich white woman - and her Haitian man, Nicholas. Oh my - it says two guards are dead. They want five million American dollars by Saturday or they'll kill the man. On Sunday they'll kill the woman if they don't get the money."

"Oh dear God," the doctor says. "Who are they?"

Trent says, "She's our mother."

I add, "And Nicholas is our friend and brother to Marianne."

Marianne has continued to cry while the doctor read the note to us. "Doctor, would you tell Marianne we'll find her brother and bring him home? Ask her to pray for us. Tell her we're at the Hotel Montana."

Our curious driver has witnessed the commotion and probably even heard the note being read. He glares at us in the rear view mirror and says absolutely nothing as we return to the hotel. When I'm back in my room with Trent, we call the family, and I try to reach Mitchell.

"Jill, listen to me carefully. Rachael and Nicholas are hostages. They want five million dollars by Saturday. Now do exactly as I say. Call Trudy to our home and tell her everything. Call Brenda Grace as well to come stay with you. And tell absolutely no one else. This cannot make the national or local news. Their lives will be jeopardized if too many people know. What about Mitchell?"

189

the way home

Jill sniffs loudly in the phone.. "Mitchell had more clout than I did in getting a charter quickly. He's already in the air and due at the Port-au-Prince airport late tonight or early tomorrow morning. How can I get word to him?" Jill openly cries now.

"Call his partner, the Goins fellow. His business card is on my desk. Ask him how you can speak privately to Mitchell while he's in the air. Just tell him it's crucial that you speak with him but don't tell him why. Get on it now. And call me back. Trust absolutely no one with this information and admonish Trudy and Brenda Grace as well. Contain your conversations within the walls of our home."

"Bobby, don't hang up yet. A kidnapping? Help me understand what's happening."

"I only know what's in the note that was given to Marianne. They are holding Nicholas and Rachael for ransom."

"Well, what happened to the guards you said were with her? How could she have been taken when she always traveled with the guards?"

"I don't know, Jill. I don't know. You're understandably upset, but I need you to pull yourself together and explain what you know to the others. Please be patient and I'll call you as soon as I know more. I love you."

• • •

Trent appears a wreck his first day in Haiti. "Trent, go wash your face and put on some clean clothes. You've perspired through those a couple of times today. We're going downstairs to the restaurant for a beer and a sandwich, and we're going to act as though everything is normal. Those people who have taken Rachael probably know we're here and may be watching us."

"Bobby, I'm not as strong as you. I don't think I can do this. They killed the guards. You didn't tell Jill they killed the guards."

"No, we are not telling the women they killed the guards. And they have names. Marcos and Andre. They have families. Now go do what I asked you to. Change your clothes and wash your face.

judy norwood enter

Meet me back here in a few minutes. Act normal. Just do it for your mother."

When he leaves my room, I walk to my washbasin and notice my hands are trembling uncontrollably. I splash cold water over my face and head and then dry them roughly with a towel.

The restaurant environment sharply contrasts with the crisis we're in, but we try making small talk. We both order beers and grilled sandwiches.

"Who is Mitchell Cummins?" Trent asks. "Is he a friend of yours, and why is he coming? Can he help us?"

I'd been wondering when Trent would think to ask who Mitchell Cummins is.

"Trent, keep your voice down. He's a protective services guy out of Arlington."

"Arlington, Virginia, where you were yesterday? Did you suspect this kind of shit could happen?"

"Trent, keep your voice down and smile. He's a friend of mine from school I've just reconnected with, that's all. He offered us his services if we ever needed him in any way, and we need him." I couldn't help but flinch at the lie that rolled so easily off my tongue.

twenty-four

Trent is still in my room at two o'clock in the morning when we hear a light rap on the door. He jumps up from the chair and grabs the door before I can stop him, thinking it might be his mother. But he opens the door to Mitchell, the big, old giant of a man who's now dressed in preppy clothes.

"Mitchell, my gosh, you got here fast. Thank you for coming." I pump his hand like it might come off. "This is Trent Crawford, Rachael's son."

Mitchell is stoic, omitting introduction and pleasantries, and tosses his small bag onto one of the beds. "I want to hear it all. Talk to me." I silently hand the filthy note to Mitchell.

Trent sits in his chair with his head down, wringing his hands. "I need you to find my mother. Do you hear me? Find my mother!"

"Mr. Crawford, you are emotional, and you shouldn't be here. Please go to your room while I discuss the situation regarding your mother with Bobby."

"Who in the hell do you think you are? My mother has been abducted by a bunch of Haitian jerk-offs, and you fly in here telling me I'm emotional."

In an unexpected, fluid movement, Mitchell grabs Trent by the fabric on the front of his shirt and snaps him to his feet. "You little prick. Your mother is in the hands of assassins who have killed her two armed guards to scare the shit out of us and prove they'll kill

193

the way home

her. They have no consciences and place no value on human life, even their own. They say they're willing to trade her life for money, but that's a lie. They're going to kill her whether they get the money or not. By definition they are not 'jerk-offs.' They are killers. And my job is to get her out from under their control before they rape and mutilate her. Now stop your whining, or I will personally put your ass on a plane and send you back to Charleston." Mitchell releases Trent and hardly takes a breath before speaking again. "We don't have much time. That's bad. We've got to buy more time to get arms and a team here. How did Marianne receive the ransom note?"

"I didn't ask her. Sorry, I've never done this before."

"It's OK. I need to talk to her. Where does she live?"

"Sorry, I don't know."

"If you keep saying 'sorry' to everything, it's gonna burn up a whole lot of useful time. Just point me in the direction you do know, and I'll take it from there. Where is Rachael's room?"

I give him the key, and he tells us to stay in our room. Trent looks shell-shocked, and I don't blame him. Mitchell just told him they mean to kill his mother. His mother's life depends on this stranger he has just met and has no idea is my half brother. I silently hope he'll not get in Mitchell's way.

In half an hour, Mitchell has returned with a few items that we identify—some jewelry Rachael left out openly in her room, some cash, and a clipping she cut out of a newspaper. It's a picture of her and the mayor of the Pétionville Commune, Pierre LeBlanc.

"The newspaper she cut this out of wasn't in her trash can. What do you know about this?"

"The article and picture ran about two weeks ago. A reporter contacted her for a photo and an article on the work we're doing here. Afterward, Mr. LeBlanc contacted her, took her to dinner, and showed an interest in the work and our family. This happened after I left."

Trent glares at me.

"Have you read this article? It describes your family as 'an extremely wealthy American family.'" He hands me the article, and

194

judy norwood enter

as I read it, the hairs on the back of my neck begin to stand straight out.

" This sounds like an invitation for extortion." I pass the article to Trent.

Mitchell's phone rings. It's now almost three in the morning. "Yes, yes. We're going to need three teams of two men each, including me. Separate planes, different hotel. I'll let you know. Your arms contact? Don't call again until you've landed."

"What? What was that?" Trent wants information.

"Sit down, and I'll tell you what I believe we have. This abduction is more sophisticated than that of a couple of street thugs. They wouldn't have known to ask for that kind of money. This smells of a top guy and hired guns. And unless you have a better idea, Bobby, I think Pierre LeBlanc is our first suspect. We're on our own here. By the time the Haitian police or the American embassy get involved, she'll be dead. I've ordered five other men to fly in on separate planes. We'll change hotels and set up an ops center in a couple of rooms. My guys can't bring in equipment like night vision, thermal imagers, guns, and grenades, but we can buy them here."

"This sounds like a war," Trent says.

"That's exactly what this is. These guys coming here were all special ops, and they're the best I know. I'll tell you up-front that they aren't cheap. They'll be looking for at least half a million each. And expenses for the guns and ordnance and anything else we find we can use here. I know your family is real wealthy, but you may be talking about four million when it's all said and done. I want nothing."

"Whatever you need or want, Mitchell, it's yours. And if I weren't wealthy and didn't have the money, I would beg, borrow, or steal it to get Rachael and Nicholas free."

"If you weren't rich, they wouldn't be there. OK, let's get some sleep. We've got four days until Saturday."

195

twenty-five

I relocate us to three rooms at the Le Plaza Hotel on the Champ de Mars square in the heart of Port-au-Prince. It's near government buildings, the French embassy, and many points of historical interest, such as a museum. Mitchell says that to hide out effectively, you should place yourself where the most people are. To do this in Port-au-Prince is not difficult. We've closed out Rachael's room and packed up all her things to bring with us.

Mitchell's covert operations team is on the ground, on its way to the hotel, and will use his room for operations and ours to sleep. Trent and I move as though in a nightmare, having been pulled surreally into the center of a hostage rescue of Rachael and Nicholas. This is as foreign to us as a ship in the middle of a desert. Mitchell demanded that we listen to him and not question or disobey any order he gives us, which we agreed to. Trent is too numb to confront any longer. And I just plain trust the man. All our lives are in his hands.

Mitchell briefs Trent and me after the teams' first meeting. "Each team has a specific job, and the first is reconnaissance. Benny and Moses are already out on the streets and down at the wharf pretending to be high and doped-up while looking for information. They're both black and speak Kreyol. Their job is to find any tracks that might lead to Rachael. I'm extremely uncomfortable not having communication with the captors. That's not a typical hostage

the way home

situation. We want to assure them we're putting the money together and not ignoring them. And I want to require that they let us talk to Rachael and Nicholas. Marianne told me a lone man delivered the ransom note to the clinic and threatened her about following him or trying to find him. In this city of almost a million people, it's hard to find one young black Haitian in ragged clothes, so he's pretty safe from detection. I'm making certain assumptions because of the newspaper article. Trace has this Pierre LeBlanc under surveillance. I'll give that two days, and if nothing turns up suspicious with him, I'll pull off and go in another direction—I don't know where—or else force his hand."

As we're novices to this, Mitchell is patient to explain. "The second team is securing arms. In a third world country, it's a little harder to obtain the equipment and arms we need but not impossible and usually a little cheaper. Harry and Bruno are our procurement team. We're using the cash Bobby withdrew from the bank account here for the children's home, and Louis Chandler is wiring more as we speak. We're using American dollars for the purchase. Harry and Bruno are looking for flash bangs, a type of grenade that blinds and deafens, as well as knives, GLOCK 9mm pistols—actually pretty easy to come by here—rifles, and anything more we can buy. The problem is that every special ops team usually has time to do some target practice with its weapons, and we can't here. A weapon is an extension of a man's hand, and not knowing how that weapon handles is dangerous. Even with a familiar weapon, we're accurate in a high-stakes operation only eighty percent of the time. That diminishes with strange weapons. But we have no other choice. Some faction in this country is always on the verge of revolution, so I'm expecting to find plenty of artillery here. We just have to locate it."

Since neither Trent nor I have any questions about weapons, Mitchell takes a long drink of bottled water and then continues. "The third team is me and Trace. We manage operations from here, and when the time comes, we're first in. So now you know what to expect. The first thing is to find a way of communicating with these assassins."

"What can we do to help?" I ask.

judy norwood enter

"Your primary job is transportation. Send the charter planes, yours and mine, back to the States and tell Jill to get busy finding two planes to lease. We need two six-to-eight-seat passenger planes. Our goal is to get in, get Rachael, and get everybody out without losing anyone. The 'getting out' is your job. Our exit planes have to be sitting on ready at the airport when we give them the heads-up that we're on our way. And we'll need vehicles to get to the airport. I don't care if you steal them or buy them, but we'll need rides for six big people as well as Rachael and you guys."

"Oh dear lord, we're stealing cars in a foreign country." Trent says.

"Your other job is to have clean clothes and some toiletries ready for Rachael. Some water to clean up with. When we show up at the airport, we need her to look like a tourist, not a hostage. You and Trent change clothes as well."

"Will this be a nighttime operation?" I ask Mitchell. Trent turns to me and mouths "nighttime operation?" incredulously.

"You'll know when I do. Night is usually better with cover, but nothing is off the table right now. We've got less than four days left unless we can find them and buy some time."

Mitchell leaves the room, and Trent explodes. "I'm a damn banker in Charleston, South Carolina. I don't know how to be a covert operator in a third world country. We can get killed or thrown into prison for the rest of our lives! Do you know what prison would be in a country like this? A living hell!"

"I've heard enough, Trent. Get your ass back on that plane before it leaves for Charleston. Go back and take care of the women. No one will think less of you for it. I got Rachael into this, and I'm not leaving without her."

Trent slams the door on the way out back to his room, where I assume he will pack. I've made notes on a piece on hotel stationery of what Mitchell has said. I know everyone's name and what they're responsible for. And I read over what I wrote about my job. It would seem like it would be a simple thing to remember, but when the lives of your family are at stake, what you hear is being filtered through fear, and it's hard to remember the exact words.

the way home

I call Jill and tell her everything, except I again omit the killing of the guards. She says she'll start working right away to get the planes we need. When I ask how everyone is doing, she tries to reassure me, telling me Brenda Grace is there and helping and Trudy has moved in. Gladys is there as well, and Jill has explained to all of them the necessity of not speaking to anyone about this dilemma. She assures me that no one knows what's happening here. She does ask why we don't just pay the ransom and get them out, and I tell her as lightly as I can that we have no assurance Rachael and Nicholas will be set free if we do.

I go to Trent's room and knock. He answers like he's coming out of a deep sleep. "I came to tell you that Jill is having that charter leave soon and you need to get on it."

"I'm not going, and I won't be any more trouble. She's my mother, and I'll do anything to get her out of here safely. I've always been a bit of a coward. Trudy was always the brave, wild one." He laughs. "But I've found my balls, and I'm staying. I couldn't live with myself if I didn't."

I grab Trent and hug him to me. "They'll get her out. I know they will. I trust Mitchell with my life and the lives of my family."

"This guy must have been some kind of school friend. You trust him like he's family."

twenty-six

Benny and Moses return to the room with news and looking and smelling like the streets of Haiti. They've picked up rumors near the wharfs of a white lady and somebody killing her guards. The informants only have sketchy details about a possible abduction but no eyewitnesses.

Trace returns with nothing. He says Mayor LeBlanc took a couple of photos with the good citizens of Pétionville and his driver took him down to the wharfs to pick up a package, but he found nothing that would tie him to Rachael. Mitchell wants to change tactics.

"Bobby, I want you to go to Pierre LeBlanc first thing tomorrow morning. Be standing on the doorstep of his office early and tell him what's happened. Trace won't be far away and will gauge his reaction. Tell him you need help in finding her right away. Be frantic."

"No problem being frantic. I am."

Trent and I go downstairs for dinner and pretend we don't know the two groups of three men entering the restaurant. They appear like normal businessmen having dinner and drinks. Trent and I pick at our meals and nurse our beers all evening long. Two of Mitchell's guys bunk with me and two with Trent. Mitchell and Trace hang in the ops room but never seem to sleep.

the way home

People in Haiti seem to rise early but move slowly throughout the day. I'm at the mayor's office at half past seven the next morning and don't have to wait long. Trace is hidden not far away. Waving the picture of him and Rachael from the newspaper article, I call out, "Mayor LeBlanc, Mayor LeBlanc. I need to speak to you right away!" Rachael has told me what a companionable dinner guest he was and that his English was eloquent. But he turns to his driver for interpretation, and I play along.

His "interpreter" relays my story to the mayor. As he does I push the newspaper photo toward Mayor LeBlanche to emphasize that he knows her and that she is missing. He doesn't take the photo and seems flat-lined throughout my frantic explanation. He speaks to his driver who tells me, "Mayor LeBlanche does not know this woman. He merely posed for a photograph at her request as he does with many beautiful women."

"You had dinner with her; you spoke perfect English and you do know her, you bastard!"

The mayor turns to walk away from me, then reconsiders and offers (through the interpreter) his advice of contacting the Police Nationale d'Haiti. "They will help you if she is *actually* missing." He turns from me again.

His phoniness and callousness pushes me over the edge, and I grab him from behind just before his driver cuffs me at the back of my neck.

"You son of a bitch! If you know where she is, you had better take me to her. I know you understand me. If one hair is out of place on her head, I will kill you. Do you understand? Tell those goons of yours if all of you want your money, we need to talk. Le Plaza Hotel, but I'm sure you already knew that."

Suddenly he remembers his English, pushes my hand away from his coat jacket, and speaks. "Mr. Chapin, yes, I know who you are. You are in my country, and your money has no power here. If you think you can come here and be treated like a king like you are in America, think again. If you believe your friend to be in danger, then go the Police Nationale d'Haiti. They may help you. Now if you will excuse me, I have a busy day."

judy norwood enter

The driver throws me to the ground and kicks me twice, once in the gut and once in the groin. I roll around on the broken concrete and try to get my breath. When I'm able to get to my knees, I try to stand. Everyone stares and no one helps. I limp back to the Le Plaza Hotel but don't want to attract attention, which is absurd to hope for because I'm the only hysterical white man clutching my gut on the sidewalk. Within two blocks, Trace approaches close enough to speak to me but not so near as to look like he's with me.

"He knows where she is. The son of a bitch is involved and knows where she is. We've got ourselves a damn good break here."

Trace gets to Mitchell before me, and everyone else is listening as I enter the ops room. "Good job, Bobby."

"What do you mean 'good job'? I lost it. I showed him my hand and lost it." I fold up in the fetal position still clutching my gut on one of the beds.

"You did exactly what I thought you would do. You got emotional and showed him your cards, but we saw what he was holding, too. Benny is stuck with him like glue right now. He'll contact his guys today."

Trent is beaming at me, and I begin to feel that my adrenaline rush is shifting from coming from fear and anger to excitement. "Hey, Bobby, looks like I'm not the only one to find my balls."

twenty-seven

Benny calls Mitchell to report. "The mayor's driver is headed down to the port and the wharfs, but LeBlanc is not with him."

"Follow him," Mitchell instructs, "and I'll send Trace back over to watch the mayor."

Mitchell tells us that Benny is following the driver that clubbed me down to the wharfs. He instructs Trace to pick up the watch on the mayor's office and report any change in his location.

"We've kicked the hornet's nest, boys; I predict that before night falls, we'll have contact. Bobby, go to your room alone and wait. They'll come to you. They don't know about us yet and maybe not Trent either. You're the face they'll be looking for."

"How will you know what's going on if I'm in my room?"

Mitchell cocks his big head to one side. "Because I can hear you fart in that room, understand?"

My room is cold because someone has ramped up the AC - probably Trent. First, I take a hot shower and massage my bruises. When I've dressed I sit on the ugly floral bedspread made too small for one of the beds. I shift to one of the two mismatched upholstered chairs in the room. I splash my face with cold water, brush my teeth, and comb my hair. I sit on the bed again. I notice spider webs in two corners of the room and pass the time by watching one of the spiders

the way home

devour a bug in its web. The window has fogged up from the AC because I can't get the temperature adjusted and I'm shivering.

The light knock comes to my door. "This is it, Mitchell. My contact is here." I speak into the cold, empty room; I partially open the door.

Two men who are dressed in full suits complete with vests, white shirts, and colorful ties are standing in the hall. The tall rangy one speaks. "May we come in, Mr. Chapin?" Perfect King's English.

"You may, but I prefer to leave the door to the hall open a bit."

"Not possible." They step in as I'm forced to step back, and his silent assistant closes the door with a soft click.

They both walk around the dull room inspecting it. The one who speaks touches the ugly misshapen bedspread on one of the beds with a disapproving swipe. His short, young assistant walks to the AC and fiddles with the thermostat. "It's too cold in here."

"Well, unless you're planning on spending the night, that's my problem. Get your damn hand off my air conditioner and talk."

Mr. Kings English speaks. "We heard on the street today that you caused a scene at our good mayor's office."

"You heard on the street today? Are you sure you didn't hear it from the mayor's driver or perhaps Mayor LeBlanc himself?"

"Mr. Chapin, you don't know who you're dealing with. We are not some heroin-stoked vagrants from the streets. We are businessmen in the bartering business and want to trade something of value that we have for something you have. It is just that simple. Please don't fuck with us, or we will have to dispose of your valuable goods."

"Don't hurt her. I'll give you whatever you want."

"That's much better. I can see that you appreciate the goods we have and do not want them damaged. There is no clandestine 'drop' of five million dollars you must make. Have it here in a suitcase on Saturday at noon, and I'll send a courier at no extra charge to pick it up."

"First, I can't smuggle five million dollars into this country that quickly. I'm working on transfers to the bank, but that much money raises red flags. If you'll give me a few more days, till, say,

judy norwood enter

next Wednesday, I could come up with enough counterfeit purchase orders for medicines, provisions, and building materials to justify that amount of money."

He contemplates this. "Very well. A few more days won't matter. Noon Wednesday in this room. And if you have us watched as we pick up our reward for her return, we will dispose of the collateral. Do you understand?"

"Yes. And the second thing is I want proof they are both alive and will be brought here when you pick up the money."

"Mr. Chapin, you have been watching too much American television. You are in no position to make demands. When we pick up the money, we'll tell you where they can be picked up. And as for proof, I guess you will just have to trust us."

"Trust you? You have kidnapped my mother and her friend for ransom, and you killed Marcos and Andre to make your ruthless point. And I'm just supposed to trust you? Proof by five o'clock today or no deal. You'll probably kill them anyway, but what you'll have is two more murders on your hands and no five million."

Mr. King's English is pacing the floor and pissed now, but I don't flinch. He wipes condensation from the fogged up window and tries to peer outside. "Very well. What is your pleasure? A phone call? A photograph?"

"Yes, both please. Five o'clock today in this room. Unless, of course, you would just like to bring Rachael and Nicholas with you so I can see for myself." And I manage a smile.

"Very well. You'll have both. Then we are finished until next Wednesday at noon."

They quickly exit the room glancing up and down the hall, and I close the door. The rap comes after I hear the elevator open and close.

"It's Trent with Mitchell right behind him. Mitchell grabs me in a man hug with Trent hanging on. I follow them to the ops room where everyone except Trace and Benny is gathered, and we're all high-fives except Mitchell, who is somber.

"No celebrating until we've got Rachael on a plane. Bobby, you bought us six days. We can do this with the extra time. May give

the way home

us time to go out into the countryside and do some target shooting. Harry and Bruno have found us some assault equipment. Better than I had hoped for."

Benny and Trace return from following the mayor and his driver with nothing new to report. Benny and Moses dress in the derelict addict garb of torn, dirty pants and ragged plaid shirts and head back down to the wharfs to pry whatever information they can find out of the indigenous inhabitants. They conclude that Mayor LeBlanc and Mr. King's English wouldn't dirty their lily-white hands with the actual holding of Nicholas and Rachael so they must have hired some wharf goons. I pray to God that's not true because rape and murder are high on my list of fears for Rachael.

At precisely five o'clock, the proof arrives. An envelope is slid under my door, and my hand shakes as I open it. The first photo is of Nicholas, badly beaten and bound. His poor eyes reveal absolute fright. The second photo is of Rachael, and it is better than I expected. She's wearing a soiled floral dress of the style Haitian women wear, her hands and feet are bound with tape, and her hair is mussed, but there's a little smirk on her lips. Her eyes tell me the tale. They're bright and relieved and convey to me the message that she has not been raped.

My phone rings, and it is Mr. King's English. "Mr. Chapin, you have your photos, no?"

"Yes, I do. Thank you. May I speak with them?"

My door opens, and Trent and Mitchell come in, taking the photos from my hands.

"Bobby, hey, sweetie. Sorry I got lost going to the wharfs and caused you worry. You're gonna find me, right? I didn't mean to worry you going down to the wharfs without you." And the phone is then taken from her.

"Boss Man, we plenty scared and hope you gonna get us out of here. Tell Marianne and Monique I love them." Then Nicholas is gone.

Mr. King's English is on the phone. "Wednesday at noon for both of them. We'll bring them to a place you can easily find after we've picked up our reward for their return. No more contact."

judy norwood enter

Trent is holding Rachael's photograph and rubbing it softly between his fingers when I tell Mitchell. "Rachael's message - she apologized for getting lost at the *wharfs* and then said she was sorry for going to the *wharfs* without me. They're being held somewhere at the wharfs. She was trying to tell me where to find them."

"You're sure?" Mitchell says.

"As sure as I am of anything else in this mess. Rachael repeated the words as a code. She's trying to help us."

Mitchell calls Benny, who's already patrolling the wharfs and following the mayor's driver, and tells him what I believe to be Rachael's code. He sends Harry, Moses, and Bruno down as well. He tells Trace to monitor the four of them to make sure they aren't followed. He says, "No sleep tonight, fellas."

Mitchell has Nicholas's photo and is placing a call to his grandmother; in Kreyol, he tells the family that Nicholas is alive and we'll have him by next Wednesday. Mitchell has confessed he's afraid for Nicholas after we leave. But his grandmother has assured him that Nicholas's brothers, cousins, and uncles will have their own kind of Haitian justice after we've gone. He seems doubtful and I suspect he won't leave them alone to contend with the captors.

Trent continues to caress his mother's photograph. "Trent, call Trudy with the news. I'll want to talk to Jill."

The family is as elated as we are to know Rachael is safe. Jill has leased two planes in Atlanta, which will accommodate us all. She took a contract for a month, and I'm thinking that when we get out of here, we'll all take them to the Bahamas for a celebration trip. At Mitchell's direction, the planes are to arrive at the Port-au-Prince airport on separate days, one Saturday and one Monday, to wait for our undetermined departure.

• • •

I turn my attention to my next assigned job of securing vehicles to transport the ops men and their weapons to the place of rescue and

the way home

for transporting all of us to the airport quickly. So I begin with the concierge. "Where can I buy a vehicle?"

I'm directed to the doorman, who I'm told has a brother-in-law who sells cars. The decrepit doorman is leaning against the front of the hotel smoking a cigarette. His smile reveals missing teeth when I ask him about buying a car. He tells us to wait while he secures a hired car for us, and when it arrives he gives the driver the address of his brother-in-law. We rumble over pot holes and dirt streets leaving town to the north. About ten or so miles outside the city, the driver slows and we spot the used-car lot. Six rusting vehicles are parked in the dust in front of an old, one-story farmhouse. The driver pulls over and I pay him while telling him to leave us.

A wrinkled, old man cooked by the sun and age looks up from hoeing his meager garden and greets us. "Bonswa. Bonswa."

"English?"

He nods. "You want car?" He excitedly throws down his garden tool pointing with pride toward his vehicles. A rather large, light brown woman in traditional floral dress comes out to the wide porch of the house and examines us.

While I talk to the farmer about his cars, Trent peruses the old vehicles and asks for keys. The farmer-turned-car salesman produces a large ring of keys and draws one off. Trent pushes it into the ignition, and with a sputter and a bang and not much black smoke, the old Nissan cranks up. Trent backs it out of its space between the other cars and drives it around the dusty yard. He pulls it back into its space, smiling. He lifts the hood and tinkers with the engine for several minutes. Trent and Jeff always messed around with cars when they were young.

He slams the warped, rusty hood. "I think it might do."

"How much?" I ask.

"Five hundred American dollars."

"Sold."

"You didn't even negotiate with him!"

"Trent, have you forgotten why we're here?"

Trent eliminates an old Chevy Caprice. "Can't trust a Chevy," he says. He passes on a Volkswagen in good condition because of its size. He zeros in on a Honda Civic, lifts the hood, kicks the tires, and drives it around the barren lot. He makes several quick, tight turns in the dirt like he's testing it for tire traction. The farmer frowns at me and I shrug. Trent wheels the Civic back into its space and slams the door.

"A Honda always runs."

"But it's so small."

In a low voice, he says, "Three in it, six in the Nissan. That's all we need. Buy it."

So another seven hundred dollars later, five hundred for the Civic and two hundred to skip the paperwork, Trent and I, like two schoolboys with their first cars, drive back in Haitian style to the Le Plaza Hotel. The skinny, cigarette-smoking doorman is grinning ear to ear at our new purchases. I kick in fifty dollars for his tip. Everybody's happy.

When we return with the cars, Mitchell declares that we're a natural at this covert ops thing. Trent swears that as soon as we get Rachael out of this country, neither he nor his mother will ever leave American soil again. I, on the other hand, know my destiny is to return to Haiti.

Trent and I sit in my room playing cards while Mitchell mans the phone and does whatever else he does in the ops room. We sleep intermittently and call for coffee as soon as the sun comes up. We hear some of the ops guys in the hall. I stick my head in their room and find Mitchell still there wide-awake. I offer to have coffee brought up for them, but Benny and Moses go to Trace's room for some sleep.

"Mitchell, when do you sleep? Why don't you use my room and catch some winks?"

"I dozed during the night. But I'll take that coffee you offered."

"Anything new last night?"

"No, brother, you would be the first to know."

211

twenty-eight

The first plane arrives on Saturday. We're relieved one is on the ground. The next is due in on Monday as planned. Mitchell doesn't want to arouse attention or suspicion by landing two American private plans on the same day. We drive our little Nissan and Civic around town, testing the engines and troubleshooting anything that could lead to problems later. Trent keeps his head under the hoods until he's satisfied one of them won't blow up on us while angry assassins pursue us as we flee for the airport.

Trent usually peppers me with questions about Mitchell when we're together - which is most of the time. "Who is this guy, Bobby? He won't talk about school or you. I heard him tell you that he won't take money for this operation, just his men. What's his special interest in this?"

Trent quizzes me again with his head up under a car hood when Mitchell comes, unnoticed, to stand beside me. "You boys talking about me out here?" He laughs when Trent bumps his head soundly on the open car hood and rubs the forming lump with his greasy hand.

"Hi Mitchell. We're not talking about you. In fact, Bobby won't talk about you at all. Who are you? How'd you get tangled up in this?"

"Well, my inquisitive friend, I'm in Haiti with you because your mother is in danger, because Bobby and I have history, and

the way home

because this is what I'm good at - no, excellent at. You need me, and that's why I'm here."

"And how about the money? You're not getting paid but you asked for pay for your men."

"Money is a private matter."

"Not if you're a banker." Trent says.

Mitchell laughs. "Like I said, Bobby and I have history. I owe him."

"Trent, let it go. Are these cars going to hold up for us. I don't want to get half-way to the airport and break down," I say.

Trent ignores me but gives up on his angle of questioning and shakes his head. "Well, I don't care who you are as long as you get us all out of this mess alive. You seem like an all-right guy and under different circumstances, I might like to get to know you better - take you on a dove-shoot this winter in Charleston."

Mitchell laughs. "Trent, buddy, I don't kill little birds."

• • •

Each day I've talked myself into believing Rachael and Nicholas are OK given their circumstances, but surveillance by the others has turned up no location for the hostages at the wharfs. I've asked Mitchell if I should be gathering five million dollars for the extortion money.

"It's not an option. They'll kill them for the sheer display of power," Mitchell tells me.

Mitchell sends Harry and Bruno into the countryside on Saturday in our newly purchased rides to pick up the weapons contraband and tells them to seek out a place for target practice. They return very late in the day and we're all called in the ops room for a meeting.

Bruno says, "The guns, ammunition, grenades, night-vision goggles - all that and more are easy to get here and cheap. A place for target practice is a little harder to locate, but we've found a desolate place north of here about sixteen miles that will do. We'll take one car and four men at a time. We may have time for a couple of runs

judy norwood enter

up to the practice site. I'll take the first group up tomorrow morning and Harry will take the second group up tomorrow afternoon."

It's now Sunday morning, and I wake up longing to be sitting with Rachael in the kitchen at the old pine table eating cinnamon buns and drinking dark coffee. Instead, I'm scheduled for the afternoon trip out of town for target practice. Trent is uncharacteristically complacent and cooperative about the afternoon assignment to fire strange weapons. It turns out he's a damn good marksman. He may have quit fishing but he hasn't given up hunting.

Monday brings in the second plane. Everything is in place with regard to air transportation, ground transportation, and assault weapons, and target practice is over. Mitchell declares, "We're as good as we're going to get."

However, no location has been found for the rescue. Mitchell calls an ops meeting at noon on Monday and declares everyone in the field should go down to the wharfs if they have to and start ripping open crates and containers and searching warehouses. Trent and I want to go as well, but Mitchell reminds us that every ops guy is black and in disguise and we white boys would stand out like a full moon in a dark sky. We're told to man the ops room — which sounds important, but not much is going on in there — and be patient. Mitchell is counting on the more aggressive approach to flush out Rachael's location. Mayor LeBlanc has been faithfully followed twenty-four hours a day, and still he leads us nowhere. Mitchell is hoping that because money-counting time is just forty-eight hours away, he'll want to see that his collateral is in good condition.

Trent and I are anxious sitting alone in the ops room while everyone else is out beating the bushes to find Rachael and Nicholas. We try to play a few hands of Blackjack. "Bobby, why'd you blow us all off?"

"What?"

"You know - after Jeff died and even before that. Why'd you stop coming around?"

"Oh, Trent. I used to have a quick answer to that question but I don't today."

"Was it because Mother married Uncle Robert?"

the way home

"It was her, it was him, and it was a whole lot of other things I wanted to run away from. Not a manly thing to admit to - running away. Being afraid to face and confront the people and their behavior that's hurt you."

"Hurt comes in a lot of different faces and forms. Dad dying the way he did - right in front of me - I never went back out on the water. I mean I live in Charleston surrounded by water and I can't get in a boat or even go to the beach with my family. I tell you the truth, if my mother gets out of this alive I'm going back out on the water. Nothing can make me more afraid than losing her in this hellhole to those bastards."

Mitchell walks into the room. "You guys talking about me again?"

"Mitchell, did anyone ever tell you what an ego you have? Not every conversation involves you," Trent says.

"As a matter of fact, I've been told that. But I couldn't do the work I do without being a bit overconfident and egotistical. It's a way of combating fear."

Trent and I look at one another. "That's just what we were discussing - fear - and what men do with it," Trent says.

"You know that old adage *fight or flight*? That's what all men do with fear. And I've seen plenty of both. They run away mentally or physically from their fear, or they refuse to entertain it and fight like hell. It's a choice," Mitchell says.

"Rachael's a fighter," I say. "She's the strongest woman I know. She won't give up on the people she loves, or bringing to justice the people who hurt the people she loves. She's going to walk out of there alive."

• • •

Tuesday morning around four o'clock, we hit the jackpot. Benny calls in to report that Mayor LeBlanc made a lone, secret visit to one of the warehouses at the port and lights came on in the upstairs office after he entered. He heard shouting through an open

judy norwood enter

window and saw a struggle. The mayor stayed about half an hour and then retreated in his shiny car again alone. Benny says he and Moses found a discreet way to enter the locked, dilapidated warehouse through a rusted ground floor window with broken locks. Only one set of stairs led to the upstairs, and they heard Rachael crying. There was no way to see into the room without being exposed, but they found the location.

Mitchell is only moderately happy because the location is at a dead end. He wants a full view of the room and what they would be walking into, but time is running out. "These guys may be strong-arm goons, but they're not stupid. They are isolated upstairs with only one way in and one way out."

Tuesday night and it's the final hour. Wednesday morning in broad daylight is too risky and too close to the deadline. By now the building has been repeatedly scouted and only one ground floor window, one door, and one set of stairs leading to the holding room are confirmed. These are less than ideal conditions, Mitchell explains to us.

Also troubling him is that there seem to be no guards outside or just inside the building. Where are they? All day Tuesday the teams switch disguises and positions, surveying the building and its surroundings. During the day the warehouse's rusted lock is broken, and some merchandise that vagrants have stolen from shipping containers is stashed on the bottom floor. One of the captors sticks his head out the window opening and shoos the thieves away but doesn't bother to come downstairs and relock the door. They and others like them continue to stash their stolen wares in the derelict warehouse while the guard upstairs seems to ignore them. Mitchell declares this is the only break we're likely to get. Leaving Benny watching the warehouse and Bruno out in back of the hotel guarding the vehicles, the Nissan filled with artillery, the rest of us gather in the ops room for orders.

All the men are dressed in camouflage, and their small bags are packed and by their sides. The only weapons I see are the GLOCKs, which are also strapped by their sides. The tension and adrenaline hangs in the room palpably.

the way home

Mitchell is somber and authoritative and begins his speech. "Every operation is different in scope, location, and personnel. But each one is just as important as every other because every time human lives are at stake—the hostages' and ours. We have simple directives and goals—get in, get Rachael and Nicholas, and get out alive. Our only obstacles to reaching these goals are the armed guards who hold them. You've had the luxury of field target practice with the fine but old artillery Harry and Bruno bought for you at Walmart." There are a few nervous laughs. "You've got some high-grade fuel charging through you now in the form of adrenaline. It jangles your nerves, and that can get you killed because it affects your accuracy. Whatever method you use to flush it out and slow your pulse rate, you need to do that now. I want calm and peaceful soldiers. It's your job, so put yourself into a position to execute what you do best. Killing is a last resort. But when you fire your weapon, shoot to kill with efficiency and without hesitation, and make no mistakes. Every shot fired carries with it the possibility of someone dying, and it could be you or the hostages. Special ops guys count their successes by the number of good guys they save from the hands of the bad guys. And that's what we're about to do tonight. Don't make the mistake of thinking this operation is small. These men are assassins and, I remind you, have killed two armed guards. They'll want to kill you, too."

Trent and I are gape-mouthed as we listen to this life-or-death pep talk. "Bobby and Trent, gather your few things and Rachael's. Leave behind anything you can do without. Wear these dark fatigues and blacken your faces with this grease stick. You take the Civic and follow me and Moses, Harry, Bruno, and Trace in the Nissan. All of the firearms and grenades are in that vehicle except the two GLOCKs I've had you practice with in the field. Keep them at your sides and don't even think twice about using them if you're threatened, or I guarantee you'll die. Some shipping containers were delivered today and stacked in front of our warehouse about seventy-five feet from the front door. A second big break for us. You'll park the Civic behind those stacked containers and wait. Don't move from there until we deliver Rachael to you and you take off for the airport.

judy norwood enter

Nicholas's uncles are waiting at the hotel, and we'll see that he hooks up with them. Then we'll be right behind you on that second plane."

Trent, the bean counter, speaks. "The old Nissan will only seat six men. Where will you put Nicholas?"

"On somebody's lap for four blocks."

We are all given headsets. Trent and I take five minutes to pack, change, and grease our faces. When we reach the Civic around three o'clock, the alley is clear, and the ops guys are getting into the Nissan. We follow them until they pull into a shrouded area at the wharf just shy of the shipping containers where I've been told to park the Civic. I get as close as possible so the gun-toting guard I've seen backlit in the second-story window can't see our car over the tops of the containers. I'm shaking like a leaf in a hurricane, and Trent is uncharacteristically calm. We look at each other in our blackface and army fatigues with GLOCK 9mm pistols at our sides.

"If our slick Charleston friends could see us now," I say.

Trent assures me. "Hell, most guys I know in Charleston own more than one of these. We would fit right in." And we manage nervous smiles.

Mitchell has seen no reason to burden, or rather scare us, with information that a sniper is going to try to take out the guard in the window with an SR75 rifle Bruno has purchased. We listen through our headsets.

"Check-in." It's Mitchell's voice.

Then we hear the guys respond on roll call. "Harry here; Bruno on your tail; Trace in place; Moses here; Benny staring at you."

"Damn! The vagrants are back hauling their shit into the warehouse." It's Harry's voice. "You copy, Mitchell?"

"How many?"

"Four. And they must be on some happy juice because they're weaving and dancing all over the place."

"Do you think they'll leave to bring back more stolen goods?"

"Don't look like it. They're passing around a bottle and look content right where they are. From what I can understand, it sounds like they're arguing about the split on the sale of their stash."

219

the way home

Harry's voice follows. "Mitch, you see that guard in the window leaning out to see the commotion?"

"Copy."

"He's an easy mark. Just give me the word."

"Harry, wait, wait. There's a guard on the ground trying to run the squatters off." This is Bruno's voice.

We hear loud arguing in Kreyol between the thieves and the guard.

"Mitch, this may be our chance if there are only two guards. We can take them both. Make a decision."

"Something's not right. Hold."

"Mitch, there's another guard in the window throwing his smoke out. That's two upstairs and one on the ground." Moses has seen the third guard in the upstairs room where Rachael and Nicholas are being held. "This one is yelling at the vagrants—can we take him?"

"Mitch, I'm closest and can take the guard on the ground quietly with my knife, but the vagrants will see and make a commotion. What do you think?" Trace is ready to move.

"Take him. They're already making a ruckus. The guards upstairs won't know the difference."

And in an instant, Trace is on the guard and quietly slits his throat. He drags him to the back of the building while the squatters stagger away, screaming indecipherable Kreyol. One of the two remaining guards upstairs hangs out the window, calling for the dead guard. He seems agitated.

"Mitchell, let's use the flash bang downstairs. One of them will have to run down to investigate, and that leaves one with the hostages. He'll be confused and deaf from the noise, and we can get in."

"Green. Go, Trace."

Trent and I disobey and crawl out of the Civic, using the containers as cover while peering around the side. We witness Mitchell and Bruno crawling on their bellies to the warehouse while the other three cover them. Trace is in position at the door.

"We're at the point of no return, boys. Cover us." We hear Mitchell through the headsets.

220

judy norwood enter

Trace tosses in the first flash bang, and the noise and light is deafening and blinding. The percussion shakes the containers hiding us. Both guards hang out the window. One of our snipers shoots one of them with the rifle, and his body plummets to the ground. The other guard almost falls out the window at the impact but rears back, and I hear screaming and yelling.

"I'm at the base of the stairs, Mitch, but no guard. I'm going up! I'm going up! There he is, damn it!" There are gunshots.

"Trace, you all right?"

"I'm all right, but guard number three is definitely not. I'm going up."

All is silent as we wait for Trace and Mitchell to come back on-air. "She's here, Mitch, but she's passed out or something. She has a pulse, and she's not hit. The percussion of the grenade might have knocked her out. Nicholas is barely alert."

We hear Mitchell. "I'm coming up. Let's get those hostages out. The flash bang has roused our neighbors at the wharf, and I don't want to hurt anybody who doesn't have a horse in this race."

We hear Mitchell telling Trace to drag Nicholas down the stairs while he grabs Rachael. Bruno meets Trace and helps with Nicholas. "We're bringing 'em down the stairs, everyone. They're a mess but alive."

When I see Mitchell running with Rachael and Trace dragging Nicholas to the Nissan with Bruno covering him, I spring across the parking lot from behind the containers along with Trent. Mitchell yells, "Back to the car, back to the car." Trent and I make a U-turn quickly on the heels of Mitchell, who's running to the little Civic. Mitchell gently lays Rachael in the backseat of the Civic, and Trent crawls into the front seat, leaning over and soothing her. "Mom, you're safe, and we're headed to the airport."

"You're safe, pretty lady. Go home to Charleston." Mitchell slaps the top of the little car as I see vigilantes from the wharfs who have heard the explosion. Some are carrying sticks and pipes. Good luck with those assault rifles, I think.

"Go, go, go. Airport. And clean her up." Those are the last words we hear from Mitchell as we tear out of the parking lot. The vintage

221

the way home

Civic sputters when I floor the gas pedal. I'm shaking so hard I can hardly change gears, but I manage to make the tires squeal as we leave that godforsaken prison for our plane. It's almost five o'clock, and our plane is readied. The stench in the car is horrible, like Rachael had been immersed in a latrine for a week. She's alert now and crying.

" I had to drink the water, and I've pooped all over myself. They wouldn't always let me go to the bathroom. And they didn't feed us very much. I'm so hungry."

Rachael is hungry, I think. She's going to be all right.

"It's OK, Mother. Bobby and I are here and taking you back to Charleston. We'll get you a doctor."

"Please clean me up," she cries.

Trent undresses his mother and bathes her with some moist cloths we brought at Mitchell's instruction. On the ride from the wharfs to the airport, he wipes down every inch of her soiled body, dry-shampoos and brushes her hair, and puts clean underwear, fresh slacks, and a light pullover summer sweater on her. He also applies a little moisturizing cream and some lipstick. I am deeply moved as I see her son do for her body what he does for his own with respect, gentleness, and lack of any shame.

Meanwhile, I'm using one of the moist cloths to wash the grease off my face and try stripping my clothes off, but it's impossible to do behind the wheel of a Civic. Trent finishes with Rachael, strips himself, and gets into jeans and a colorful T-shirt. When we park at the airport in the early morning light, I jump out and strip my fatigues off and slip into jeans and my own T-shirt. Trent inspects me and says I need to take another swipe at my face.

Rachael is weak but looks like a hungover tourist rather than a woman who had been held hostage for almost ten days. We're in the portion of the airport reserved for private airplanes, where boarding is easier. I tell the woman at the gate that my mother is very ill and I need to get her to a hospital in the United States. She's sympathetic and allows us to board immediately. Mitchell has already taken care of contacting the pilots so they could clear with the Port-au-Prince airport.

judy norwood enter

Within twenty minutes, we're in the air, and Rachael is in a clean lavatory. Trent has already taken medication from his bag and given her Cipro with some crackers and a Coke. But she's thin, dehydrated, and disoriented, and we decide she needs to go to the hospital.

"Thank you, Brother. Without Mitchell I don't know what we would have done. I wonder if they're on their plane." Trent is relieved.

"Whatever Mitchell says he'll do, he does. They've delivered Nicholas to his family at the hotel and are on their plane headed back to Arlington."

"It's lucky for us that you and Mitchell 'have history'. I hope I get to see him again to thank him for saving my mother's life."

I regret I can't tell Trent the truth about Mitchell. I want so much to tell him that my brother saved his mother's life.

twenty-nine

The Chapins and the Crawfords spend Thanksgiving and Christmas living large between Charleston and Pawleys Island, decorating all their houses with the smells of greenery, candles, and homemade goodies like Charleston pralines and pecan pie. Turkeys ooze buttery marinade, and decadent breads emit fierce smells from their ovens that make mouths drool and stomachs anxious.

Jill's Christmas gift to me is the redecoration of the bedroom where my mother and father used to sleep. This is the bedroom in which I suppose my brother and I were conceived. The colors are vibrant peaches, corals, and yellows that match the dynamic colors of the sun. Our king- size bed is covered in a thick, luxurious comforter of the purest white I've ever seen. The warm room is full of good memories and promises new ones to be made. Jill tells me before Christmas that she wants to create a new life here: she wants to conceive a baby in this room and raise it in this city and this house with scores of family members all around. And I tell her this will be my Christmas present to her, a baby born into this family with so much love. I don't mean to sound so poetic, especially since my giving her the gift is as much fun as her receiving it. I calculate that if I'm as good as I used to be, we'll hear the cries of a new baby in the halls of this house by next fall.

the way home

I invite Mitchell and his family here for a portion of the holidays, but he declines. He's still unsure if he should occupy a place in this family, even after Rachael's rescue. We speak regularly, and I've made two visits to Arlington since the kidnapping. Each time I get to know him better and invite him to Charleston. I've told him of my plans to return to Haiti after the first of the year. Of course, he always admonishes me to be careful and offers to accompany me.

A near-death experience changes a person and it changed Rachael. She didn't sleep well and refused a prescription sleep-aid after her five-day hospital stay in Charleston. She sleeps better now, and we continue to fatten her from the weight loss. Mack Longworth has been a friend and medical resource for her to talk through the experience. She speaks passionately about returning to the children's home, but is obviously reluctant. And since she learned from me (and I learned from Mitchell) that Pierre LeBlanche has disappeared, she frets of his whereabouts and if he'll resurface. I'm more apt to believe, as Mitchell has inferred, that we will never see him or hear of him again. A more positive outcome of her captivity is that she is even more of a free spirit, buying more gifts than Santa Claus and working tirelessly in the homeless shelters in Charleston. At Mother's wing at MUSC, we put on the grandest Christmas party, with families of the residents coming and enjoying good food and gifts and bringing encouragement to these brave women who are in the fights of their lives.

Marcos and Andre's families become special projects for Rachael after her rescue. "Those men died senselessly because of me," she says. "I'm going to take care of their families."

I learn that Marcos has four children below the age of eight years. And he supported his mother since his father died a few years ago. Andre never married and had no children but helped support his siblings and parents. He was the oldest of nine brothers and sisters. Their families depended on them since they were primary income providers. So she and Louis designed a generous trust fund for the families of these lost young men. And during the holidays, she played Santa Claus in a big way and splurged on lots of presents for those families robbed of their family members. Our Rachael, that indefatigable champion of children and the poor, provides regularly for all of Nicholas's family, including his grandmother, Monique, and Marianne. Gifts for all of them were sent at Christmas. She says she looks at them as extended family. When she and Nicholas were being threatened and held hostage, a bond formed between them, she says, like they became brother and sister.

I travel back to Haiti prior to Christmas with all the gifts for these beautiful families who have sacrificed for us. So little makes them so happy — not that Rachael sent a little. Rachael doesn't know how to do "little." She wanted to return with me for the Christmas party, but the family nixed it. Still, she put us on notice that she will return with me in January and nobody can stop her because she misses her children in Haiti.

Our entire family travels to Brenda Grace's in December to throw the biggest dry Christmas party ever at Jeff's clinic with the residents. We invite their families and give out gifts to all their children and spouses. Trevor's family comes, and he looks well - brighter and more peaceful. Rachael is right in believing there is no medicine like a family's love.

thirty

Bobby and Rachael departed Charleston for Port-au-Prince on the chilly morning of January 12, 2010. He had scheduled a meeting with government officials for the following morning about furnishing steel buildings and structures for public parks. Rachael was going to spend time at the children's home with Monique and Marianne. This would be her first visit since her kidnapping in early September, and she had seemed nervous. In such a short time, Bobby had developed a profound love of the Haitian people. But after the completion of a children's medical clinic near the children's home on the outskirts of the city and the funding of a foster-child program that put children back into their extended families' care, the glass was still half empty for Bobby. He and Nicholas were designing a new plan and trying to find a more suitable location for the medical treatment center in Jack's memory. Contractors had been hired, and construction was due to begin in the spring. And Brenda Grace and I were becoming adept at handling the trusts for various projects and constantly pursued ways of investing in these people. This park was one of our latest ideas.

Bobby would return from his trips to Haiti calling it "the Land of Never Enough." He would recount his experiences to anyone who would listen about the deplorable living conditions for these tenderhearted Haitian people in hopes of inciting them to action. He kept journals of his experiences there.

the way home

"Haiti is the Land of Never Enough. Not enough food, clean water, electricity, plumbing, jobs, medicine, transportation, education, or money and all it can buy. But what is plentiful are hungry children and adults, dirty water, primitive living conditions, filth and garbage, children with no expectation for a better future, and young men begging for jobs that don't exist."

In particular, the young men and children found a special place in his heart. On one trip, Bobby and Rachael flew into Cap-Haïtien in the north from Port-au-Prince to explore possibilities for other clinics or any project that might help alleviate some of the suffering. He wrote the following in his journal:

"Begging children at the airport in Cap-Haïtien are relentless. 'Mister, give me a dollar, just a dollar.' They've learned enough English to beg any Americans who might reward them with a dollar. The air in the city smells of burning wood, dust, and filth. Raw sewage runs freely in the river out to the ocean, and garbage lies piled in the streets. The poverty en masse is staggering. Thousands of dilapidated shacks cover the hillsides and streets. The UN soldiers patrol the airport and streets with their guns, a frightening reminder of the instability of the government and its people."

On this first trip to Cap-Haïtien, Bobby and Rachael ventured into the countryside twenty miles outside the city. They had received permission to stay at the small mission in the village of Cahesse. The mission's founder lives in the United States but built this mission on land given to him by his grandmother. This is from one of Bobby's entries in his journal:

"Traveling miles by bus into the country along mainly dirt roads, we leave the overcrowded, foul streets of Cap-Haïtien behind. Scrawny goats, cows, donkeys, and horses are grazing on dry grass in barren fields. Shrunken pigs amble along the roadside. And the smells of burning wood and dust constantly hang in the air. The mountaintops in the distance are barren of trees where Haitians have stripped them to make charcoal.

Even with its meager offering of a small school, our barracks, an outdoor cooking hut, the church, and a very small clinic open only two mornings a week, this place is an oasis for the people in

judy norwood enter

nearby rural villages. A community well has been dug at the mission's gates for the villagers, and here where they gather, I meet some women and children.

I'm told that the mission offers free education for 114 children and one hot meal a day of beans and rice. The women tell me through our interpreter that these children will not eat again at home in the evening so that other family members may eat. I cannot fathom my own children eating once a day and depriving themselves at night so I may eat.

After a refreshing, cold shower, I climb into my cot on this first evening and stare back in the dark into the eyes of the children peering into our open-air windows. They're looking for more jelly beans, but I distributed them all right after we arrived. Lying here in very frugal conditions—but with much more than the typical Haitian—I think of the luxury of my life…my home in Charleston, a big, clean, comfortable bed and furnishings, electricity at the flip of a switch anywhere in my home, clean water and hot showers, plumbing, refrigeration and the food—the sheer wealth of food."

After the kidnapping, every trip Bobby took to Haiti left me challenged to function normally at home. He consoled me by saying it was an isolated incident and they were taking precautions. But fear would wake me in the night, and I would cry out his name. During the nine months that he made frequent trips to Haiti, I became accustomed to these timorous feelings, but they never left me.

At approximately 3:50 p.m. on the afternoon of January 12, 2010, only an hour after Bobby and Rachael had arrived at the Hotel Montana in Port-au-Prince, the finger of God shook the earth beneath Haiti. Bobby had texted me at 3:30 p.m. to say they might move hotels the next day but gave me no reason. This was my last communication with Bobby. Two and a half months later, Bobby's wallet along with his body would be found buried under tons of debris that was once the five-story Hotel Montana. He was the last American found.

Within twenty-four hours of the 7.0-magnitude quake, Bobby was officially listed as "missing," and I was given a telephone number by United States representatives that I could call each day

the way home

to hear a list of Americans who had been located, dead or alive. I called faithfully each day and waited to hear his name. The number of people on the conference call dwindled until only I remained. I waited another two weeks alone to hear the expected, dreaded news that they had found his body.

A page on Facebook called "Haiti Hotel Montana" had been set up and managed by some wonderful volunteers. I met two women on that page whose husbands were missing and whose bodies were found before Bobby's. I attended both of their funerals, one in Montana and one in New Mexico. I remain friends with them today. Shared loss has its way of binding people together.

Rachael's story is a miracle. While Bobby had gone down to the lobby right before the earthquake, Rachael, older and tired, went to her room on the fifth and top floor to rest. She tells that the ceiling collapsed onto the floor and threw her from the bed.

From her hospital room in Florida, she said, "I couldn't see anything except a little light through the dust, so I crawled on my hands and knees up onto what turned out to be the concrete roof of the hotel. When I stood up, I was literally standing on the roadside!"

A stranger picked her up and took her to the airport where they had heard medical help was available. She was cut, bruised, bleeding, and confused. A doctor from Miami who heard the devastating news took his private plane into Port-au-Prince that night, went into the airport, and took the first seven people he could load onto his plane. Miraculously, Rachael was one of those people and in the hospital in Miami that same night. As I watched the news on *Good Morning America* the next day, I saw Rachael being boarded on that plane. It was a miracle the doctor's plane could get in that quickly, as the airport at Port-au-Prince closed to all except emergency traffic the next morning.

When Bobby's body was flown home almost three months later, the girls and I were at the airport, waiting on him one last time. At my instructions, the hearse drove slowly by the old Chapin home in Charleston that Bobby had grown to love so well. Our portico, our yard, and the streets were lined with friends and strangers who had followed our story. Some were carrying flags or waving white handkerchiefs, crying, and cheering his name. And others carried banners and signs reading *Welcome home, Bobby! We love you!* Other people had heard of the "Anyway" poem and knew that Bobby had it inscribed on a wall in the children's home in Haiti and were carrying signs and banners that read "Anyway." Bobby had come home to a hero's welcome.

My prayer is that at the very moment the world came crashing down on top of Bobby, God sent his father, his mother, and his brother to meet and welcome him into paradise—and that finally Bobby had found his way home.

epilogue

On Memorial Day weekend in 2010, Pawleys Island is filled with families flocking to rented beach and creek houses, all gathering to play in the sun and sand, eat fresh seafood, and make some memories. Ours is gathering at my beach house like our two families have done so many times. Together in this place of history and happiness are Trent and Gladys and their two children, Trudy with her husband Mark and their three children, Jill and the girls, Brenda Grace and Jeff's son and daughter, and, of course, me, Memaw Rachael. The absence of our men—Jack, Robert, Jeff, and especially Bobby, since his death was so recent—weighs heavily on us adults the first day, but we make a pact that evening on the porch overlooking the dunes with their sea oats waving at the ocean to find a place for all their memories, to speak of them often with laughter and stories, but to also live the day for one another and our children and not pass on a legacy of grief to them. I'm so proud of Trent. He's our only man in this family of women and steps up to the cause to take care of us like a good southern son. My grandsons Grady and Hardy say they're the men of the family, too, and will take care of us. "We got three men left in this family, Memaw Rachael. We'll take care of you girls." You understand, taking care of us strong but genteel southern women is an illusion we allow our good men, but we enjoy the attention, and they relish the job.

the way home

Trent, Grady, Hardy, and Memaw Rachael—I completely underestimated how much I would love being a grandmother—untie the Jon boat from our dock and head out on Pawleys Island Creek to net the shrimp for the evening meal. I think to myself that these shrimp we're going to harvest in our casting net and make supper out of may be offspring several generations down the line of "the four chickens" that were caught and cooked in a magical time now cast only in my memory. I love watching these new, little beach souls, Grady and Hardy, learning to do what their two families have done most of their lives in this very creek. And just like Jack, Robert, Mary Elizabeth, and I did, we gather on the back porch to drink a little beer (the kids have Kool-Aid), peel the shrimp, and watch the next generation bury its feet in the pluff mud. Trent chases them down with a hose to wash off the fetid muck dear to our noses. You have to love the creek to savor the smell. It punches your nostrils with the smells of tides and fertile, rotten growth in the saturated earth where clams, oysters, shrimp, flounder, and crabs make their home. In this tidal creek, we harvest what we have not sown and appreciate and value every good thing the sea has to give.

The kitchen is alive with the smells of the past, the homemade biscuits Mary Elizabeth taught me to make, and the buttery grits cooking over the open flame until the grains meld into one another and form a smooth, sticky consistency. And those big, juicy, succulent creek shrimp marinated and cooking in spices are simmering in the pan. From the living room, we hear the kids screaming, "I got Boardwalk. I'm gonna win!" Brenda Grace is supervising the children, but the smells of warm bread, spicy shrimp, and adult laughter entice her to the kitchen. She puts on "What Kind of Fool Do You Think I Am" by Bill Deal and the Rhondels and solo-shags with a pretend partner into the kitchen. "Anybody want a glass of wine?"

Trent says he'll open us girls a bottle, and Jill exempts herself. We all smile, sweetly acknowledging how she's almost five months pregnant with Bobby's son. Trent mixes purple Kool-Aid and takes frosty glasses to the living room, where all the kids are sitting around the Monopoly board on the sandy, scarred, hardwood floor. There is something symbiotic about the scene; we've brought

judy norwood enter

back together remnants of the loved ones we've lost, gathered them here in this same beach house to continue in this life we lead painfully without them and yet happily together. Everyone feels it and speaks of the sense of familiarity with the past and continuity for the present and future.

Brenda Grace and Jill are sisters of a sort, both struggling with the death of husbands and the young children they left behind. What they don't have to struggle with is money, as so many single moms in this country do. I silently thank Robert for that. Even after all these years, Trent and Trudy still miss Jack and say what a wonderful, playful grandfather to their children he would have been. And I silently thank God for my missing ones: Mary Elizabeth, Jack, Robert, Jeff, and Bobby. I have had the good fortune and blessing to have had these complicated, compassionate, and altruistic people shape my life. And I have enjoyed the odd combination of having both Jack and Robert as friends and husbands, men who both loved me and loved each other.

At the large, familiar kitchen table bulging with the savory food, we speak of the desperate need in Haiti, and I tell them of my plans to continue the work there but to perform it at a different level because so many hundreds of thousands of people remain homeless since the earthquake. Trent and Trudy are skeptical about my returning. "Mother, you have been a hostage and an earthquake victim in that awful place. How can you possibly want to return there, and what about your responsibility to this family? We buried Daddy, Aunt Mary Elizabeth, Uncle Robert, Jeff, and Bobby. We don't want to bury you, too."

"Some things are worth sacrificing your life for, Trudy, and for me those precious homeless children are. I have some professional protection with Mitchell Cummins lined up, so please don't worry about me. He and one of his associates will accompany me on every trip I make and not leave me alone for even a minute. I plan to be around a long time for my kids and grandkids."

Trent is both pleased and surprised. "You mean Mitchell has agreed to work for you on these trips? I'd like to see him again."

the way home

I explain that Brenda Grace and Jill will continue to administrate the money for the work and perform investigative research on the new needs and opportunities from the safety of their own locales. The money is still well invested and ready to be put to work. They want updates on what I know of the loss and destruction and aid to the victims as I remind them how blessed we are that Nicholas, Monique, and Marianne survived the quake. The children's home is still damaged and uninhabitable, but Nicholas already has repairs underway. Be reminded again, I say, how fortunate we are that not one child in the home at the time of the quake was killed. Thank God.

Jill already knows the surprise ending for the night, but the others do not. Mitchell and his family are due any moment, and so now is the time. Over the mellow, sentimental strains of "Hello Stranger" by Barbara Lewis, I stand at my place and clink my glass with my fork. "Family, I have an exciting announcement to make that will change our lives." Bobby always said that I am given to the dramatic. But it gets people's attention.

Trent speaks with his mouth full. "Mom, we don't want any more change, and we surely don't need any more excitement. The kidnapping and rescue in Haiti last year, the earthquake, and Bobby's death only a few months ago have worn us a little thin for excitement and change."

"Well, this will make you happy. Instead of this family grieving another loss, we are celebrating the arrival of someone lost to us whom we have found. He and his family are joining us for homemade ice-cream tonight, and you will be seeing them often. In fact, they will be instrumental with regard to the family's work in Haiti. My protection will be assured, and the administration of the work there will be furthered. Bobby's right-hand man, Nicholas, will welcome the assistance." I stop to look at the quizzical faces and then make my announcement. "We will welcome him along with his wife and two sons into our family because he is Mary Elizabeth's son, born to her in 1976. Because of circumstances, he was given up for adoption, but Bobby and I located him living in Virginia with his family last year. He is Mary Elizabeth's sole surviving son."

judy norwood enter

Trudy, as always, is the first to speak. "What? What are you saying, Mother? Bobby and Jeff have a brother we didn't know about?"

Brenda Grace wears a stunned look. "Did Jeff know he had a brother?"

"No. No, he didn't. And Bobby only learned of him after his father's death. He has been reluctant to introduce himself to this family because he fears that he might create problems for us. But I will tell you that unknown to most of you, except Trent, he has already been a savior to us. He put his life on the line for me and for Bobby."

Trent wears a puzzled look. "Mother, I have no idea what you're talking about. I know something of this stranger the others don't?"

"Wait, Trent. Children, we'll bring your ice-cream to the living room. Go and play games until then. And, children, when your uncle and his family come, they may look different than us to you, but they are family. Respect them as you do us, and be nice to your new cousins. So run along."

Children are curious and inquisitive, but ice-cream and games trump family meetings. Trudy checks on the two churns of ice cream on the porch that have been hand-cranked, one peach and one strawberry. She packs burlap on top of the ice in each old wooden churn so the ice cream will continue to freeze until Mitchell and his family arrive. We work together and clear the dirty dishes from the table accompanied by the groans from the dishwasher of the grits pot, Brenda Grace. "Who left the grits pot on the stove? This stuff has set up like concrete."

There's a light knock at the old screen door, and when I open it, Mitchell and his family are nervously crowding the doorway. I hug Mitchell and Betsy and pull them all into the kitchen. "Kids, this is your brother, Mitchell Cummins, and his beautiful wife, Betsy. And these two handsome young men are Blake, twelve, and Andrew, nine. Make them all welcome. They have traveled a great distance from the great state of Virginia to visit us. But we'll forgive them right off the bat for not living in the real South!"

Jill springs across the room to where the Cummins family is still standing and hugs Mitchell. "Thank you for coming all this way to

the way home

visit us. We're glad you all are here. This is Trudy, and you already know Trent. Meet Brenda Grace, Jeff's wife. All our children are in the living room playing games."

"Happy to meet you all," Mitchell speaks for his family. "Rachael and Bobby brought us photo albums. We feel like we already know you."

Trent seems to move almost in slow-motion from his place at the table toward Mitchell. The two stare at each other for a long moment, and then Trent reaches out, grabbing Mitchell in a man's strong embrace. The two men remain with their arms wrapped around each other for a minute, sharing in the connection that first brought them together. When they release, Trent's tears are falling.

"This is the man who saved our mother's life in Haiti. He and his men risked their lives for our mother. I didn't know who you were, Mitchell. Why didn't you tell me?"

"I thought your knowing I was Mary Elizabeth's son would complicate an already dangerous situation in Haiti. All our focus had to be on Rachael and the operation to free her."

Trudy moves across the room to join Trent and Mitchell. Without a word—it's unusual for Trudy to be speechless—she grabs the big man and holds him in her arms. Crying into his big shoulder, she can only whisper, "Thank you."

The children hear the commotion and run to the kitchen where Hardy sizes up the new additions to our family. "If you guys are in our family now, that means we have three more men. Do you like Kool-Aid and Monopoly?"

That seems to break the spell that has been cast over us all by the wonderful knowledge that Mary Elizabeth had a son thirty-four years ago who was destined to save my life. God does indeed work in strange ways.

Jill speaks up on the important issue of barefootn'. "Well, Cummins family, there is one way you are very different from us. Show him, family!" Following Jill's lead, we adults and children stick our feet in the air, wiggling our naked, tanned toes. And on cue, I crank up the familiar strains of "Barefootn" by Wilson Pickett, transporting us back to the free-spirited sixties.

judy norwood enter

"Everybody get on your feet; you make me nervous when you in your seat.

Take off your shoes and pat your feet.
We're doin' a dance that can't be beat.
We're barefootn', we're barefootn'.
We're barefootn', we're barefootn'".

Andrew and Blake have shed their shoes and been drawn into the children's playful dance to the music. Jill with her baby bump begins a solo, slow shuffle, shag edging toward this handsome, broad-shouldered, gentle giant of a man.

"Well, take off your shoes and put them into the family shoe basket along with ours. And Mitchell, do you and Betsy know how to shag?"

Made in the USA
Lexington, KY
12 September 2012